Business With Pleasure

A Gwen Arthur Novel

Olivia R. Burton

Edited by: Alexis Arendt
www.wordvagabond.com

ISBN-13: 978-0-9976333-3-7

Peacock Deceiving a Suitcase
www.PeacockDeceivingASuitcase.com

OTHER TITLES

Gwen Arthur Series

Mixed Feelings
Business With Pleasure
Cold Feet
Hollow Back Girl
Change of Heart

~

Bone to Pick
Flesh and Blood
The Writer's Overnighter
Gut Feeling
Suckered In
Split Second

The Preternatural PNW

Rattle
Metal
Knell

~

Throb
Murmur

COLLABORATIONS

Passage Through Moonlight
The Godfather's Naughty Daughter
Song of the Argyle Goddess
Belladonna Clasped
Cash Grab

CONTENTS

One

Finding a corpse outside a grocery store was a terrible way to start the day, but at least it got me out of exercising. Had I been given the choice between being dragged to the gym and having someone die, I would have absolutely chosen the former. The universe decided for me, however, and that's how I ended up in the parking lot of the Wallingford QFC with my best friend and a dead man.

Minutes before we knew what was waiting for us two spaces down, Chloe Warren pulled her car into a parking spot and detailed our plans for the grocery store like it was a precision military op.

"I'll hit the baking aisle and get the sugar, since you always get the wrong bag. You steer clear of all things sugary and pick out a few boxes of tea. We'll meet at the registers and be out in five. Got it?" I grunted in response and she pretended I'd answered clearly. "Excellent. Also, get a variety of tea this time. Not just the mint chocolate. You're six months off with that."

"But it's good," I insisted.

Knowing I'd follow her orders despite my argument, she continued as if I hadn't spoken. "Oh, we also need another bag of candy for the dish. I'll get that too."

"I can get that," I said, bolstered by the idea of visiting the candy aisle.

"I don't trust you." She was up and out of the car before I could muster a protest. Truth was, she was right; when it comes to sugar in any form, I am not to be trusted.

I fought off my urge to throw a tantrum and climbed out to find her frowning at something beyond me.

"What's that guy's deal?"

"What guy?" I asked, turning to scan the long parking lot. Without hesitation, I extended my power, poking at all the psyches I could find within range. My empathy picked up the emotions of a couple kids, three parents, a dozen or so birds, and one squirrel.

"What guy?" I repeated, seeing nothing out of the ordinary.

1

"This one." I glanced back just quick enough to see that Chloe's eyes were focused on a place I hadn't inspected. Trying to follow her line of sight, I shifted the sphere of my empathy, focusing on the building in front of the car. I still felt nothing interesting, but I did catch sight of a man hunched over the steering wheel of his car.

"Is he sleeping?" Chloe asked. I blinked at the man, wondering for a moment why I felt nothing from him. I'd come across creatures my supernatural power couldn't read before, but they hadn't looked human. This guy looked nothing but. Chloe realized what was wrong a split second before I did. "Shit."

"Shit!" I squeaked, stumbling back and bumping my butt against the car. Chloe was already on her way past, moving toward the truck. "Don't go over there! He's dead!"

"I know," she agreed calmly, her phone already in her left hand as her right reached toward the door of his truck. "I need to make sure."

"I'm sure!" I insisted. I had very little experience with dead bodies but I knew what one felt like. Even sleeping people have some emotional signature. This person was a void, like there wasn't anyone there at all. I'd been able to feel the emotions of others for as long as I could remember, and the absence of emotions in the presence of a human body was nerve-racking.

It didn't help that the last time I'd been in the presence of a dead person, a demon and a vampire had been involved.

"I still needed to check," Chloe said as she shut the door to the truck and turned back toward me. "We can't tell the police you knew he was dead because you're magical."

She had a point. The world at large isn't aware that people like me even exist. If you were to pick a random person off the street and ask them to tell you about magical powers or vampires, you'd probably get a lecture on poofy-haired, teenaged blood-suckers with boundary issues. Most humans just don't know there's a world of werewolves, fairies, and gifted humans within our own. I'd barely known until last year.

I couldn't tear my eyes away from the body as Chloe made the call to the police. Noticing my discomfort, she gestured vaguely toward the grocery store. I felt the pity inside her expand in a fizzy mess, like dumping vinegar into baking soda.

"Go, shop. I'll handle everything here."

"Are you sure?" I asked, though I was already scooting along the side of the car, aiming to get far away as soon as I could.

Instead of answering me, she turned her attention to the phone, explaining that she had to report a body. I fled.

I felt somehow safer inside the store. I'd seen Chloe in action, and could vouch for her being a badass, but being inside a building with a bustling group of strangers still seemed more secure. Without a thought to the tea Chloe had suggested I buy, I went straight for the snack aisle, visions of chocolate dancing in my head. I'm never particular about what type of chocolate, though I prefer the sweetest of milks to most any dark. Even white chocolate will do. Chocolate milk, chocolate bunnies, orange chocolate, mint chocolate: it's all good in my book.

I was hoarding a large variety of crinkling candy bags when I felt a familiar sort of emotion waft over from somewhere behind me. It was inhuman, that much I could tell, and the intensity made it feel like it was maybe an aisle away, no more.

To my empathy, human emotions all tend to feel the same. They'll vary slightly person to person, but I can always tell when a human is sad, happy, annoyed, what have you. Humans aren't the only creatures that feel emotions, though. I was acquainted with a very attractive werewolf who was wholly dedicated to feeling horny.

I knew the pattern of these emotions, though I hadn't felt this particular mixture of them before. Instead of the usual spring breeze, this was overly warm, even scalding in places, like campfire embers being flung at my skin. It took a few snaps of pain before my brain resolved what I was feeling into a clearer meaning: frustration.

"Madel—" I started to call out, aiming to ask what had my favorite café owner so out of sorts, but I barely got half her name out before the bag of peanut butter cups slipped from my hands. "Dammit."

Unwilling to leave any candy behind, I crouched down, shifting the contents of my arms and wishing I'd been smart enough to grab a basket. Or a cart, come to think of it; the basket might not have been big enough for all the chocolate I'd probably need to get over the shock I'd gotten outside. As I tried to keep my precarious candy balance, I felt the emotions move away.

"Madeline!" I called as I finally managed to get all the bags wrangled. I glanced forlornly at the wall of chocolate again before heading to the end of the aisle and turning the corner. The breezy, burning irritation had moved on, and I saw no sign of the woman I was sure I'd felt just minutes before. My phone dinged once in my pocket, startling me into dropping the peanut butter cups again.

"You slippery assholes," I grumbled, crouching to grab them. Three more bags plummeted to the floor as Madeline moved far enough away that I could no longer feel her at all.

"Do you need some help, ma'am?"

I glanced up at a young woman approaching and shook my head.

"Just tenderizing my chocolate, thanks." Turning back to my suicidal sweets, I gathered the bags into a pile in my arms and paused to consider my options. From the feel of it, Madeline had already left and in order to catch up with her I'd have to abandon the candy, something I wasn't willing to do. Sighing out my guilt, I booked it to the registers. I only remembered once I was there that Chloe had tucked a reusable sack into my pocket and I could have saved myself a lot of trouble.

Just as I'd suspected, Chloe had been the one buzzing my phone while I'd been making small talk with the cashier. The police had already arrived, along with an ambulance and a curious crowd of onlookers. I was only able to get back to Chloe's car because she'd told them to expect me. I'd torn into the bag of daredevil peanut butter cups within seconds of purchasing them, and I offered one to the officer who let me by. He declined, but I didn't take it personally. I probably looked like a crazy person, digging into a sack of candy and trying to unwrap several at once without dropping any. You'd think with all the candy unwrapping experience I'd had over my lifetime I would've been able to do it blindfolded, but then I probably would have run into the cop instead.

I caught sight of Chloe at the center of the hustle and bustle, despite the fact that she was the shortest person there. Chloe Warren is slim, almost slight in her build, though I promise you she's stronger than she looks. I'd once watched her garrote a vampire and go toe-to-toe with a demon. Her blond hair is short, her face heart-shaped. She's got round blue eyes and an infectious smile. She's the greatest assistant and best friend I could have ever asked for, and not just because she's saved my life.

The next forty-five minutes passed at a clip, filled with questions, statements, and the words 'cardiac arrest' mentioned gravely. In the end, Chloe stood with me watching a pair of EMTs loading the body into the back of the ambulance. Once the path was clear, we climbed into her car and I settled the bag of candy into my lap.

"There's no tea in that bag, is there?" Chloe asked. Defensively, I shifted the sack so she couldn't see inside it and shrugged as if I didn't have a satisfactory answer. "You're hopeless."

"I'm hungry," I argued.

"You're always hungry."

"Is that a crime?"

"No," Chloe pointed out as we headed through the neighborhood toward our office building. "But it is why I make you work out."

"We can't make it today!" I realized, feeling a bit of cheer muscle in on the stress that was still making my insides rumbly.

"Nope. We have to go straight to your first appointment." Chloe's smile was wicked and, when I realized why, I unwrapped another peanut butter cup as consolation.

"The morning just went from bad to worse," I sighed as Chloe pulled up against the curb around the corner from our building. Chloe laughed but didn't speak until we were out on the sidewalk.

"Mrs. Q isn't worse than a dead body."

"The dead body doesn't call me names and make me want to tear my hair out."

Choosing to ignore my perfectly valid complaints about my least favorite client, Chloe grabbed for the sack of candy. I refused to let it go as she pulled it up to inspect it. She probably wouldn't chuck it into the path of an oncoming car, but she's been known to go to greater lengths to keep me healthy.

"You see?" She shook her head, pointing to my bounty. "This is why I didn't want to let you alone in the candy aisle."

"I wasn't really alone," I said as we approached The Internets, the café that takes up nearly the entire bottom floor of our building. "Madeline was there."

"And she didn't stop you from slowly rotting your insides?"

"I didn't actually talk to her," I sniffed, offended that Chloe assumed our favorite latte pusher might object to my eating habits. Sugar as all four food groups is a very valid life choice, I think, and Madeline's never objected before. "But I will." Letting Chloe take the weight of the candy bag, I made a beeline for the café.

"You don't have time for—"

"I can't hear you!" I said, shoving open the door. "I'm going through a tunnel!"

I felt Chloe's frustration spike, like having a handful of tacks dropped on my spine, but I knew I could count on her to get upstairs and open the office before Ellen Quottrich arrived for her nine o'clock therapy session.

"Gwen!"

I paused in the doorway, swinging my head around to see who had called me and finding an attractive blond in all beige standing just out of arm's reach. His eyes were wide behind his rimless glasses, his pale brows high. I could feel his shock and it was, all things considered, pretty mild. I knew who I was looking at—I'd recognize my ex-husband anywhere—but my brain went dead the instant I saw him.

We stared in silence at each other for much longer than was polite and, when it got too much for Stanley to bear, I felt his shock shift toward worry.

"Gwen?"

"Oh shit," I breathed as a decade of guilty thoughts lit up my mind and made my knees go weak with shame. Stan flinched at my oath, but I was still paralyzed in terror and didn't have the mental faculties to apologize.

"Excuse me!"

I turned at the sound of another voice, blinking against the hot, prickly feeling of anger, and found a man in a nice suit standing to my right.

"*Excuse me*," he repeated, yanking the door out of my grip and pushing past, determined to exit the building even if he had to knock me over to do it.

"Gwen," Stan said gently, grabbing my wrist to pull me out of the way. I twisted to watch the man go, not realizing his frustration and irritation had leaked inside me and taken over. Seeing Stan had short-circuited my self-control just enough that I'd lost all control over my psychic shielding and left myself open to sponge up whatever my empathy might rub up against.

"Jackass!" I called after the suit. He didn't turn back, already distracted by his Bluetooth headset and unaware that Stan was the only thing keeping me from running after him. His anger twisted inside me, writhing and thrashing like a cat fighting its own tail.

"Please."

I whirled on Stan, a snarl fixed on my face, rational thought beaten briefly back. At his worried expression, though, my mood shifted drastically. My own emotions took over, chasing out the stranger's frustration and swamping me in guilt. We stared at each other again for a few more moments before the sloshing remorse splashed up through my chest and out my lips.

"I am so sorry," I babbled, intently meeting his blue eyes as I reached out to grip his arm. "You—I—it—I am *so sorry*."

Discomfort fluttered through Stan, making him glance around at the people nearby, before he patted my hand. "We should sit down."

I stayed silent as he gestured with the handle of the cup-holder in his right hand and let him pull me to a table against the back wall. Stan set the holder and its two cups down before moving to pull a chair out.

"Please, can we sit?" His request sparked something in my brain and I shook my head.

"I can't," I said. Stan frowned, disappointment threading through him. It made my regret harden into jagged balls of shame and lodge in my throat.

"I underst—"

"No!" I argued. "It's not—"

"Gwen, it's okay. I—"

"I found a corpse!"

The tables around us went quiet in an instant and I flinched as a dozen shards of interested shock jammed into my rib cage like shrapnel. I absolutely had not meant to say that so loud. My phone rang.

"Son of a bitch," I snapped, resentment at the day screaming up my spine and tightening every muscle I had. "Mother fucking Friday morning."

By the time I dug my phone out of my many jacket pockets, our audience had gone back to their own discussions, though I could still feel the creeping grip of curiosity from at least three of them. Crestfallen, Stan continued to watch me as I answered my phone.

"I'll be late." I didn't wait for Chloe's response before hanging up and stuffing my phone back in my pocket. I returned my attention to Stan, reaching forward as if I might touch him but unable to force myself to make contact. "I want to talk to you but I have an appointment that I'm late for. My office is right upstairs and I'll have time free in about an hour, okay?"

Still looking unsure, discomfort fluttering gently through him, Stan nodded, and reached for the to-go cups he'd set on the table.

"Here," he said, handing me one.

"I can't take your—"

"It's yours. Why do you think I'm here?" He smiled softly and it squeezed my heart tight in my chest. Unable to speak, I nodded as I took the cup. We stared at each other for a few seconds before my phone started to ring again and I realized Chloe wasn't going to leave me alone until I explained what was going on. Although there were a few dozen people in my office building, I was willing to bet I could pick her emotions out of the din, even from two floors down. It got me moving again.

I waved once awkwardly and then dashed toward the back door of the restaurant.

OLIVIA R .BURTON

Two

My eyes strayed to the clock on the wall and I felt a jolt of giddiness rocket through my limbs. I had three minutes left until I could politely inform Mrs. Ellen Quottrich that our time was up. Despite the fact that I hadn't looked away from her for longer than an instant, she'd caught me.

"Am I distracting you from something?" Her voice was brittle, but her words were steely and I could feel the insult like a punch to the gut.

"No, ma'am. I'm just checking the time."

She scowled my way and I felt it. While her body was frail, her emotions were tough. I could admire that, at least. When she didn't say anything else on the subject, I gestured vaguely with my right hand.

"We still have some time, so please continue. Your son couldn't come out for—"

"*Wouldn't* come out for my birthday. He *wouldn't* visit. Justin claims it's because Harold's working so much but I just know he doesn't want to see me. I'm surprised they even invited me to their wedding."

"Which you didn't go to, if I remember?" I physically flinched when she sucked in a breath. It was like being pelted with rotten oranges to feel her guilt and the outrage that I would bring that up.

"I couldn't fly all the way to Massachusetts. I'd just had my surgery."

"And was he hurt when you declined?"

Mrs. Q didn't respond, sitting across my desk with a sour look on her ancient face, her bony hands clenched into fists on the arms of her seat. We watched each other in silence for maybe a minute. I kept my face pleasant, even though I wanted to jump to my feet and cry, "Begone, foul creature!" Maybe I could find a stool to jab her way and a whip to crack in case she needed some real encouragement to leave.

I don't know why she insists on coming back to me every week. I can, no matter what she's talking about, always feel an undercurrent of loathing within her. I generally consider myself to be pretty genial in the face of her rudeness—Chloe laughs when I mention this, but what does she know?—but I can tell she despises me. I can literally feel it, and it's difficult not to

9

absorb it and throw it right back.

"Our time is up," she said finally, lifting her nose in the air. "We can discuss this later."

I nodded as if I agreed, though I knew she just didn't want to talk about her estranged son anymore. She only enjoyed it so long as I didn't imply any culpability on her part. Pushing herself to her feet, she glared at the clock on the wall and turned to move toward the door. I knew she would refuse my help if I offered, so I waited until her back was turned before hopping to my feet and rushing to the door. Despite feeling her thumping insult against my skin every time I do it, the petty satisfaction of annoying her is worth holding the door as she hobbles past every week.

It took her longer to cross my small office and move into the lobby than it should have, and I wondered briefly if stalling was her way of getting me back. Unfortunately, I couldn't probe her emotions to tell for sure; her irritation and unhappiness melted under the spastic, scalding sparks of emotion coming off the werewolf entering my little lobby. I was surprised I hadn't felt it the second he stepped onto our floor, though I was grateful. Mel Somerset was the first werewolf I'd ever met, and I'd known the instant I'd felt his emotions that I didn't want to meet another.

He shut the outer door and did his best to catch my eye. I studiously ignored him, smiling tightly at Mrs. Q as she hobbled out toward Chloe's desk. I watched her tense as she caught sight of Mel, and I wondered what I would be feeling from her if he hadn't been around to suffocate my empathy.

After a moment, I started to wonder instead why his emotions seemed to be crackling and popping more than usual. It was less a steady stream of discomfort, and more like being tagged repeatedly by children in wool socks running around on thick carpet. His emotions had a nervous tic. I felt it when Mel seemed to notice he was the sole male in a room full of women, and I watched bemused as he fixed his gaze on Ellen and let loose a stunning smile.

I can't stand him, but he's a good-looking guy, tall and muscled like a movie superhero, with a square jaw to match. His eyes are a blue that rivals the afternoon sky, and that morning his dark hair looked like he just rolled out of bed after having fantastic sex. To listen to Mel talk, he'd probably rolled out of bed after fantastic sex, then had more fantastic sex in the shower, while driving in the car, and maybe in the elevator on the way up to his office. I was betting that any day now he'd run out of legal, available women to bed and he'd have to move out of state.

It would be the happiest day of my life.

Chloe had hopped out of her seat to help Ellen through our little waiting room, despite the fact that the old biddy fought her every damn time she did so. I swallowed my own irritation, walled up my empathy, and tried to stand tall. It was tough in the face of the morning I'd had and the fact that just being around a werewolf is physically painful.

Momentarily, at least, Mel was distracted by my elderly client. When Mrs. Q slapped at Chloe for trying to take her arm, Mel stepped in. Despite his defective emotions, his body language was typical, like he felt he was being heroic and charming.

"Here, miss. Let me help you. I was just on my way out, myself—"

"Get your hands off me," Ellen ordered as she craned her fragile neck to challenge his lie. "I know what you are."

The explosion of shock that came off of Mel vaporized every scrap of lust and yearning that I had come to expect and dread from his emotions. As a werewolf, he's forever hungry. I hadn't quite narrowed down the list of what he was hungry for, but sex was always at the top. Despite the fact that he could have literally snapped her in two if he really wanted to, Mel fell back a step as Ellen jabbed her finger toward his sternum. She didn't quite make contact, her arm shaking and jerking like getting that close to him was painful, but he reacted like she'd punched him right in the gut.

"I've seen you with dozens of young women through here," Mrs. Q continued before shuffling toward the door once again, cradling her hand against her chest as if he might try to grab for it. "Creep! *Cad!* Don't touch me. I can walk on my own. Get away from me."

We all went silent as Mrs. Q hobbled ever so slightly faster toward the door. She reminded me of an electric toy car that was working its hardest, despite being nearly out of juice. Chloe, whose eyebrows were in her hair, stood by the open door as Ellen hit the hall, turned the corner, and finally disappeared. I could still feel her moving at a snail's pace toward the elevator, but I tuned her out and turned my attention to Mel. I shouldn't have been able to feel her at all with him around, but she'd really done a number on him.

Closing the door, Chloe looked to Mel with wide, curious eyes, her mouth quirked up in half a grin. Neither of us had ever seen a woman react to Mel so viciously. Usually even married women were charmed when he so much as smiled their way.

"Wow," I mumbled, looking him up and down.

"That was weird," Chloe agreed. Mel turned to her, his eyes a bit glazed over.

"Did she just—"

"Tell you the old lady equivalent of 'fuck off?'" Chloe offered with a small grin. "Yes, she did."

"I—is she married?"

"She was, but her husband died years ago," I said, trying to decide if I wanted to find him a fainting couch or laugh in his face. The events of the morning had faded into the background, behind the joy of being able to think straight this close to Mel. It had been months since I'd been able to stand him, and that had only been because I'd been magically blocked from his feelings.

"But she wasn't even a little bit interested in me," Mel said, his voice barely above a whisper.

"Well, she is pretty old," I pointed out, as if it was possible he'd missed her age. Chloe stepped forward, rubbing her hand over Mel's shoulder. She was gentle, pity greasing the edges of her psyche, though I could tell from the grin on her face alone that wasn't all she felt for him in the moment.

"You need to sit down, big guy? Has it been a hard day?" she asked. Mel didn't seem to notice that she was teasing.

"No woman's been that mean to me since high school."

I considered his words. I didn't like the fact that the more his emotions flickered pathetically, the less I was enjoying his bewilderment. Mel takes almost daily joy in making me miserable; I wanted to enjoy every second of his unhappiness. Feeling bad for him was not allowed.

"I don't … I can't …" He trailed off, staring down at me. I raised an eyebrow as something new tried to spark to life in his chest. It wasn't the painful current of electric lust that usually grabs for my bare skin, but it badly wanted to be. His face changed slightly, the usual lust and hunger within straining toward the surface as he leaned into me and waggled a brow. I jerked back, expecting his pure and agonizing Mel-ness to flood back through him and drown me.

"What are you doing?" I demanded, a little flutter of panic jumping in my chest. I didn't want him back to normal. I liked him better sad. "Stop. You're being weird."

"How you doin'?" he asked. I stood tense and terrified for what felt like a minute before realizing things weren't getting worse. He wasn't as cocky and persuasive as usual; not even a horny sex worker would have accepted his offer just then.

"Stop it. You're creepy," I said, looking him up and down. I wondered briefly if maybe he wasn't Mel at all, but some broken, robot facsimile.

When he realized I wasn't giving in or running off, Mel's face fell. Chloe leaned around his shoulder to see his face and dissolved immediately into a fit of giggles, leaning against him to stabilize herself.

"This isn't funny," Mel pouted. "It makes no sense. I need to see if she's—Maybe she didn't get a good look at me. That has to be it."

"Yes," Chloe said, snorting out one last laugh before controlling herself. "That's the only explanation. It can't be that she's three times your age and has seen you rubbing up against the entire single female population of the office building."

Mel didn't seem to hear her, focused on the door. Without so much as a goodbye, he rushed out into the hallway toward the stairwell. Delighted that his usual slick demeanor had been ruined by a few nasty comments from a nasty woman, I didn't even flinch when the door slammed behind him.

"That was awesome," I said as Chloe closed the door after him.

"It was pretty funny," Chloe agreed, swinging her gaze to mine. "He was so confused, though. I felt a little bad for him."

"I didn't," I insisted, refusing to admit that I might not entirely loathe the man. "If only because it shut him up."

"Shut him up?"

"You know," I said, as if that would clear up what I'd meant. Chloe continued to watch me expectantly. Unsure how to explain myself, I waved my arms spastically around my head. "You know, with … his emotions."

"Really?" Chloe asked. Her smile was intrigued, though the greasy pity oozed a little faster through her, thinned out by her concern over his well-being. I nodded.

"Once she called him a creep, everything went, like," I dropped my flailing arms in front of me slowly like a wilting flower, "and then it was nice, quiet. I wish that worked with me. Why doesn't it happen that way when I tell him no?"

"Because you don't entirely mean it."

"Allow me to give you the young lady equivalent of 'fuck off.'" I flipped her the bird.

Chloe snorted out a laugh, indulging herself for a few seconds before settling back against her desk and crossing her ankles. As if in apology for the accusation that I would ever let Mel touch me, she pulled a handful of peanut butter cups out of the dish on her desk and held them out to me. I made a happy squealing sound, going at the foil-wrapped candy pile immediately.

"So, tell me why you were late."

As if on cue, I felt Stan approaching from the stairwell. I can't always tell each individual person by their emotions, but Stan was easy to recognize. Even in the throes of puberty he'd been calm, sweet, special. It was why I'd gravitated toward him in the first place. Using the candy as a distraction, I decided to let his presence speak for itself, leaving Chloe hanging until he knocked lightly on the door and opened it to lean in.

"Gwen?" he asked.

"Oh my god!" Chloe yelped, shock and elation going off like a nuclear bomb through her psyche as she slammed the dish of candies down on her desk. I grunted against the explosion of glee, stumbling back and dropping my last, freshly unwrapped candy to the floor.

"What?" Stan asked, his worry a minuscule vibration compared to the atomic cloud of Chloe's excitement. I groaned against the feeling, staring down at my lost treat. Chloe keeps the floors pretty clean; she probably wouldn't lecture me if she caught me eating it. "What's wrong?"

"You're Stanley Sneedley!" Chloe shrieked, rushing toward him fast enough that I could feel Stan's panic at her approach. Deciding I could live without the candy, I looked up to watch them both, my own pity welling to the surface. Unlike with Mel, I didn't try to tamp this down. I might not have spoken to Stan for the last third of my life, but I knew I'd always care for him deeply.

Chloe seemed to catch on to his discomfort as well and reconsidered the grab she was making for him. I think she'd been planning to hug him but realized he might not like the intrusion. "I love you!"

"Oh," Stan breathed, flustered. "I … thank you."

"I'm so excited for *Airship!*" Chloe said, grabbing Stan's hand as she twisted to face me.

"*The Floating Airship,*" Stan elaborated automatically. Chloe was watching me, excitement naked on her face.

"Gwen! This is Stanley Sneedley!"

"We've, ah … met," I said, not really feeling up to explaining that once upon a time I'd briefly been Gwen Sneedley. It would have been difficult enough explaining our history without Chloe being a giddy fangirl. Her enthusiasm only strengthened my desire to be swallowed up by the earth.

"He writes books!"

"I know," I said, with a nervous laugh. I'd never read any of them, but I still bought them compulsively. I had no idea (because I'd seriously never counted) how many copies of his novels I'd stashed in the back of my closet over the years. It was a guilt-based action, of course, considering the fact that we'd only been married a year before I'd cheated on him and left. Run, actually. Fled. Scrammed like a cartoon, leaving a Gwen-shaped hole in Stan's heart. "In fact, he's here to see me."

Chloe's body language changed minutely and I could tell she'd caught something in my tone that piqued her curiosity. Still holding Stan's hand, she nodded once my way before turning back to him.

"Could I get you to sign for me?"

"Of course," Stan said, his cheeks going a bit pink. I had the sudden urge to pinch them. "I'd like to talk to Gwen first, though. If you don't mind?"

"No! Go ahead! This is so exciting!"

Gently, as if worried she might try to keep it, Stan slid his hand out of Chloe's grip, shuffling sideways to move around her without losing sight of her. It reminded me of an explorer who'd stumbled on a sleeping jaguar. Chloe just watched him happily as he closed in on me. I gestured to my office.

"In here," I said. He nodded once and moved quickly toward the doorway. I caught a whiff of him as he passed close, and it brought back a ridiculous flood of hormonal teenage memories. His soap, shampoo, and maybe deodorant were different, but he still smelled the same underneath. I bit my lip and swallowed thickly, leaning away. Stan didn't notice.

Chloe noticed, though. Suddenly feeling like my mom had caught me sneaking a boy into my room, I spun to rush after him, slamming the door. Relief rushed out of me in a sigh, but it was sucked up into a sudden vacuum of discomfort when I realized I was standing alone in my office with my estranged ex-husband.

"Oh god," I heaved out, the words riding on an uneven laugh. I felt a puff of amusement and the slimy slide of sympathy from Stan but I tried to ignore it as I looked him over.

He did the same to me, his gaze doing a quick run from my sensible heels, up my legs, over my slightly pudgy curves and to my square jaw, round nose, and green eyes under thick bangs. My dark brown hair was chin-length and had been for years, but the last time we'd seen each other it was considerably longer.

Possibly as a procrastination technique, I gave him another once-over, slower this time. He looked really good, slim and proper in his khakis and sweater vest. I felt a dozen impulses rise up from the parts of my brain, all of them rooted in sweaty habits formed with him when we'd both been teenagers. Embarrassment joined the guilt in my stomach and I felt it start to ache.

"When ... did you get in?" I asked, my mind a blank. What does one talk about with one's ex-husband when one doesn't want to bring up what a colossal jerk one is?

"I took the train in on Tuesday. I haven't been up this way in a while and wanted to take time to ... relive some things." His eyes darted off to the side and I felt discomfort jump out of him. I knew about a dozen things he likely didn't want to relive, and they all involved me. Clearing his throat, he smiled, tried to lighten the mood. "Did you enjoy the drink?"

"What drink?"

I felt a wriggle of embarrassment as Stan explained, "I bought you hot chocolate. I was going to bring it up to you earlier but then ... I didn't need to."

"Hot—Dammit!" I snapped, realizing Chloe had taken my drink before shuffling me in to see Mrs. Q.

"Excuse me?" Stan asked, taking a small step forward. "Was it bad? The woman behind the counter said it was your favorite."

"No, it—I didn't drink it. Chloe took it away." At Stan's puzzled expression, I waved my hand jerkily in the air. "She does that. She thinks I eat too much sugar."

Stan's lips twitched and I felt a pleasant roll of fuzzy nostalgia envelop him. "You? Too much sugar?"

I met his gaze and, though it is my habit to glower at disapproval over my eating habits, I couldn't manage it with Stan. We shared a laugh and he turned to inspect my office for a moment before gesturing to the couch.

"Can we sit now?"

"Yes," I said, crossing toward him. "Now I have the time. And sorry about earlier. It's been a bad morning."

"What's happened?" he asked as he settled into the couch, angled so he could face me as I sat next to him.

"Well, I had to get up early, for starters. Chloe was going to make me work out—she does that too." I rolled my eyes. "We found a … body, though. And then I ran into you." I felt my eyes bug out as I realized what I'd said. "Not that you're like a corpse! I like you. I mean … We're … It's just—"

"Awkward," Stan supplied. I nodded and we went quiet for a few moments. I wasn't sure why he wasn't bringing up the disastrous end to our marriage, but I wasn't sure how to get into it, or even if he'd want to talk about it. He'd been the one who'd been hurt and abandoned, and if he didn't want to relive what I'd done, I didn't want to force the issue.

When the silence got too much to bear, Stan took a quick breath, straightened minutely and reached down to the fawn-colored messenger bag hanging by his hip.

"I actually was hoping you could help me with something."

"Anything," I said. Though Stan is the nicest, least vindictive person one could ever meet and I knew he wouldn't demand something embarrassing or painful of me, I would have gladly agreed if he had.

"I'm having an issue. I'm guessing you know about my books?"

"Yes." I didn't go into detail about my embarrassing and expensive habits.

"Well, my fan base isn't large, but they're very loyal. And they're always very nice, though one of them is …" He seemed unsure of how to say it, so I gestured like Vanna White.

"Crazy? Obsequious? Purple?" I quirked my lips, unable to resist the reference. "Clairvoyant?"

On a soft laugh, Stan shook his head and continued simply with, "Off." He lifted the flap on his messenger bag, pulled out a manila envelope, and held it in his lap. "I've been getting worrisome letters. The last few have been talking about being excited to meet me."

"Are they threatening? Have you gone to the police?"

"No, nothing like that. I don't want to get anyone in trouble if there's no problem. But, there's a convention this weekend," his cheeks pinked, "for my work, and she—Norma is her name—she says she's going to be there. I wouldn't ask if—I mean if you don't—"

"Don't. Whatever it is, I'll do it. I owe you at least … something."

"I don't—" Shaking away the argument he'd been about to make, he continued. "I appreciate it. Since she's going to be there, I was hoping you would be, too."

"At the convention?"

"Yes."

"Because …?"

"Because I don't know who she is, and while I'm sure she means no harm, I'm still just a bit concerned." He handed me the envelope carefully, as if it was might spontaneously combust. "Your empathy isn't the only reason I thought you might be able to help. You're trained, you know people. You'll be able to tell me there's nothing wrong. Perhaps she's just more enthusiastic."

He went quiet for a moment, his eyes straying to the door, and I knew he was thinking of Chloe's explosive greeting. I fought off a smile and tapped the envelope in my lap.

"This is …?"

"Oh, her letters are in there." Focused on me, Stan continued. "You can look them over, and if you think I'm overreacting, just let me know and I'll drop it. If you see something that concerns you, though …" Worry spurted out and smacked me in my chest. I gave my most encouraging smile.

"You're the nicest person I've ever met. I'm sure no one wants to hurt you. I will absolutely look these over and come make sure no one's interested in keying your car or something."

"Thank you, Gwen."

"It's no trouble." I thought about it for a moment. "This convention, is it big?"

"Oh, no. I'm not that popular." The fact that he felt no shame or envy at his assessment of his popularity made my heart melt a little. Sweetest guy I'd ever met and I'd run him off. "It's no more than, at most, two hundred people."

"That's not big?" I'd never braved a convention before. The idea of standing in the middle of a sea of emotions didn't appeal to me.

"I don't think so," he stated. "It's entirely fan-coordinated, and people are coming from all over. I don't get to attend many of these, only four over the last few years. Please, though, if you're not comfortable—"

"I'm fine. I'll be there."

"Okay." Relieved, Stan smiled. "I've included my contact information and directions to the hotel in the packet."

"Thanks," I said, turning my attention to the envelope. I was curious, but I didn't want to tear into it with him sitting there. Ignoring him to read when we'd only just made contact again after so long would have been rude. Stan said nothing further about his predicament and, at a loss for further questions on the subject, I lifted my gaze to his. This time the silence got to me. "How are your parents?"

"They're very well. They finally got themselves a farm. I can't count the number of animals they've got now."

"That sounds like them," I said with a grin.

"And your family?"

"Good!" I grinned at the thought of my sister and her kids. Before I could elaborate, Chloe knocked on the door twice before pushing in and smiling down at us.

"Sorry, Gwen. Ian wants to know if you can see him early?"

"What time? How early?"

"As soon as possible." Her eyes strayed to Stan, and I felt a jolt of giddiness shoot out of her. Her shameless fangirling made me roll my eyes.

I nodded. "That's fine. Let me just … um, finish up here."

"I'll get my books out!" With an excited wiggle, Chloe twisted and left the office, leaving the door ajar. I laughed and turned back to Stan.

"You must be used to that by now."

"Not really," Stan admitted, sheepish. "She's a different sort of fan than I'm used to."

"She is pretty unique."

"Thank you again for the help," he said as he pushed to his feet.

"Really," I said, getting up as well. "Anything you asked me to do, it wouldn't be enough."

Stan's lips tightened and, for just a moment, I felt a splash of embarrassment squirt forth. I shook my head, wanting to tell him he had no right to feel that way, that he'd done nothing wrong. Instead, I hopped forward and yanked him into a hug. He hugged me back without hesitation, and I felt the tension I'd been holding since he walked in seep out of my shoulders. I held onto him for a few seconds, surprised when he didn't push me away and when I felt nothing unpleasant in his emotions. I pulled back, intent on apologizing again, maybe throwing myself at his feet and wailing, "I'm not worthy!" at the heavens. Chloe rushed in before I could speak, a stack of paperback novels in her arms.

"I just happened to have these in my desk. I read them over and over. This one?" Chloe waved a copy of *Murder in a Time of War* wildly in the air, which made Stan's eyebrows draw together. I got the feeling he would have only reacted more harshly if she'd been shaking an infant. "My favorite!"

"Thank you," Stan said, trying his best to be gracious in the face of her enthusiasm. I felt his embarrassment and it made me sigh wistfully. He was proud of what he'd accomplished, but I could tell he wasn't sure what to make of Chloe's unmitigated glee.

Three

Stan made it to the door and out of the office without too much harassment, which I took to mean Chloe was saving it all up for me. I stood by the door, took my time in shutting it, and then tried to work up the courage to turn around. When I finally did I found Chloe standing next to her desk, fixated on me like a laser.

"So. Next client, right? Any minute now," I offered, hoping she would let it go.

"How do you know Stanley Sneedley?"

"Yep," I said instead of answering. "Next client. Any time. Ian'll be here. Any minute—in fact. I should go prepare." I cleared my throat and walked toward my office as casually as I could, despite my desire to run and slam the door like a horror movie cliché.

Chloe just reached a hand out and took my arm gently as I passed her.

"Dammit," I whispered. I turned to Chloe and found her watching me with both brows up. Curiosity was rooting around inside her like pigs looking for truffles, but I could feel concern, too. I flailed my hands at my sides for a moment and then shook my head. "It's going to take a while to get through it, okay? We can talk about it after work."

"After Ian," she said, reaching out to tap the phone on her desk. "I rescheduled your last appointment for the day. I figure you could use the break."

Torn between relief and guilt, I squinted at her.

"You're serious?" I asked, despite the fact that my empathy would have told me if she was lying. "This isn't a ploy to lure me into a false sense of security and then drag me to the gym? It's still early. I know you; just because I don't have my two o'clock doesn't mean you won't make me spend that hour lifting weights."

"I've never made you lift anything heavier than a bran muffin," Chloe said, placing a hand to her heart as if she was insulted by the implication. "And I'm not lying. Does that sound like me? Would I stuff you in a burlap sack, shove you in the trunk of my car, and then handcuff you to a treadmill for forty-five minutes?"

"That's suspiciously specific," I pointed out.

Sucking in a quick breath, Chloe snapped her fingers. "Perhaps I've said too much."

Despite the fact that I could feel Ian closing in on the office door, I glared at Chloe and reached past her to grab the bowl of peanut butter cups off her desk. "Just for that, I'm going to each every one of these."

"Certainly not *ninety-five* minutes."

It occurred to me as we stepped inside The Internets that Madeline was absent from the building. I wondered as Chloe and I made our way toward the end of the line if she'd been gone that morning as well, but I couldn't remember. The shock of seeing Stan had stopped my brain from forming proper memories.

"No Mad?" I asked Holly as we got to the front of the line. She shook her head and handed a receipt off to a girl behind the counter who I didn't recognize. She had no nametag yet.

"Nope. I got a call this morning asking me to come in and take her shift. I'm not even supposed to be here today."

"Dante Hicks is just like you," I said in a sing-song to no one in particular. Chloe glanced at me, unsure about my reference. Realizing no one found my joke funny, I moved on. "She's really not here? Just ... not at all? She didn't explain herself or anything?"

"She doesn't really have to," Holly said with a casual shrug. "She's the boss."

"But she's always here," I insisted. "Always. From six in the morning to two the next morning she's here. Right? But she's not here at all? And you're not even curious?"

"I'm curious," Holly said, punching a few things into the register. "But no one cut off her pinky finger and sent it in with a ransom note, so I'm not worried. She's a grown woman."

She was something else, too, though I'd never had the guts to ask what. As I stewed in silent curiosity, Chloe nudged me out of the way, sliding a fifty-dollar bill across the counter. Holly nodded, knowing Chloe's generous tipping habits better than to try to give change, and turned her attention past us. "Morning, can I help you?"

"I didn't order," I said, despite the fact that Chloe was already steering me out of the line.

"She knows what you want. It's fine. Come on."

"But I wanted cake!"

"You always want cake. You have a desk full of candy; you don't need cake. You'll survive."

"I don't have a desk full of candy!" I protested, reminded of the mystical sugar thief that had been sporadically haunting my every stash since November. I'd never actually seen the creature, but I knew from its stealing habits that it had as big a sweet tooth as me. "Not anymore."

"Come on." Chloe ignored my complaining as she pushed me toward a table along the back wall. I realized as we closed in that it was the same one Stan had chosen that morning. I let her sit me down and stayed quiet as she slid into the seat across from me. "Now. Tell me about you and Sneedley."

"Of all the things that happened this morning, that's not really the most important," I said, hoping to avoid the subject entirely. Chloe lacks my empathic powers, but she can still tell a lie from the truth. I couldn't fib, but I certainly didn't want to tell her about my past. "Let's talk about the dead guy instead! Heart attack, right? That sucks, man. You just never see it coming." Chloe just continued to watch me seriously. I cleared my throat and tried again. "Or, hey Madeline's missing. She was at QFC this morning but she can't make it into work? What do you think's up with that?"

"She's not missing. She's probably just taking a day off. Even a succubus needs time away from work."

"Even a—" Realizing what I was about to parrot back to her, I gasped. "She's a succubus! Let's talk about that!"

"You're changing the subject."

"You bet I am! Do you know how many times I've sat in this place trying to figure out why just drinking a hot chocolate made me so horny?"

"That's probably just because you refuse to date. Madeline's very careful about her influence. Now." Chloe snapped twice in front of my face. "Stan. Explain. Or I'm going to have them dump your triple chocolate mocha down the sink and bring you an apple instead of a cherry muffin."

My carbohydrates in jeopardy, I gasped, sitting up straight as an arrow. "You wouldn't."

Chloe just smiled. I wanted to take up arms at the idea of Chloe forcing me to eat fruit, but I caught sight of the new girl bringing over our order. I gave her a stiff smile as she slid the muffin in front of me, and surreptitiously gripped the side of the plate in case Chloe got any ideas.

Chloe thanked her with a grin before looking appreciatively down at the plate of vegan donuts she'd gotten. I considered snatching one in case she tried to feed me broccoli later. Once we were alone again, I forked off a chunk off my muffin and lifted it to my lips before speaking.

"You know how I was married?"

"Mmhmm," Chloe responded through a bite of her lemon-scented Mighty-O donut.

"Stan was him," I said, finally sinking my teeth into the delectable crumbly morsel. If I had to talk about the most shameful thing I'd ever done to another person, at least I got to do it while packing my face with sugar-topped breadstuffs.

Chloe watched me normally as she chewed, but when she took another bite I felt shock spike out of her and jab me hard right in my left eye. I winced and rubbed at my eyelid. She blinked hard, swallowed, and then carefully set her donut down.

"You?" She didn't continue, just stared.

"Me what?"

"*You* were married to Stanley Sneedley?"

"Don't make that face."

"*You were married to Stanley Sneedley?*" she repeated, her voice barely even a shocked hiss. "That's what you just said? I thought I was imagining it for a second. You? And Sneedley?"

I squirmed in my seat, taking another bite to distract myself from how uncomfortable I felt.

"It was … you know," I said around the muffin before swallowing the lump that had formed in my throat below my snack. She was right to be shocked. From the outside, from the point of view of someone who really knew me, it must have seemed ridiculous for Stanley Sneedley to have even been interested in Gwen Arthur. And yet, we'd been each other's first everything when it came to young love. "We were kids, okay?"

"Were you also two different people? Because that's the only way this scenario makes any sense," Chloe said, still watching me with her mouth agape. There was a grin pulling at the edges of her lips, though, and her emotions spoke of affectionate teasing. I blew air out in a raspberry.

"Okay, look. We met in high school and he was *adorable* and I was kind of an idiot and we dated for three years. Then we got married at eighteen and I cheated on him and ran away like a coward."

Chloe flinched like she'd been slapped, her brows drawing together in confusion.

"You—"

"Cheated! Yes! I'm awful!" Even though I felt no disgust on her part, I had enough for the both of us. "It was—I was—I don't want to get into it. He deserved better than me, always has. But I saw him and liked him and decided he was better than any other boy because have you *met* teenagers?" I let out a groan of disgust at the memories of being a sixteen-year-old empath sitting in the roiling stew of hormones that had been high school. After a second, I let out another, louder sound of revulsion, and Chloe laughed.

"He was different?"

"He was … quiet, you know?" Ever unsure how to describe my empathy, I wiggled my fingers next to my forehead. "He was calm, pleasant. He wasn't sure of me at first, and I don't blame him. But I'm very persuasive and, well, he was too polite to say no."

Chloe snorted at my statement and I smiled at the mental image I'd conjured of chubby teenaged me and bony, over-polite teenaged Stan.

"So what's he doing here?" Chloe asked as time passed and it became clear from how I was going at the muffin that I didn't know what else to say. "Did he just come to say hi because the convention is in town?"

"Um, not really. Well, sort of—no." I shook the stammers out of my mouth. I didn't want to assume he'd only shown up to ask for help, but I couldn't fathom him wanting to see me socially after what I'd done. "He asked me to go to the convention to help him with something. He has a wayward fan—"

"A wayward Sneed?" Chloe asked, leaning in to test the temperature of her drink. "I doubt that."

"Sneed?" I blinked over at her. She waved a hand and set the soy latte down.

"His fans, they call themselves Sneeds."

"Are you a Sneed?"

Chloe smirked at my question. "I'm too wild to be a Sneed. If you're going to the SneedCon, you'll see."

"It's just for him?" I asked, thinking of the conventions I'd read about on the internet and seen on posters stapled to telephone poles around the city. "Is he that popular?"

"He is and isn't," Chloe clarified with a shrug. "He's no Stephen King, but his fanbase is very loyal and … um. Unique. They're a little old-fashioned, too, so a few years ago, they started talking getting together for an in-person meet-up, thinking it would be better than chat rooms and mailing lists or whatever. Then someone realized they could use it as an excuse to organize this and coordinate that and, when one of them politely inquired if Stanley would be willing to join in on the fun, boom. Full-on convention."

"He couldn't say no to the request?" I asked with a sappy smile.

"Nope, though you can tell he's not sure what to do about the attention."

I winced at the reminder that I'd be stuck in the middle of a bunch of strangers, figuring they'd all be as giddy and over-excited as Chloe. Pushing on, I patted my bag.

"He gave me some of the letters the fan's written. I'll read them over tonight. He thinks he might be overreacting, but that's patently impossible. I once dragged him into the girl's bathroom at lunch to make out, then accidentally dropped his pager in the toilet, and his only response was, 'Oh dear.' I could probably light his house on fire and he'd just look sort of—" I made a face like I'd taken a sip of tepid tea expecting it to be the perfect temperature. Chloe laughed, and I pressed on.

"He wants me to hang around the convention and see what her deal is, like if she comes up to say hi or something." I perked up slightly, realizing Chloe had known about the convention without my mentioning it. "Will you be there?"

"I'm out of town, remember?"

"Oh, right." I nodded, thinking of Chloe's parents in Bremerton. Every year on the same date since we'd met, she would take a few days off to go see them. Delight possessed me in an instant when I realized she wouldn't be able to drag me to the gym on Sunday. Pleased that the weekend wouldn't be a complete disaster, I stabbed at the last bite of my muffin. While I chewed, I eyed the plate and considered that I could probably scrape all the leftover sugar granules into my mouth before Chloe could stop me.

Knowing me better than I know myself, Chloe grabbed my plate, sliding it to her side of the small table without a word. I scoffed and reached for her last donut. She didn't stop me. Halfway through, I remembered our earlier conversation and spoke around the cinnamon-sugar mass in my mouth.

"You know, I just knew Madeline wasn't human."

"You never mentioned it," Chloe pointed out. I shrugged.

"I didn't think you'd know, and it seemed rude to rock up and ask her, 'So what are you?'"

"She wouldn't mind," Chloe said with a shrug.

"Did you ask?"

"Didn't have to. She's not the first succubus I've met, and I kind of figured it out from the way she disappears with customers every so often and comes back with her fly down and her hair messed up."

I considered for a moment that Mel often did the same thing, but their emotions felt so much different I never would have assumed Madeline was a werewolf. Sensing Mel is like lighting yourself on fire, regardless of his mood. Madeline was more like a spring breeze most of the time.

"So she feeds on sex, right? Her and Callum?" I asked, referring to Madeline's rarely seen brother.

Chloe shook her head once. "He's an incubus, but he doesn't feed on sex. She does, he doesn't. It's like you and Amy, right?"

It took me a second to figure out what she meant. "Police Amy? From Bellevue?"

"Yes. You're both fa—" Chloe seemed to catch herself before she said something but corrected so smoothly I wasn't sure I'd actually heard the hitch. "Humans with powers, but you sense emotions and she can heal. Not all succubi and incubi feed on sex. Just depends on what they're born to, you know, go after."

"I don't understand how you're monster Wikipedia," I observed. "I'm the one with the powers, I should know more than you."

Chloe shrugged, brushing off my concern. "I've just asked a lot of questions, grown up around the right people."

I made a noncommittal sound. She'd been open about growing up around other kids with powers like mine, and about having known creatures like Mel. It didn't entirely explain some of the skills and knowledge she'd busted out the previous year, though. I let it go, knowing that I could trust her no matter what and figuring that I should just be grateful that her learning about the preternatural side of things had worked out so well for me. Chloe smiled suddenly, meeting my eyes.

"I know what you're thinking."

I doubted it, but gestured loosely with my fingers on the table. "Shoot."

"You're wondering why Madeline looks the way she does."

Her statement made me laugh and I sat back in my chair. "Now that you mention it, it is a little weird. But I guess there's a key for every lock, right?"

"She's the key, and she's a master. Doesn't matter that she's ugly," Chloe said. I felt my brows go up at her blunt assessment. I'd often thought the same, but it seemed somehow crass to vocalize it in the woman's own restaurant. "Mel needs to be pretty and charming to lure someone into the back and toss up her skirts. Madeline just has to look their way and they're game."

I shifted uncomfortably at the idea of overriding consent in that way, but wasn't really sure what to say. Chloe pressed on after a few seconds.

"I've never asked Callum, but I'm pretty sure he doesn't feed on lust. I mean, he's turned me down for a date, which is crazy."

I laughed, thinking of Madeline's slightly awkward, grumpy younger brother. "You do make it pretty clear you're open for business," I agreed.

"Hey, I stopped wearing the neon OPEN sign, didn't I?"

OLIVIA R .BURTON

Four

It had been seven months since the candy thief first showed up to invade my cabinets and leave me a string of wacky messages in magnets on my fridge. My life had gone back to normal since my twenty-ninth birthday, but the creature still felt the need to make itself known occasionally. Luckily, though, it was just to steal my stuff, not to warn me about any more vampires or demons.

I had moved past worry that the creature might mean me harm and settled into a general despair over the fact that I was no longer able to keep candy or sugar around my house without seeing half of it disappear within hours. I'd even tried stashing a bag of caramels in my fire safe, and woke the next morning to find a bag full of empty wrappers locked inside.

When I stepped into my bathroom that night and found a pink sticky note in the center of my mirror, I just sighed, wondering what the creature wanted now. Usually its notes were pleasant, sometimes they made no sense for days, and occasionally they made requests.

As if Sonny, my pet sun conure, was perched on my shoulder solely because he was interested in what the candy thief had to say, I read the note aloud.

"'You'll want to dress pretty tomorrow.'" I frowned at the message. "Because I usually dress like a prison inmate?" Scoffing at the implied insult, I yanked open my medicine cabinet to grab for my face wash and found another note stuck to it. Figuring Sonny was invested now, I read it as well.

"'I just mean don't wear your sloppy jeans.' I don't have sloppy jeans!" I protested, though I was pretty sure I knew the pair the thief meant—they had a hole in the left knee. I didn't mention it aloud, but I wouldn't have worn them anyway. I certainly wasn't trying to impress Stan the way I had when we'd been dating, but I felt a certain responsibility to look presentable around him.

I plucked both notes down and set them on the counter as I went through my nightly routine. I don't know when I decided to start keeping all the thief's notes, but I had a box in my office that was slowly filling with brightly colored squares of paper covered in scribbled handwriting and curious doodles.

After I was brushed and washed and Sonny was tucked into his cage, I headed in to bed early, setting my alarm for seven so I'd have plenty of time to clean up, dress pretty, and get tea before meeting Stan at the hotel. I'd been asleep maybe twenty-five minutes when the terrified barking of a small dog jolted me awake.

I yelped involuntarily when my empathy swung outward toward the sound, picking up three distinct sets of emotions somewhere in front of my home. Immediately sucked into the panic and frustration coming from outside, I bolted upright and jumped to my feet. Consciousness hadn't fully claimed me yet, but I was mobile. I had no real direction for a minute or two, wandering in anxious circles around my bedroom until I stopped long enough to realize where the sound was coming from. I clipped my arm on the doorjamb as I rushed toward the front door. In that moment my empathy was screaming that something was wrong, that someone I cared about was in danger, and that I had to stop it.

I made it to the door, still barefoot and barely awake. I spent some time fumbling with the doorknob before I paused, blinked down at my hands in the dark, and woke up just enough to ask myself what the hell I was doing.

"Oh my god," I mumbled, scrubbing my hand over my face. "What is— What's—Sonny?" I looked around my living room, at a loss as I took in my surroundings for the first time. The dog was still barking and had now added in some long, panicked, howling whines. I wanted to be irritated at the sound, but there's nothing like empathy to make you empathetic. I was worried about the dog, wondering what could make any creature so terrified.

I unlocked the door as I stuffed my feet into my sneakers and then bolted out onto the lawn, heading straight toward where I felt the dog. It wasn't far, just at the end of my driveway, shifting foot to foot as it stared anxiously at something on the ground and barked spastically. When the terrier noticed me it yelped, suddenly caught between the desire to flee and the need to keep loudly announcing that it was distressed by whatever was hidden from view by my car.

A man yelled from across the street, "Shut your dog up!"

Irritation at his callousness burbled up inside me just as I stepped around the bumped enough to see that the dog was barking at a corpse.

"Oh shit," I said, dancing back a step. The dog let out a howling whine, pushing forward just enough to nudge the woman on the ground. Despite the fact that I could tell from the void of emotions that she was dead, I found myself waiting for her to move, to pat the dog on the head and say, 'It's okay, pooch, I'm fine.'

The dog started barking again, unable to keep still as it tried in vain to get its master's attention. A door slammed across the street and I looked up to find an older man I'd seen a time or two marching over.

"What the hell is—" he cut off as he saw what I was staring at. His emotions shifted like a sharp twist on a roller coaster, and I felt my stomach turn. "Oh my god. Linda?"

"I don't—" He didn't seem to hear my protest, already at a jog.

"Oh my god, Linda! What happened?" His eyes flicked to me as he closed in. I shook my head, but he wasn't in a state to listen. Worry spurted from him like an inner city hydrant on a hot day. I took a step back as he dropped down next to the woman. "Wake up, Linda."

Evidently placated by someone coming to the aid of its master, the dog stopped barking, letting out a long whine and dropping to its belly as the man tried to help Linda sit up.

I took another step back, shaking my head. She was dead, but I didn't want to be the bearer of bad news. I wanted to run back into my house, settle my churning stomach, and pretend I hadn't seen any of this.

"Greg?" I heard from across the street.

"Call the police, Helen!" Greg called back toward his wife.

"What's— Oh my god, Linda?"

"Helen, call an ambulance!" Greg insisted, shifting to lay Linda out as if he might revive her with CPR.

"I'll call," I offered, turning and rushing into my house without waiting for a response. The sounds of Greg and Helen worrying for the well-being of a corpse followed me over my threshold.

My first instinct after the police had left, and poor dead Linda had been carted off in the ambulance, was to call Chloe. She'd left for Bremerton maybe six hours before and I knew she wouldn't have minded the call, considering the circumstances. I also knew from her previous trips that she was unlikely to answer.

It took me over an hour to get my brain to calm down enough to go back to sleep, and when I woke up to my screeching alarm I was convinced I hadn't gotten more than ten minutes, tops. I considered hitting snooze, but the candy thief's suggestion that I dress well crept into my brain. Sighing as I realized that my promise to Stan trumped my desire to sleep away my emotional trauma, I hauled myself out of bed and toward the shower.

A mere two hours later, I was grumbling about the cost of parking as I maneuvered the hallways of the massive hotel, heading toward the meeting room in which the convention was being held. Mid-sip of my tea, I flagged down a woman in all black with a silver nametag, and gestured vaguely with my free hand.

"The convention?"

"You're a bit early," she said, irritation spiking behind her pleasant expression.

"I'm a friend of Mr. Sneedley." I wasn't sure if that was exactly true, but I was sure she didn't care about our past. The irritation burbled with cynicism, but her expression remained the same.

"I can show you back to the lobby and you can speak with the desk."

I wanted to be frustrated, but I got where she was coming from. Without my empathy, I probably would have assumed I was lying too. Nodding, I took a step back.

"I'll figure it out. No worries."

Without waiting for her to answer, I turned back toward the lobby as if taking her advice, and pulled my phone out of my bag. Stan answered on the first ring.

"Good morning, Stanley here."

"It's me," I said, stopping and stepping out of the center of the hallway. "I don't know where to go."

"I'll come get you, just give me a few minutes. Is that okay? Are you in the lobby?"

"I'm … not really sure where I am. I left the lobby and just started walking like I knew where I was going. I figured it would become apparent from there."

Stan let out a low chuckle. "I'll find you. Just stay out in the open."

"Don't jump into any dumbwaiters, got it."

Stan was quiet for a moment before saying, "Just a few minutes," and hanging up. His tone indicated he was worried about my potential behavior, and I felt a little ashamed. Deciding I was going to be good if it killed me, I leaned against the wall and slipped my phone back into my bag. Since I had the time, I set my tea on a stack of plastic chairs against the wall next to me, pulled the letters out and gave them another look-see. It was a little hard to concentrate with the events of the early morning swooshing in and out of my brain, but I managed to at least get my focus back onto what Stan had asked of me.

Norma Laby's letters were all hand-written on lined paper, her writing messy but legible. While her words weren't threatening in and of themselves, the girl made it clear she spent more time than one normally would thinking about Stan's books—and Stan.

She had entire essays about what she believed the significance behind certain names or characters might be. Even though she'd never asked for anything in return, Stan put sticky notes on some of the letters, saying he'd written her polite thank-you letters for her thoughts. These stopped a few months ago, and I was guessing that his agent or manager or someone had told him to stop encouraging her.

I didn't read all of the essays in depth, but the talk about Jameson James from *Murder in a Time of War* was particularly enlightening. She didn't seem to like him very much. She much preferred Moira O'Mara, the love-interest-slash-accidental-murderer. That was probably what had gotten to Stan, and I had to agree with his assessment that Norma was a little off.

"Good morning, Gwen."

I looked up and smiled as Stan walked over. He looked good today too, and part of me sighed wistfully. The teenager in me was quite taken by the pressed slacks, the corded sweater vest, and the white button-up shirt. He looked bright-eyed, well-rested, and very cute. Shuffling the pages into an uneven stack, I grabbed my tea and stepped close. To my surprise, Stan leaned in to kiss my cheek before gesturing down the way he'd come.

"It's this way, in the ballroom."

"Sounds fancier than I'm prepared for," I said as we started walking. Stan took a moment to look me over, and I felt myself straightening slightly as if the inspection was an important test.

"You look lovely," Stan said after a moment. My insides bloomed warm with glee and I considered that it had been much too long since a man had said something like that to me. Oh, Mel tells me frequently how attractive he finds me, but he doesn't count. I could be Madeline's ugly twin sister and he'd still consider me hot. If you consider yourself a woman, Mel is attracted to you. He's a rather simple creature when it comes to sex.

"When do they start letting people in?" I asked, before I could do something stupid like suggest we find a broom closet and relive the sweatier moments of our youth.

"Usually they open the doors a few minutes early. I'll be up on stage at the beginning, answering questions. I'm most excited about later, when I'll be doing a reading from *The Floating Airship*, my newest novel." Adorable pops and fizzles of mild excitement sparked off his skin like failed firecrackers, and I had trouble not pinching his cheeks.

I made quiet sounds of interest as we walked, and he continued.

"I'll sign things while some of the panels go on without me, but I will join in on a few of the others." He stepped forward to open a door into a short hallway, where I was greeted with a quietly bustling behind-the-scenes area. As we made our way down the hall, I was handed a little card with "Backstage Access" printed on it. I tucked it into my bag.

"Will you be able to stay for the whole con? Tomorrow will be mostly a repeat, but there will be different panels and likely different questions from the audience. Not everyone shows up both days, I find."

I wanted to go home immediately after and pass out to make up for the sleep I'd missed the night before, but I nodded.

"If you want me to, I'll clear my schedule for the rest of the weekend." I didn't mention that my schedule probably would have just been a solo trip to the movies, junk food, and the internet. "I read these, by the way." I gestured with the pages in my hand and leaned against the short staircase that led to the backstage area. Setting my tea down, I flipped through them.

"First, I'm going to confess that I don't read your books." Stan had no opinion on this, positive or negative. I kind of loved him for that. "So a lot of her essays don't make much sense to me. However, you're right to think something's off about her. I'm good with eccentrics," I wiggled my index finger in the air near my head, "so I should notice her if she gets close and be able warn you she's around. Though, if she's dressed up or something, I won't be able to give you a face to watch out for."

"Dressed up?" Stan tipped his head, reaching out and holding my tea steady as someone rolled a large table out onto stage nowhere near enough to put the cup in any danger.

"Don't people usually dress up as their favorite characters or something at these things?"

"Oh." Stan blinked, briefly deep in thought. "Perhaps. I don't have any outlandish outfits in my previous books, so perhaps I just haven't noticed. I can think of a few gentlemen who might have been Alan Allen or Valentina Valentine, but it was never specified." I cocked my head at the names, but they somehow made perfect sense for Stan. Distress was leaking out of him, but it was so mild I was in no danger of taking it in myself. I reached out to pat his shoulder, enjoying the fact that, just like in high school, his emotions were no more intense than a half-flat cup of soda water.

"I'm sure it's fine and you didn't miss anything. I'll just trust that everyone out there will be wearing their own faces."

A man stepped up next to Stan and asked politely if he could speak to him about the stage setup. I nodded, told him to go ahead, and then gestured back down the hall. I wanted to make my way into the con with everyone else, to get a feeling for what was about to go down.

Five

They might not have been robots, but I was willing to bet the Sneeds were cyborgs at the very least. Sneeds bustled amiably through the giant hall, waiting in well-coordinated lines, watching the low stage, or sticking to small cliques and chatting politely. Regardless of where each Sneed stood, they all managed to be just about equidistant from each other, as if there was a grid of personal space and everyone knew the boundaries of their square.

There were a few food booths, each serving low-fat, vegetarian food with a bevy of vegan options. I considered buying myself some cookies, but they were touted as sugar-free, with gluten-free options available, and I was suddenly less interested. You can take my life, but you'll never take my sugar!

Gluten, I could take or leave.

I had armed myself with various types of painkillers for the weekend, anticipating debilitating headaches from being surrounded by hundreds of people for two days, but it was proving to be quite a pleasant experience. Somehow Stan had managed to write books that only people very similar to him were interested in buying. The emotions floating around the room were calm and collected, with little bits of nerdy glee shooting into the sky here and there. No one was arguing, shouting, fighting, or waving a sword around and screaming about fake revenge.

The items on sale were all handmade: stickers, sweaters, scarves, buttons, and the like. One woman did get a few heads turning with an amigurumi squid holding little Scrabble tiles in its eight arms. She was courteous when I asked to see what the tiles said, but I didn't ask her to elaborate when I read the letters: INNOCENT. Apparently I was one of only a few attendees who didn't have an opinion on her craft.

At the end of Stan's first panel, he excused himself to the back for a short break, and I decided to move toward the edge of the room again. I still hadn't a sense of anyone acting strangely, but I thought maybe if I stuck to the edge I'd have a better shot. Really, I was just out of ideas.

As I took up residence next to one of the scarf booths, I felt a peculiar set of emotions off to my left. I glanced over and found an attractive man smiling at me from near a booth that was selling shirts with quotes from Stan's books printed on them. I smiled back and the stranger took that as an invitation.

The closer he got, the more I wondered what the hell he was doing here.

"You don't look like you belong," he said as he walked up. I shrugged a shoulder, looked down at my outfit and then back up at him. I'd chosen a bright red skirt, a sleeveless white blouse and red heels. My messenger bag was black with cartoonish expressions of onomatopoeia across its surface, and I'd gone with dramatic eye makeup.

"I was going to say the same to you, actually."

He raised a brow, stepped back, and looked down at his own outfit. His slacks were well pressed, but his t-shirt was a bright blue that brought out his eyes. Other than having the same coloring as Stan—blond and blue—he looked as out of place as I did. We were the only two in the hall besides the hotel employees who weren't wearing plain beige or white. It must've been a Sneed uniform or something.

"I think I look nice."

"You do look nice, but bright blue?" I made a sound of admonishment with my tongue. "For shame."

"You're one to talk, Red."

"Well, I'm here for work, so to speak. What's your excuse?"

"Oh, I'm just here to start trouble."

I smirked and shifted my weight subtly closer, looking up into his eyes. Not quite a head taller than me, he was narrowly built, his physique a slim invitation beneath his sensible clothing. He had good looks and charm, blue eyes to kill for, and dark blond hair. His face looked sweet, but there was something puckish about it: his angled jaw or full lips, maybe. I had no problem believing he was here just to be a nuisance.

"Trouble? Here? Good luck with that."

He winked at my sarcasm before moving to stand next to me and pointing toward a group at the center of the room. They were all munching on the undecorated, sugarless cookies I'd seen in one of the booths, their conversation quiet. I let myself smile at the fact that my new friend had violated the personal space grid and was pressed nearly against my shoulder. He smelled pretty good.

"Ten gets you twenty I can get them arguing in under five minutes."

I let out a short bark of laughter, sure from their emotions that I'd be making twenty bucks. "Bet's on."

A sneaky sort of pride snuck into the lust I could feel curling through him and he smiled down at me, reaching his hand across his body to offer his palm to me. I took it, shook, and let my fingers caress his skin when he pulled back. Pleased I was returning his flirting, he gave me another wink—with the other eye this time; ambi-ocular, oh my—and then stepped away toward the center of the room without another word.

It was entertaining watching him make his way into their midst. It reminded me of a group of bunnies seeing a fat, well-fed wolf walking toward them. They weren't quite willing to scatter, but they did subtly try to close ranks. He just used it as an excuse to sling his arms over two pairs of shoulders and lean between them.

I couldn't hear what they were saying, but the bunnies—ah, Sneeds—got steadily less nervous and more agitated as Mystery Man spoke. Whatever subject he'd brought up was clearly not a happy one, and I briefly wondered if he was cheating and just calling them all vicious names. Within minutes the two he'd stepped between had set their cups down on the edge of a nearby booth and begun chewing their cookies more hastily than was polite. Soon there was frustrated head shaking and ever so slightly elevated voices.

Another minute passed and my new friend stepped back, murmured something with a nod, his expression dire, and then slowly backed away. Unconcerned by his departure, they took the cause up amongst themselves. While there wasn't going to be a full-on brawl, he had certainly managed to start something. Satisfied they were as riled up as they could get, I was guessing, he headed back my way. There was extra swagger in his gait.

"If you don't have cash, I'll take your name and number instead."

"Hmm," I responded, grinning at his confidence. There was an electricity to him that I hadn't felt around a man in a while. Again, Mel doesn't count, as his interest isn't a pleasant undercurrent but a downed power line in a lake full of electric eels. Giving a small nod, I broke eye contact and glanced past him to the still-squabbling group as I dug into my bag for a business card.

"How did you do that? I'm new to this whole scene, but I didn't think something like that was possible with this lot." He shrugged, but it was cocky, faux humility. Before he could answer, I jerked my chin toward the group. "Up to six now, very impressive."

As I slipped my card out of my bag, he stepped up next to me again, making sure his arm pressed against mine. We stayed silent for a bit, both taking the time to watch the heated—well, warmed—debate. Other fans stepped up to watch, whispering about it in hushed tones; I wondered if they were worried they would be noticed and pulled in. I focused my senses on the Sneeds nearby and found a collective crackle of interest and apprehension. Finally breaking the silence, my new friend lifted a hand again and pointed to the left side of the group.

"There are two schools of thought about *Drowning in a Sea of Water*. One—"

"Which book is that?"

"The one about the aquarium and the Scrabble tournament."

"Aquarium. Schools. Nice."

"Thank you," he said, his arm still up and pointing. "Some of the Sneeds posit that the squid didn't actually do it. They think there was foul play afoot—atentacle?—and that Stanley will bring the squid back for another book in order to redeem him. Her. It? I don't know squid anatomy."

"And the other Sneeds?" At my question, he shifted his hand slightly to point at the other side of the squabble.

"Oh, *they're* convinced that Stanley's books are perfectly clear and concise just as they are. His grammar, of course, is impeccable; how could one misunderstand his meaning?"

"Ah, that explains the Scrabble tiles." I peered around, looking for the girl with her little knitted cephalopod. When I didn't see her, I glanced up at the stage and saw Stan had reemerged. He was setting up with two other people for another panel.

"I'm a little surprised you don't know how big this controversy has gotten. Which side do you fall on?"

"Oh, I don't read the books."

His brows went up, intrigue puffing out of him in a misty cloud. He wasn't quite as temperate in his emotions as those around us, but I appreciated the way he felt just the same. I'm willing to admit that was partly just because I like the way he looked in those pants, though.

"You're not a fan, then? And yet you're still here. I take it you're some sort of spy? An infiltrator? A traitor to the cause?"

"A traitor, sure," I agreed, thinking of how my marriage had broken up. Without elaborating, I stepped around to face him head-on. "I'm Gwen, Stanley Sneedley's ex-wife."

I jolted as shock stabbed out of him, embedding itself in my chest like a half a dozen heated knives. I managed to avoid the grunt that wanted to wheeze through my lips, but I found myself stepping back as if it would help with the pain. Despite the fact that my confession had surprised the hell out of him, his pleasant expression remained until he saw me stumble.

Before he could ask about my strange behavior, I smiled tightly up at him and forced out an uncomfortable laugh, trying to play my behavior off as if it were perfectly normal.

"But don't be jealous; he's not really my type anymore." I hoped he wouldn't notice the strain in my voice.

"Well, clearly," he agreed, still watching me, but letting me have my dignity. The mild curiosity that had been woven within his lust before had grown to take over his psyche, but he didn't ask why I'd reacted the way I had. "Otherwise you two would still be married."

"Touché." I smiled, gesturing with my business card toward his chest. "And you?"

"Oh, I'm exactly your type." His easy smile was back as he reached out to pinch the card between two fingers. He didn't take it, though, watching me to make sure I still wanted to hand it over. When I let go and dropped my hands, I felt a pleased little thread of delight soothe away the last of his shock. Within seconds it was like the only thing he'd felt at all was attraction.

"I'm Owen." He pocketed the card with his left hand and offered his right. We shook again, and this time it was he who refused to completely break contact.

The announcer on stage called politely for quiet, and I turned my attention forward and then briefly over to the little group Owen had disturbed. They went silent immediately, but there were a few contrary glances thrown around before they let the fight go. Two of them exchanged handshakes, murmured something that seemed to relax the shoulders of the others, and then they all turned to the front. When the room went silent, Owen and I stepped away from the booth we were haunting and watched.

"As you know, Mr. Sneedley has finished his latest novel." The crowd gave a well-mannered cheer. "While it won't be out until the end of November, he has graciously agreed to answer questions about it and do a short reading from *The Floating Airship*. So, those of you interested in asking questions, please feel free to come to the front, take a seat, and when the microphone goes out to the crowd Mr. Sneedley will answer them."

Owen looked toward me and gave a smile when I met his eyes. "I take it you and Sneedley remain good friends?"

"Um, sort of." I dropped my gaze as I let out an embarrassed laugh and couldn't fight the smile that pulled at my mouth. Unsure how to explain our relationship without actually explaining what an ass I'd been, I took a slow breath, looking back to Owen and hoping my silence wouldn't be taken as insult.

"You said you were here for work, earlier?" he asked after a moment, letting me have my secret shame. I nodded, and he continued. "What's a mid-level, milquetoast author need with a beautiful therapist, anyway?"

From lovely to beautiful in just a few hours; I was doing pretty well for myself. I shrugged a shoulder, remembering as he'd asked that I really was there for a reason and that it wasn't to flirt with attractive troublemakers.

"It's sort of a personal favor."

"A dirty favor?"

I laughed, giddily amused at the idea of Stan ever asking me such a thing. Even had we remained friends over the last decade, it still would have been a ridiculous notion. Owen laughed with me, pleased at himself, and I realized I was going to have to get back to work before I let my hormones and his emotions take over. I had a backstage pass, after all; it probably wouldn't have been difficult to find a dim, private corner. Chloe's comment about how I won't date came to mind and I felt my sex drive perk up and remind me that it had been a really long time since I'd felt anything more intense than Madeline's aura. I could tell Owen would happily help in that regard, but I forced good sense to stuff my hormones into a dark closet, and sighed.

"Not dirty, but important. In fact, I should get back to it and you're kind of a distraction."

"A good one?"

"I think it would depend on the situation," I said, shaking my head as I fought off a smile. "Right now, no. Not a good one. "

"Does that mean you want your card back?" he asked. I considered him, making a show of it. I ran my gaze slowly down and then back up his body, and let it rest on his face, on his mouth. The lust that had been a curling, soft twist within him grew, strengthened by arousal. I found it was aggressive, like being felt up in the backseat of a tiny car by an excitable and ham-handed first boyfriend.

Something about his inherent confidence made me want to turn things around and press against him, grab him inappropriately and demand we go find that dim corner. I was sure it was partly because it had been a long time since I'd had sex, and partly because a little piece of my brain said I shouldn't let him think he was in charge.

"No, you can call me." Sighing out a breath like I was getting bored with him, I lifted my hand daintily in the air and gestured to nothing. "I can't promise I'll answer."

"Fair enough." He nodded. I took a step back as I looked toward the stage.

"Since Stan has everyone's attention, I think it's a good time for me to get back to my work. It was nice meeting you, Owen."

"Likewise, Gwen. I hope you answer when I call."

"We'll see," I said with a coy smile, before turning and putting distance between us.

Six

Sunday at SneedCon was very similar to Saturday. I came across most of the same people, heard a few of the same questions, and ate most of the same bland food. Owen didn't make an appearance on day two, and I was an even mix of relieved and disappointed. I'd barely been able to keep my empathy to myself the day before, seeking him out whenever I could until he left an hour after we'd met. He wasn't always easy to spot from his emotions alone, but any time I caught sight of him across the ballroom, I'd felt myself blush.

He'd caught me looking a few times, but hadn't engaged me past winking or smiling my way.

Stan was finishing up the last panel, about to start setting up for another round of book signing. I sighed, irritated that I had essentially wasted two full days standing around and being of no help to him. Absolutely no one seemed like the type to have written the letters that Norma had sent. The people who'd asked questions or approached Stan had all been polite, with nothing untoward lurking in their psyches. No one seemed odd or threatening, or even rude. It was like being surrounded by Canadians.

Part of me wanted to shove someone down just to see if *they* would apologize for it.

I spent the rest of the con near the stage, watching the signings, staring mostly at my ex-husband. It made me feel good to see him so fulfilled, doing something with his life he enjoyed. It said something unpleasant about me that a little part of my brain had, prior to our reunion, been convinced that my leaving had ruined his life. I chose to ignore my egotism and focus on how happy for him I was in the moment.

By the end of the convention, when the Sneeds were all exchanging information and helping the vendors clean up their booths, Stan and I left out the back together.

"That was nice," I commented. He nodded, and I felt an exhausted kind of contentment puff out of him. I reached out and rubbed his shoulder. "You want to get dinner?"

"I am pretty hungry," he said, before smiling. "But you knew that."

I nodded. "Come on, I know a really great vegetarian place."

"You do?" he asked, genuinely surprised. I hooked my arm into his and steered him toward the parking garage.

"Not because I want to; I still eat everything." I gave him a wink, making sure he knew I half-meant it in a dirty way. He shook his head over a smile. "Chloe's vegan."

"Oh, that's nice."

"It usually is, yeah. Sometimes she makes me eat vegetables and I have to threaten her with bodily harm, but a lotta times there are cookies."

"Well, no wonder you don't mind."

We idly chatted about his parents as we got to my car, got further in depth about my sister's perfect family as we drove, and paused the conversation as we entered the restaurant. The waitress seated us quickly out in the atrium and Stan took in the scenery with a sort of brain-dead pleasure that I'd never seen on him before. I ordered a pot of my favorite tea and Stan asked for the same. With the sound of the burbling fountain to my left, I reached across the table to touch his hand. He looked up at me blankly for a second and then shook his head.

"I'm sorry. I'm always a little drained after conventions. I adore them, but I'm not really built for all the attention."

"Oh, don't worry. I just wanted to make sure you weren't falling asleep." I pointed at one of the menu items. "Don't waste brainpower; that's the tastiest sandwich on the menu."

"I don't know if I should trust your judgment, Miss Eats Everything, but I'm going to for now. What are you getting?"

"Pizza." I snorted. "I'm surprised you even had to ask."

"Right, silly me." Stan smiled and watched me as I folded and stacked the menus, setting them at the edge of the table. Finally I felt a spark in his emotions and he perked up. "I got a list of the attendees yesterday evening. I don't think I remembered to mention it before you left. Norma wasn't on the list for either day. Did you catch anything unpleasant?"

I thought of poor deceased Linda in my driveway, but didn't mention Friday night at all. I didn't want to distress Stan when he was riding happily on a wave of post-convention bliss.

"Sadly, no. I did laps around that place, bought food, harassed vendors, wore red, and no one got my radar buzzing."

The waitress brought our tea and Stan poured his, ignoring the sugar packets on the table. I upended six of them into my pot, stirred it, and waited as Stan ordered. Once the waitress left the table, I closed the teapot lid and started to speak. Stan interrupted my intake of breath, which I blamed on his sleepiness.

"Someone got your radar buzzing, but I'm fairly certain his name wasn't Norma."

I sat there, my mouth still open as if my question had gotten backed up somewhere behind my tongue and I was just waiting for it to wrestle its way out. Stan let out a laugh that bordered on a snort and then sipped his tea, possibly to cover it up. I shut my mouth and tried to fight my unnecessary embarrassment.

"No. His name wasn't Norma."

"You two looked like a pair, the only spots of color in the room."

"Yeah, what's up with that?"

Stan shrugged, set his tea down. "I'm not really sure. I just attract a certain type of fan. I mean, I guess I don't really use a lot of colorful clothing in my books, though that's changed in *Airship*."

"Are all your fans vegetarian?"

"Possibly. I don't see any meat talk on the forums."

"You actually participate there?"

"Occasionally." He leaned back in his chair. I watched him let go of his strict posture, and it made me think of high school again. "They're all so nice, and a lot of their conversation isn't even about the books. If someone asks a question, I do my best to answer."

"How many people ask about the squid?"

Stan's lips pulled up in a crooked smile and I felt a little slice of smugness in him that surprised me.

"No one. They're too polite."

"So, you just let the controversy go like that? For shame!" I teased, leaning back in my own chair.

"Right now I'm fine with it. It doesn't cause too much trouble, and ... who knows." He shrugged. "One day I may want to settle the debate. Right now, I haven't decided. To be honest, I hadn't even considered there was another way to interrogate the text. I wrote a story and hoped people would like it."

"Well, that's all you really need to do."

"True."

Our food came, and we both dove in. As Stan ate, he seemed to wake up a bit, getting more animated. We exchanged stories from our ten-year radio silence, and as we finished eating, I decided it was time to bring up the elephant in the room.

"So," I said as he lifted his napkin to dab at his face as if he were as messy an eater as me. "It's been ten years."

"It has indeed," Stan said. His gaze drifted to the table as he realized what my tone was really saying. "And you want to talk about it?"

"You don't?"

Still watching the table, he took a deep breath and straightened up, as if perfect posture could ward off unpleasantness.

"I wasn't going to bring it up."

"How could you not?"

"I ... didn't want to be rude."

I watched him, a smile pulling hard at my mouth. "You didn't want to be rude? Oh, Stanley. I never deserved you."

Stan's expression went sad and I felt a soft sort of pity pool inside him. "Don't do that to yourself."

I held up a hand. "I did enough to you." Though the pain wasn't fresh, the guilt seemed to renew itself any time I thought too hard about what I'd done. "I'm not sure why you don't hate me— No." I shook my head. "That's not true. You don't hate me because you're a better person than that."

"I don't hate you because I'm sure I share the blame."

I blinked up at him. "For my adultery? I made that decision on my own. It was cowardly and weak and every time I think about ..." My nose stung, my lip trembled. Stan just lowered his gaze to the table again while I fought off the urge to sob. "I did everything wrong. You were wonderful and I just didn't appreciate it."

"I don't think that was it," Stan said, his tone surprisingly forceful. "After you left I thought a lot about what had happened, how we had been doing. With time came clarity and I realized that we weren't happy, not how we'd been in high school. We shouldn't have gotten married, just because we were young. I agree that your decision to run without trying to work things out was cowardly, but it would have ended anyway. We were too different. Please, I don't hate you, and I don't think you should hate yourself."

I watched him and, though I could feel myself tearing up, it wasn't the same forceful wailing that had wanted to push through my lips shortly before. I was sad for what we were, and that I hadn't given it the respect it deserved. After a few silent seconds, I nodded once.

"Okay then. But I'm paying for dinner."

"I should at least—"

"Nope. Don't argue or I'll make a scene."

Distress passed over Stan's features at the idea, and he nodded. I laughed and pulled out my debit card to make sure the waitress didn't have a chance to charge him. Once we were paid and on our way through the parking lot, Stan checked his watch. Surprise gurgled within him.

"I can't believe how early it is. Is your place far? I'd love to see it," he said. I arched a brow at him across the hood of my car. I couldn't see the blush across his cheeks, but I felt it. Before he could start backpedaling or explaining that he hadn't meant anything intimate, I yanked open my door and climbed in. When he was seated next to me, I patted him on the leg.

"I'm teasing. I'd love to show you my place. You can pet my bird."

"I'm immensely glad right now that you don't have a cat."

I laughed as I started the car, glad that what little mischief I'd been able to rub off on him in high school hadn't disappeared.

Stan never made it back to his hotel, but it wasn't for salacious reasons. We spent a long time catching up, and I put him to bed in my guest room, passing out in my own bed shortly after. I dropped him off at his hotel before heading in to work, late for a Monday morning. I had just under an hour until my first appointment, but Chloe still teased me for being tardy.

"Please tell me you're late because you had a torrid one-night stand." Chloe followed me into my office and waggled her brows at me when I turned to face her after I dropped my purse on the couch. I sighed, but put a small smile on my face as if I was trying to hold in a secret. Chloe followed me out of my office and to the records room, poking me rhythmically in the back as we went. I remained silent until she finally made a whining sound. I laughed and poured my tea, upending the sugar container over the cup.

"I did have an overnight guest."

"Oh, do tell."

"It was Stan," I said, putting the mug to my lips as if to hide a smile. It was still too hot to drink, but the tea smelled good. Chloe rolled her eyes and snorted, turning away from me. I wasn't sure at first if she thought I was joking, but she shook her head.

"Your ex-husband doesn't count. I know you."

"You know me what?" I followed her out into the waiting area

"You're not gonna dip your toe in that pool again, come on." Chloe took a seat at her desk, spun in her chair to face me as I followed her. I stood there, annoyed that she knew me so well.

"I could. I could be dipping! There could be dipping—and not of toes! Dipping of dirty things!"

"Uh huh," Chloe said, dismissively. I sighed and gave in.

"Fine, no dipping. He slept in the guest room after we talked. We had ten years to catch up on."

I took a sip of my tea, regretted it instantly and felt stupid for not remembering how hot it still was.

"I wouldn't mind having sex, though. Not," I clarified, "with Stan. That pool has sailed. But sex, all the same."

Chloe ignored my mixed metaphor and jerked a thumb upward, in Mel's direction. I glowered at her and shook my head rapidly, hoping she left it at that and didn't verbalize her suggestion. Eager to change the subject, I moved on to more pleasant topics than sex with Mel. "I found another dead body Friday night."

Chloe went tense, all trace of humor disappearing. "Where? Is everything okay?"

"I wasn't in danger. A neighbor had a heart attack practically on my lawn. Her damn dog woke me up and I ran outside to find her, just ... well, like the other guy." I shifted uncomfortably at the memory. Chloe was watching me, alarm flaring within her.

"Two in the same week? That's weird," she said, her gaze going distant. Her alarm settled into grim determination. I wondered what she was thinking, and why she felt like she was preparing for something.

"I'm not in any danger," I pointed out. "I know it's called a heart *attack* but I don't think one's going to jump out of a dark corner with an axe and yell 'rawr!'"

Chloe's eyes snapped to my face and she snorted out a laugh like my comment surprised her. After a moment, she shook her head.

"You're right. You can't die from someone else's heart problems. But I'm restricting your sugar intake, just in case your heart gets any ideas."

"What?" I demanded, stomping my foot. "You can't do that!"

"Too late. I'm getting rid of the rest of that candy you bought Friday, and you can't stop me."

"I'll eat it first," I threatened, whirling to rush into my office. I set my tea down and opened the bottom drawer where I normally kept my purse, aiming to devour as many handfuls of chocolate as I could. The plastic bags I'd stashed there before leaving for the weekend sat empty and flattened, under a sticky note that just had a smiley face drawn on it.

Chloe didn't bother to ask about the screeching string of cuss words I let loose. She'd stopped consoling me about losing sugar to the candy thief back in January, and no longer considered my rage over the creature worth addressing.

My first two appointments went off without a hitch. My Mondays had become significantly less horrible since my least favorite client moved our appointments to Fridays. Granted, my Fridays were now worse, but the fact that they led into the weekends made seeing Mrs. Q marginally more tolerable. I was bent over a drawer in the squat filing cabinet in the records room when Chloe yelled out to me from her desk.

"Gwen, you have a visitor!"

"Just a minute!" I yelled back, finding the file I needed and pulling it out just enough to peel back the front and check a date.

"In some parts of the animal kingdom that position would be

considered an intimate invitation."

My brain recognized the voice and the rest of my body flooded with bashful excitement. I jerked upward, turning to face the source, and found Owen standing just inside the doorway. The folder I'd been holding had come with me as I'd twisted, and its contents now littered the floor. I looked down at the paperwork, swore, and then crouched down to pick them up.

Before I could say anything, Owen was already on his way over, crouching down to my level to help me clean up. We didn't say anything until the paperwork was secure in its folder again, at which point we looked at each other.

"I would have called, but you did threaten not to answer," he explained as he stood up and extended a hand toward me.

I grinned up at him for a moment before squeezing his fingers. He pulled me to my feet with a subtle tug toward him, and I followed it. There was a certain bold directness to him that I really enjoyed. I broke the stare after a bit, letting go of his hand and moving to set the folder back in the drawer. He was quiet as I knocked the drawer shut and then gestured past him to the hallway.

"Did you come to avail yourself of my services?" I asked as I walked past him toward my office. Chloe pretended to be very busy at her desk—shuffling papers, clicking pens, moving the mouse around like it accomplished something—as we stepped out. I paused next to her desk and Owen did the same, tucking his hands into his pockets as he answered.

"That depends on what you'd be willing to do for me."

"For you? Or to you?"

Owen smiled toothily, and I caught the excitement sparking off his skin. Chloe gave a fake cough, and Owen tried to hide his laugh. I gestured to my office and took the moment he glanced over to turn and stick my tongue out at Chloe. She just winked obnoxiously and moved her seat to give us our undivided attention.

I sighed and hissed, "Oh jeez."

Turning my back defiantly on Chloe, I gripped the back of Owen's elbow so I could lead him into my office. Once we were alone and I'd knocked the door nearly shut, I slid my hand down his sleeve before letting go, making sure he noticed the lengthy contact. He stayed close as he looked around the room, turning slowly before landing his gaze directly on mine.

"Nice place."

"Thanks. The couch is good for stretching out on, sharing all your darkest secrets."

"And desires?" Owen asked, his voice low. I bit my lip, wondering if he was this bold with all potential dates or if I was just sending out all the right signals.

"If you like." I considered kissing him then, just grabbing his collar and pulling him close in a frenzy of lust and excitement. I could tell from the way he was watching me, the way his emotions rubbed against me like a cat in heat, that he would have been game.

I could feel Chloe out in the waiting room though, her amusement tinged with a bit of worry that I didn't quite understand, and it kept me grounded.

"So," I said, shifting my footing slightly to step back without making it obvious that I felt the distance was necessary to my self-control. Owen mirrored my action. "Had you called, what would we have talked about?"

"I would have invited you to lunch in, say," he lifted his wrist as if to check his watch, but didn't look away from my face, "now?"

Chloe's chair creaked out in the waiting room, and I considered that she was probably leaning in to get an earful of what we were saying. Sighing, I rolled my eyes and held up one finger, silently asking Owen to wait. Grabbing the knob, I yanked the door open and found Chloe twisting with a yelp to face her desk as if she hadn't been eavesdropping.

I smiled at her and said, "Oh Ms. Warren, is my lunch hour free?"

"Well, hmm." Chloe said, masking her face in innocence. "Just give me a moment while I check."

I rolled my eyes to Owen and found him grinning at the show we were putting on. Chloe hummed as she opened my calendar on the computer and then turned back to me. "You have a one-thirty and then a three-thirty after that. Will you need more than ninety minutes for lunch?"

I turned back to Owen and lifted a brow, hoping he'd caught Chloe's meaning. He just shrugged, lifting his hands to waist level, making it clear it was up to me how much time we spent away from the office and what we did with it. I sighed, tempted but determined to keep my head on straight.

"One-thirty is fine. I'll be back by then." I reached out and offered my hand to Owen, pulling him out into the lobby when he took it. Chloe watched us quietly as we headed out, but called after us as we stepped out into the hallway.

"You hear that, Owen? She's got a curfew! You bring her back in one piece."

I wasn't sure if the threat I'd heard in her tone was serious or imagined.

Seven

Usually an early lunch saw me invading The Internets café for some of their hot beverages and internet-themed pastries. I wanted a mellower atmosphere, though, so we ended up at a little Thai place down the street. Once the menu small talk had been exhausted and we both knew what we wanted, Owen leaned back in his chair, watching me. His curiosity was back, grabby and determined as it had been right after he found out I'd been married to Stan. I thought I knew what he wanted to talk about, so I gestured toward him as if to say, 'go ahead.'

"There's something different about you," he said, surprising me.

"Different good or bad?"

"Oh, definitely good, but not necessarily human."

Swallowing hard, I stiffened, unsure if he meant that metaphorically. Chloe had quickly picked up on something different about me, but she hadn't asked about my empathy it until I'd brought it up. If Owen knew about people like me, he was being surprisingly candid about it.

"Meaning?" I asked when I was sure my voice wouldn't squeak.

He tipped his head, gave me a look that said, *Oh come now. Don't play that game.* Out loud, he said, "Meaning you've got a little something else going for you. Mind reader?"

"Not quite," I said, still unsure how I should feel over him pegging me so easily. There were many reasons I didn't talk to strangers about my empathy, but I felt no malice in Owen. He was curious, but not in a worrisome way. To him, my irregularity was no more unusual than someone being able to roll their tongue. "I read emotions, feel what people are feeling."

"Ah," he breathed, leaning forward. The curiosity was turning to something else, intrigue mixed with delight, maybe. I thought I could sense a note of nostalgia in him, but I couldn't fathom why.

"You're not going to ask me to prove it, to tell you what you're feeling?" I asked.

"Well, I already know, don't I?" He was teasing me. I rolled my eyes over a laugh and nodded.

"Fair enough. Do you ..." I waggled my fingers toward him. "Do anything special?"

"I do plenty," he offered with a wink. "But nothing preternatural. I've met a lot of people like you, though."

"Way to make a girl feel special."

"You're special, Gwen. Not just because of your powers."

"Oh," I said, before a flustered giggle snuck through. Had it really been so long since I'd been interested in a man that I was turning into a teenager at the slightest compliment? Chloe was right; I needed to get out more. "That's a good line."

He laughed and shook his head. "It's not exactly one you get to use a lot, is it? But you gotta go for it when you get a chance to say something that cheesy."

"I'll give you that," I said. He met my eyes intently, and his smile said very clearly that he hoped that wasn't all I'd give him.

The waitress came by, brought our drinks, took our orders. He sipped his tea until she was out of earshot again and then mirrored my earlier gesture, giving me the go ahead.

"How'd you know?" I asked.

"That you're special?"

"Yeah. You don't—I don't really talk about what I can do. Chloe—my assistant knows. Family, one or two friends. Usually the men I date have no clue."

"Oh, is this a date?" he asked, feigning shock. I shrugged my shoulders.

"Well, you're the one paying."

"Am I?"

I narrowed my eyes and leaned in close. "One way or another, yeah."

He laughed, genuinely amused by my false threat. Leaning forward, he propped his elbows on the table and linked his fingers.

"It's my job to notice, to know about people like you. And ... those who might not be people."

My brows jumped, though I wasn't sure why I was surprised. If he knew about humans who could read minds, it shouldn't have shocked me that he knew we weren't the only oddities running around.

"So ... what sort of job requires a specialty like yours?" I asked.

"Well, I don't work in a nice office with a couch and a lovely assistant. Essentially, I handle problems the police can't. There are creatures out there that can do a lot of damage if they set their minds to it. There are even people whose powers far exceed yours—" He paused and held his hand up as if worried he'd insulted me; it was a courtesy, I could tell. He didn't actually think he'd hurt my feelings. "I'm assuming."

"You assume right. I'm just a notch above a stage magician, really."

"I handle those problems."

"And you're handling a problem right now?"

"Oh, I don't consider you *much* of a problem," he teased.

"Careful," I said, realizing his tactic was to avoid the question. I let him. "Or you won't get to handle me at all."

Sitting up straight as if chastised, he held his hands up in surrender. "Please, forgive me."

"Maybe," I said. "If you buy me dessert."

Back at the office, we stood outside the door in my second-floor hallway and finished our conversation about authors we liked and books we'd read. On the end of a sentence, he slid a hand around my waist and pulled me in close for a kiss. He was slow, giving me the chance to lean away or tell him no. His lips were soft, his arm warm against my back. I put a hand to his cheek and then up into his hair. Taking that as further invitation, he brought his other hand to rest on the side of my ribs, his thumb teasing the side of my breast.

I smiled, not sure if I was feeling ticklish or embarrassed, and it broke the kiss. His eyes stayed closed a second longer than mine but he watched me step back, keeping a hand on my waist.

I cleared my throat daintily and spoke. "We should have dinner tonight, really see where this is going." He smiled, and I knew we were both well aware where things would end up.

"I'll pick you up. Here, if you're not comfortable giving out your home address."

"Such a gentleman," I purred, deciding I trusted him enough to tell him where I lived. Like I'd told Stan, I'm good at sniffing out crazy, and there wasn't a trace of it on Owen. The only things he wanted to do to me I knew I would enjoy.

"I'll pick you up and cook you dinner. I'm renting a house while I'm here."

"You cook?" I asked as I pushed open the office door. "I may not let you leave Seattle." Owen's hand stayed on my hip until I walked through the door.

Chloe looked up from a book that I was sure she'd just grabbed to cover any eavesdropping she'd been doing, and smiled at us. She'd left a pen and a notepad on the desk in easy reach. I rolled my eyes at her, but she just winked cheekily.

As I bent to write my address, I dipped a little lower than was normal before turning to face Owen.

"When in the animal kingdom …" I said as I handed him the sticky note.

He smiled and gripped my hand deliberately as he took the note. "I'll pick you up at eight?"

I nodded and he looked past me to Chloe.

"Ma'am," he said, miming the tip of a hat. Without another word, he turned and left. Chloe pounced as soon as he was out of earshot.

"Spill it, every detail down to you two sucking face outside the office."

I can't tell you why I started blushing at that moment. I've never been shy about men or talking about dating before. Chloe and I could get pretty raunchy in our descriptions of gentlemen callers and their various parts. Something about Owen, though, made me feel embarrassed. Chloe's excessive suspicion wasn't helping. She didn't trust him, and I wasn't sure why.

"Well, we met at the con, and then he showed up here."

"Coincidence?"

"No, no. He won my business card in a bet."

"A sexy bet?"

I snorted. "No. He started an argument for me, between some Sneeds."

"The squid thing?" Chloe asked, surprising me. I nodded.

"Does everyone know about that except me?"

"If you actually read those books in your closet instead of keeping them under layers of shoes, you'd know."

I went stiff as a board, shame flooding through me in a tingling rush. Chloe nodded, a knowing smile parting her lips.

"Oh yeah. I've seen them."

"I've got to get ready for my one-thirty," I squeaked, twisting and fleeing to my office, all the giddiness I'd worked up over Owen gone in a flash.

Despite Chloe's teasing, my good mood returned and hung around right up until I got into the elevator at the end of the day. Mel stood inside, his emotions still an unusually mild fizz.

"You're still being weird," I said as the doors shut. He blinked at me as if he hadn't realized I'd gotten on the elevator.

"Oh, hey Gwen. Come to give the security guards a show?" Mel sashayed the short distance to me but I stood my ground and just waved a hand in front of his face as if I was testing his sight. It wasn't the fact that our building doesn't have security guards that confused me.

"What is this? What's happening here?"

"I'm suggesting we have elevator sex. What else could be happening?"

"No," I said, before smiling. "That's not happening. Your mojo is broken. I think I actually like you better this way."

Mel's head snapped back, his thick brows furrowing. As faces went, his was pretty spectacular, but with the pout on he was no more alluring than a grumpy cartoon Batman.

"My mojo is fine. You shut up about my mojo." Without warning, he pushed against me again, locking his arm around my back and pressing me to his sculpted chest. "I'll show you my mojo," he murmured. His voice broke, making him sound like a teenager trying to seduce someone on a bet.

Normally something like this would have probably caused me to vomit right into his mouth, but whatever Mrs. Q had done to him three days before had made him not only tolerable but actually somewhat pathetic. His emotions were benign, the worst part about them being the occasional, spastic jump against my skin.

The doors to the elevator opened and I just shook my head, shoving him away. He barely fought me, his grip breaking like a wet strip of paper.

"I've got a date to get ready for. You ..." I was backing out of the elevator and halfway to the back door to The Internets as I tried to decide how to finish the sentence. "I don't think there's any help for you, but if there's a mojo doctor, you should go see her."

"You and I should play doctor!" he called after me. I waved a hand dismissively back at him as I pushed into the café and headed straight for the counter. The place was packed with college students dressed in all manner of strange outfits, all inspired by pop culture. There were Starfleet uniforms, cowls and capes, all genders and body types rocking the slave Leia outfit, and enough noise to wake the dead.

"Yo," Holly said as I approached the counter. The weary look on her face wasn't half as bad as the brick-heavy swamp of exhaustion surrounding her. I could tell she wasn't exactly unhappy about being so overworked, but she still needed a break. She enjoys her job, but she's only human.

"Still no Madeline?"

"Oh, she thinks she'll be back tomorrow. Said she had to take care of something this evening, that she's sure it'll clear her schedule."

"But she's okay?"

"Far as I know." Holly jerked her attention past me and raised her voice as she called firmly over my shoulder, "You hit anyone in the eye with that and you're out on your ass."

I twisted to find a young woman in cut-off jeans, a t-shirt, and a Stormtrooper helmet aiming a plastic water pistol at the table next to hers. I snorted and turned back.

"You have nothing to worry about."

Holly laughed and gestured lazily at the pastry case. "What'll you have?"

"Just a small Slimer," I said, though I did eye the case full of geek-themed sweets. "I just want something sweet to slurp on while I head home."

"You said a small, right? Have you suffered a head injury?" Holly asked as she punched my order in. I shook my head as I handed her a five.

"I've got a date tonight. He promised to feed me."

"Right, and there's no way a sugar-packed mixture of Kool-Aid and green dye will ruin your appetite."

"You see?" I said, waving away the change she tried to hand me. "You really get me."

Eight

Owen had picked me up from my house exactly on time, and I was pretty impressed. I felt like I shouldn't be, since who gives props for someone doing exactly what they said they would? I think his pretty face played a role in my feelings on the matter. He had an intensity in his eyes when he looked at me that was most definitely backed by a heady lust. I was very into him.

He drove a practical car, a basic, boring sedan you wouldn't look at twice. Our conversation was about what you'd expect from two people on a first dinner date: movies, music, hey-did-you-hear, oh-no-tell-me-more. The usual. Despite summer looming, Seattle will be Seattle and pulled one of her many rain cards. The weather was warm, but drizzles were lurking in the many grey clouds, waiting to drop and possibly ruin a perfectly good date night. I was reserving judgment to see what Owen had planned and if it would require being outside at all.

It was warm enough for a picnic, though I spotted no wicker baskets or checkered blankets in the back seat.

We drove north into Edmonds. Sweeping out of a small area bustling with businesses, we crawled through neighborhoods, up some winding, hilly streets. At the back of a large cul-de-sac, we pulled into a driveway. The house seemed completely out of place, if only because it sat in the middle of what should have been three full lots. It had a smattering of old, well-kept trees, a stone fence around the property, and a spectacular view of the water beyond. The houses around it looked years older, though no less classy.

"You can afford to rent this place?" I asked, suitably impressed. Owen shook his head as he turned the car off, unbuckled his seat belt.

"It's a friend's place. She doesn't spend a lot of time in one location, so she lets me use some of her homes when she's not living in them."

"Plural 'them?'" I asked, slipping out of the car.

"I don't know what other kind of them there is." Shutting his door, he smiled at me over the roof of the car.

I adjusted my long pencil skirt, self-consciously tugged at my vintage-style jacket, and took a peek down to see if my cleavage was still as spectacular as I hoped.

Of course it was.

"How do you two know each other?" I asked as he gestured for me to move first up the porch steps.

"We've never dated," he said, as if worried I was jealous. I shrugged as he unlocked the door and leaned in to punch a complicated series of numbers into the alarm system.

"I wasn't asking because of that, I'm just wondering how friendly you really are. How far does that trust go?" I asked, affecting a serious, James Liptonesque tone. "She isn't even a little bit worried you'll put on one of her many suits of armor and take a rapier to the priceless tapestries?"

"Suits of armor? Priceless tapestries?" he said, smiling at me from just inside the doorway. "Do you assume I'm friends with Queen Elizabeth?"

"You're friends with someone fancy. I was just wondering how you'd met. You've told me a few good stories at lunch, I just figured maybe this was another."

"She's not royalty-levels of fancy. Now, come on, let's get inside lest a neighbor get nervous about what we're doing and release the hounds," he said. I realized in that moment that he was pretty good at being charming as a way of not giving me the information I asked for.

I dropped the subject, following him inside as he crossed the tiled foyer into the living room. The house looked big, but that might have just been the impression given by the high ceilings. The kitchen was to my right, stretching out of my view. In front of me, along the left wall, was an expensive grouping of electronics that would have been hidden by modern shelving had someone not left the doors to the entertainment center open. Across from that, a plush couch and two matching chairs flanked a curving coffee table. I walked in further, glancing up briefly when the lights came on and then over when an electric fireplace in the center of the room burst to life.

"Wow," I said.

"That's what I said," he agreed. It was a lie, but I could tell it was a habitual, social fib, something to say because it fits the moment but doesn't matter.

He left me to my perusing and headed in to the kitchen. The lights in there came on and I heard the sounds of pots and pans being moved around. Something occurred to me and I fought the urge to say 'wow' again.

"You're actually cooking?" I asked, incredulous. "You weren't lying just to get me into bed, huh?" The rest of the house forgotten, I hustled into the kitchen. It was long, which made it look narrow, and done in slate gray, white, and black. Touches of red in the forms of expensive-looking appliances dotted the counters. I had to hold my jaw shut to keep it from smashing into the lovely tiled floor.

"Yes, is that a problem?" Owen set down two pots—one big, one small—and a pan as wide as my torso. I shook my head, moving around to the opposite side of the island that held the stove and watched him unpack the things he would need from around the kitchen.

Within minutes, he had gathered a bag of fancy pasta (bow-ties are always fancy, even when made of semolina and salt), a pile of brightly colored vegetables, some cream, butter, and various utensils.

"So, it's not a problem?" he asked again, reminding me I had been staring instead of answering.

"No, why would it be? What lady doesn't like to have an attractive man make her food? I mean forget the potential coupling part; everyone likes food." I tried to ignore the fact that Mel was an attractive man who'd cooked for me just months earlier. I also tried to ignore the fact that apparently I put out some sort of signal to available males that screamed, "Cook for me and I'll take my pants off."

"I thought maybe you had some sort of dietary restrictions we'd forgotten to go over."

"Oh no," I said, watching his hands. "I have a feeling there will be very few restrictions where you're involved."

Owen smiled, glanced up to meet my eyes and then pulled a large glass cutting board from under the island. As he slid a very sharp knife out of a block of wood next to the stove, he said, "I like you, Gwen."

"Drat," I mumbled, snapping my fingers and leaning a hip against the counter. "There goes my plan of seducing the EMTs when you poison me."

"Wait," he said, going at the ingredients like the star of a Ginsu knife infomercial. "Who's calling nine-one-one in this scenario? Am I poisoning you and then regretting it instantly and calling for help?"

"Maybe I overpower you and tie you up and call the paramedics myself. It's very dramatic and heroic, part of what makes me irresistible."

"You've really thought this through. It's just too bad one of us has to get poisoned for there to be bondage."

A giggle slipped through my lips as I reached for the mound of matchstick carrots. Unsure what to say, I snagged three and stuffed them into my mouth, crunching on them obnoxiously as I tried to remind myself that if I jumped him so early, all the food would go to waste. *Change the subject, Gwen*, I thought with all the conviction of an untrained puppy trying to talk itself out of chewing a shoe.

"You said you're here for work, right? To," I wiggled air quotes, "'take care of something the police can't'?"

"I am, indeed."

"So, how's that going?"

"A bit stalled. The task is proving harder to accomplish than I'd hoped," he said, turning to grab the bag of pasta off the counter. The water was edging on a boil and he brought the pasta closer, sliced the top open and set it down.

I glanced around, looking for a chair. Spotting a stool at the far end of the island, I dragged it around so I could sit down and still watch him work.

"What sort of task is it?" I leaned forward, resting my chin in my hands. I caught his gaze as it hit my face and then slid to my cleavage, and felt another swell of arousal. For a moment, I couldn't be sure if it was me feeling attractive or if my empathy was picking up him being attracted.

"Nothing I can't handle," he said, moving to prep the pain with oil. When he didn't elaborate, I felt a bit of my natural stubbornness well up. I wasn't really asking difficult questions, but he didn't seem to want to answer them, and that made me want to make him. I ignored the urge and made a joke instead.

"You're in town to challenge Timberlake to a dance-off, aren't you?"

"Yes," he answered without hesitation. "I just haven't found the perfect sequined vest yet."

Owen upended the full cutting board into the oiled pan, but kept a curl of bell pepper trapped by his thumb. When all the veggies were sizzling, he picked the pepper up and moved close to me, holding it out. I smiled, sat up straight and took it from him. Our eyes stayed locked as I popped it in my mouth and chewed.

"Thank you," I said, and he nodded.

"Welcome."

He spent the next few minutes in silence, working at turning the food from raw veggies into what I hoped would be a sauce-covered masterpiece that my childish palate would tolerate.

"You want a tour?" he asked as he finished putting away the half-empty pasta box and spices.

"Sure," I agreed, impressed as I always was that anyone trusted cooking food enough to leave it unattended. Any time I step away from the foods I stick in the microwave, they inevitably burn. One day I'll teach myself to cook properly, but I'd so far not gathered the initiative to even open up any of the cookbooks my sister buys me every year. Besides, they all have vegetables on their covers; I suspect they're meant to remain closed.

"Let's go," he said, gesturing toward me.

He didn't take my hand, but as I passed by he put a palm to the small of my back, leading me into the living room and then off to the right. We moved through the house at a casual pace and I made interested noises here and there, most of them genuine. The place was nice, and he stayed close the whole time, taking every opportunity to lean close or steer me with a hand on my body. Upstairs, there were only two doors. The one on the left edge of the balcony was closed.

"That's Elisha's room," he said, by way of explaining why we went immediately to the right and into the other room. "And this is her office."

It looked similar to mine, but I was betting Ms. Owns-Her-Own-Business didn't have crackers and cookies stuffed in the drawers of her desk.

"And is that it? I didn't see a single suit of armor, and the tapestries all look pretty new." I turned to face him and found the way he was looking at me matched the lust I could feel curling out of him to wrap like velvet around my limbs.

"No metal knights, no." I watched his mouth as he spoke, realizing he didn't have to pull me in for the kiss I could tell he was angling for. I was already closing in, overpowered by the way I felt just being this close to him. Sliding his hand behind me again, he offered me his mouth.

I slid my hands up under his shoulders, tucking my elbows around him to hold him against me. I felt one of his hands slide to my butt, while the other moved up into my short hair. Lightning shot through my limbs, that delightful, "Oh wow, a boy is touching me!" response that had been showing up since high school. I suddenly felt like my insides were fluttering and my legs were jelly.

On a small sound, Owen pulled back, moving both hands back to an appropriate spot along my spine. I licked my lips as we separated, and slid my gaze up to his. My heart had started pumping quicker and, as I took a deep breath, I did my best to separate my feelings from his.

To break the silence, he grinned down at me and murmured, "You taste like peppers."

"Spicy, that's me."

He gave a polite laugh and stepped back, letting his hands linger as they slid along my sides. We watched each other for a few moments, and when he didn't yank me against him again and go at the buttons of my jacket, I figured the sexy times had at least been postponed until later.

"Back to the food?" I asked. He nodded and backed out of the room. I moved past him to the stairs and took them slowly, glancing around the living room again. We parted at the bottom of the stairs as he went to check the food, and I veered off toward a sunroom he had neglected to show me as part of the tour.

"Oh wow," I said, loud so he could hear me. "This sitting area is beautiful."

"We can eat out there, if you'd like," Owen responded. I stepped out to watch the rain splat against the ceiling for a minute, before turning back into the kitchen.

Owen was shaking the massive pan, moving veggies around as I walked back into the kitchen. While I'd been exploring, he'd added the cream and butter ingredients to the smaller pan, along with flecks of things I couldn't identify. The kitchen smelled amazing.

It didn't take long for him to finish cooking and ninja everything onto the plate in a colorful, beautiful pile of deliciousness. In an adorable attempt to make me feel I had helped, he handed me a hunk of basil and told me to pull off a few leaves. I tore two of them before I realized I had to pull from the stems, not the leaves themselves. I tucked the torn ones under the crusty bread set off to the side on the counter and hoped he didn't notice. When the food was ready to go, I offered to grab the wine off the rack.

He looked to it as it he hadn't realized it existed and then nodded and took two wine glasses before leading the way to the sitting area.

The food was so good I had to remember to eat like a human female and not just cram the entire plate into my mouth, grunting and growling. Owen ate slowly, and we talked about travel. I hadn't grown up excessively well-off, but I'd managed to travel to Europe once in my mid-teens with my maternal aunt. Owen had been all over, it seemed, but recently he'd spent a lot of time in the States.

I'd polished off my entire plate of food and a half a glass of wine when I started to feel groggy.

Nine

I woke up in a bathtub, one leg flopped over the side and missing a shoe. My neck was bent at a very uncomfortable angle, but at least—I squinted at my body in the dimness—yep, I was clothed.

Unsure where I was, how I had gotten there, or where my other shoe had gone off to, I let out a grumbling sigh. I wanted to yell out and demand to know what the hell had happened. Instead, I shifted to get my arms under me so that I could push myself up over the lip of the giant tub. I recognized the hallway through the door as Owen's place, but it was too dark to tell exactly what was going on.

I did my best to ignore my sore neck, glancing around and then taking a deep breath to listen for any telling sounds. When I heard only the falling rain outside, I shifted back into the tub, pulling my leg in as well so it felt less exposed, and then opened my empathy outward. At first I felt nothing, but after maybe three seconds I realized could in fact feel a familiar presence.

Owen was feeling irritated and a little disappointed, but no more so than if he'd accidentally dropped a freshly baked bran muffin on the floor. I couldn't figure out in the moment what the hell was going on, but something inside me was jibbering quietly, wondering why I'd passed out and woken up in a dark bathroom. I didn't want to think Owen had anything to do with it, since he'd been nothing but decent so far, but I couldn't fathom any other explanation.

"What the hell?" I mouthed, climbing out of the tub as gracefully as I could. I stumbled at the last moment, catching myself on the ground and tweaking my wrist as I did. Instead of risking walking upright, I crawled toward the door, popping up to lean in close to the mirror. There was just enough light from outside that I could see the sharp outline of my dark hair around my face. I couldn't see if I'd been bruised, or if some enterprising frat boy had drawn genitalia along my forehead. Grunting out my annoyance, I dropped back down to the floor.

I found my shoe about halfway between the tub and the door, but I only grabbed it and put it in the corner, along with my other shoe. When I hit the doorway, I leaned out as little as I could, peering right—noticing the curtains had been drawn on the hall windows—and then left.

Owen's face didn't change when he caught sight of me, but I felt surprise splash out of him. Glowering, I let him know as I crawled closer that I wasn't happy with how the night was going. I only realized, as I rose to my knees, about to demand an explanation, that he was holding a gun.

Eyes drawn to it, I felt my mouth open but no sound came out. His expression stayed dead-eyed, but he leaned up to put his lips near my ear.

"We've got company, and they're not friendly."

"What?" I did my best not to squeak but Owen moved a hand from his gun and pressed a finger to my lips.

"They cut the lights after you passed out. I put you in the tub hoping it would keep you from getting shot up."

"I like the amount of holes I have, thank you very much," I whispered. Traces of amusement puffed into me, but he didn't laugh or smile.

"I need to find where they are and deal with them. Get back in the tub and keep your—"

"Where they are?" I asked. Owen pointed back toward the bathroom. Before he could reiterate his order, I realized what my lizard brain had been tuned into without telling me: I could feel other human emotions within my range. They were similar to his, so slight I hadn't consciously realized I was feeling them until he'd mentioned they were there.

"I can help," I whispered. He watched me blankly for a few moments before I realized I'd been waiting for him to ask how or be surprised at my offer. Unperturbed, he gave me another few seconds before impatience crinkled against my skin and he gestured for me to get on with it. "Oh, right."

Extending my senses out as far as I could, the first thing I noticed was the spastic emotional din of a bird above us. Opposite that, in the office, was a person moving carefully closer to us—or, more likely, closer to the office door. As I followed his progress, I realized there was someone else, too.

The man to our left had almost no emotional signature. I could tell he was human, but he just didn't have any feelings on the situation one way or another. Concentrating on him, I tried to get a picture in my head of where he was.

Turns out he was in the kitchen, just past the doorway that led to the hall, so close that he might've heard me breathing. Feeling a stab of panic, I opened my eyes and clapped a hand over my mouth to hold in any more squeaks. Owen only watched me, curious about my obvious panic but unfazed. Shoving my hand past his shoulder, I pointed at the door and then adjusted, pointing lower. The man was crouching.

Without hesitating, Owen turned his back on me and duck-walked toward the door. Shifting his grip on the gun, he slipped the door open and leaned in briefly to grab a quick glance toward where I'd pointed. Sure he wouldn't be seen, he moved into the kitchen and out of my sight. I didn't hear anything, but suddenly I felt an explosion of shock from the other man. In the silence, pain and anger bled out and then I felt nothing.

Pain is a tricky emotion, one I can feel from some, though not all. People react differently to being hurt, but I'd come to recognize the distinct feeling of injury from another. I would never be able to identify exactly what accompanies the jagged, sharp emotion that I know to be pain, but regardless of if someone stubs their toe or slices open their finger, I know when some people hurt.

Panic had flooded my brain in response to that feeling. Adrenaline was dulling my senses and making my limbs feel light. Was he dead? Had Owen just killed a man? Had I come here tonight intending on making whoopee with a man who had just killed someone?

When Owen duck-walked back through the door closest to me, his face was blank, untouched by the gravity of the situation. It took my empathy a few false starts before I realized that my fear was making me stupid. No one was dead; I was getting to be old hat at running up against corpses which meant I could be certain the man lying where Owen had hand-fed me vegetables wasn't one. He was out cold, though, and Owen looked no worse for wear.

"Where else?" he asked against my ear.

"Um," I mouthed, keeping silent. I took a shaky breath and opened up my senses again. My brain was fuzzy with adrenaline, but I had to at least control myself long enough to make sure I got out of this alive. I stretched my empathy as far as I could, this time avoiding concentrating on every available small animal psyche and just looking for human emotions.

I found two more people, both of whom felt no worse about the situation that Owen. I was the only one in the house freaking out about the situation. Even the bird on the roof was only mildly uncomfortable, and I was betting that had nothing to do with us being in danger.

One was the man from the office, who'd since made it to the top of the stairs, and the other was outside, at the far end of the house. Swallowing, I shifted to sit back on my heels. Owen followed me, keeping his ear close to my mouth and his body folded over mine in an odd parody of intimacy. I thought back to his comment about me not getting shot full of holes, and I forced the sound I made into helpful words instead of letting it turn into a wail of fear.

"One moving down the stairs, one at the far end of the house. Um, out to the left of the sun room."

Owen didn't say anything else; he pushed to his feet, gestured for me to stay low, and then moved toward the kitchen doorway again. Though I couldn't see a body, I watched Owen take a wide step before he disappeared, as if he was stepping over the unconscious man rather than going around. I kept a bead on him through my empathy, tracking his movement.

I was staring at the carpet, but seeing a fuzzy vision of the two other people in the house instead. Owen was just inside the kitchen, presumably hiding around the corner. The other man—it might have been sexist to assume it was a man, but I wasn't worried about political correctness in that moment—had reached the bottom of the stairs. Both were still for a few seconds before I felt the stranger jolt with surprise, heard him grunt, and then felt his emotions drop away like a bowling ball off a cliff. No pain this time, which could have meant any number of things.

I let out a breath that might have become a nervous laugh if I hadn't clapped my hands over my mouth.

Owen moved back through the kitchen toward me, and when he appeared again he kept his gun up as if making it clear he wasn't aiming at me. I found myself staring up at him, grasping at his emotions somewhat desperately. I sensed Owen's confusion and then his sympathy, faint but there. He realized I wasn't taking this as easily as he was, but he wasn't about to gather me in his arms and try to soothe away my fear. Crouching down, he leaned in and put a hand on my shoulder.

"Go into the guest room, stay low, and I'll come get you when it's safe." He moved to touch my cheek. "I promise, you'll be fine."

I gave a small nod and crawled into the room; my skirt rode up enough to leave my knees to scrape over the rug, but it wasn't so bad. Owen's landlord had immaculately soft carpets.

As I pressed myself into the hollow behind the bedroom door, I turned my head to stare at the wall. Using Owen's emotions and those of the man outside, I formed a rough idea of what was happening. Owen went into the bathroom, then slid outside. The sound of rain hitting the outside of the house stayed louder as he disappeared, making it clear he'd left the window open. He moved along the side of the house, paused, moved again, paused.

Then, as he came upon the other man, I felt shock, anger, another surge of pained outrage, and then just Owen.

It was a while before my date made another appearance.

I had been huddling on the floor behind the bedroom door, thinking about the last few minutes of my life, trying to decide how to feel.

"Gwen?" Owen was looking down at me. I realized I'd been staring blindly upward when he'd pulled the door away from me. When I only continued to stare silently, he dropped down into a crouch, putting a hand out to wave it in front of my face.

"I can see you," I said. He cocked his head.

"Are you okay?"

"Are … they?" I asked, my eyes drifting toward the kitchen, even though I couldn't see it from my spot in the bedroom.

"They're not dead," he assured me. "Just unconscious." He dropped his hand down onto my knee. It was warm and dry, despite his tussle in the rain. I glanced down at his long fingers and thought about them tangling in my hair earlier that evening. Then I thought about how he'd handled the knife in the kitchen. When I stayed silent, he leaned in, catching my eye again.

"Remember, they started it, knocking you out and all."

I frowned his way and laid my fingers over his. He upturned his palm, grasped my hand and stood, pulling me up with him. I let him tug me close to his chest and wrap his other arm around my back. Staring into his face, I tried to find some bit of remorse or worry in him.

Nothing came except … pride?

"You're not bothered by how the evening has turned out?"

"Not particularly. I mean, there are better ways to end up alone in the dark with an attractive woman, but what's done is done."

"Wow," I said, feeling myself tense. He smiled, trying to keep it soft and comforting. He couldn't quite manage the latter.

"You keep using that word."

"Well, you're not exactly … like anyone else I've met."

When the memory of Chloe garroting a vampire sprang to mind, I tamped it down, refusing to think of my candy-hiding best friend as a violent killer. Things were bad enough in the moment; my stupid brain didn't need to make them any worse.

In lieu of responding, he shifted his arm to pull me to his side and walk me out of the bedroom. We moved out into the living room and he led me to the couch. Stepping back, staying purposefully slow and non-threatening, he gestured for me to sit. I did so, and he dropped onto the coffee table, his knees flanking mine.

"Are you bothered by how I handled things? Your safety was my first priority. I wasn't going to leave you slumped over the table and run off shooting wildly in the air." He sniffed as if the idea offended him. "I'm a professional."

"But …" I trailed off. He had a point. He hadn't gone after these men for fun. He'd hauled my chubby, unconscious ass into the bathroom, tucked me into the tub to make sure I was safe. He'd only gone after the other men after I'd pointed him in their direction.

I let out a low whimper, considering that it might have been my fault that three men were spread out unconscious. Would things have gone differently if I hadn't been around? Would Owen have fixed them some tea and suggested they all use their words instead of fists and guns? I squinted at that idea, knowing logically that it was ridiculous, but unable to convince my greasy guilt that I hadn't done something wrong

Worry for my state of mind poked through Owen's calm, and instead of embedding itself into my psyche like so many emotions usually did, it relaxed me somewhat. He was only human, after all. Maybe the situation wasn't as nuts as my panic insisted. Those unconscious assholes had shown up, drugged me, and broken into the house on their own, after all. Owen had taken care of it and he'd managed to do so without shooting the place up. He wasn't lying when he'd said my safety was his first priority.

"Okay." I said, feeling myself relax somewhat. "But why didn't you just call the cops?"

"It's a nice neighborhood, but they wouldn't have been here in time. Plus, these guys are well-trained, and it could've put them in danger."

"Well-trained for what? And, what could have put the cops in danger? They're the police!" I protested, tension singing through me again. Owen frowned like he pitied my naiveté.

"Empaths, you can tell when people lie, right?"

"Yes," I agreed without thinking. He nodded, sat up tall as if trying to appear as straight a shooter as possible.

"I have no intention of hurting you or anyone you care about. I did what I felt was best for all involved. I like you. I was enjoying myself, and I would like to continue to enjoy myself." He leaned in, and I felt an almost intangible curl of lust from him once again. "If you're still up for it." His hands slid up my knees, outside the cloth of my skirt. Despite my misgivings, my hormones appreciated the action, seeping through my mind before I could stop them. I could feel a delightful tingling start where his hands touched, and it drove away the little worms of fear trying to root into my brain.

Despite the fact that I wanted to remain resolute in my suspicion, I just couldn't manage it. Everything he was saying was the truth. I was out of danger, and Owen had made that happen. He slid forward, making sure my gaze was locked on his.

"Was I lying?"

I shook my head, appreciating the closeness, the warmth of his hands.

"No," I said. "I'm just being silly."

"Not at all," he said with a shake of his head. "I would be a little bit suspicious if none of this bothered you at all. It wouldn't be the first time a beautiful woman tried to seduce me in exchange for information or my pretty head."

I laughed at the idea of my being some femme fatale sent by his enemies to lure him into a false sense of security. Glad the tension was breaking, he pressed on.

"This isn't my first time subduing intruders, but I'm guessing therapists don't have to choke out strangers on a regular basis."

I shook my head, but the laugh I let out this time wasn't completely genuine. It always looked so cool in the movies when the hero locks rippling biceps around his nemesis and squeezes until other guy passes out. Picturing Owen doing the same—and after I'd pointed him straight at his victim, no less—seemed way less cool, considering the circumstances.

"What now?" I asked. He raised a brow and glanced past my shoulder. I heard a shuffling coming from somewhere behind me in one of the bedrooms. It worried me so much I felt myself jerking forward—only a little spastically, I swear—as if I could get away.

"You're fine," Owen assured me, squeezing my arms gently before I could get up. "He's probably conscious. I didn't give him very much."

"Who is?" I asked, without thinking. "Very much of what?"

Ignoring my questions, Owen tipped his head, that curiosity of his groping once again. When he smiled, I squinted at him suspiciously.

"Do you think I could use your gift for a second?" he asked.

"My empathy?"

"Yes. You're much sexier than your average polygraph test." Pausing, he got to his feet, pulling me up with him. "Come on."

I caught sight of the man passed out at the bottom of the stairs, and it made me jolt. Owen ignored when I crashed into him in my moment of panic, and put his finger to his lips when I started to speak. I swallowed the racket I wanted to make and spoke quietly.

"What if the others wake up?"

"I made sure they're not going anywhere, don't worry. Now," he said as we stepped into the hall. "I don't want him to know you're around. Don't touch anything or make any sounds. As far as everyone's concerned, you're still out cold in the bathtub."

"Should I still be?"

"I don't know about 'should' but I'm glad you're not. Just stand back, but stay where I can see you. I'll ask him questions, and you just nod or shake your head to let me know if he's telling the truth." Owen's voice came through a smile; he liked that he could use me like this. I wasn't sure if I felt helpful or exploited.

I decided to reserve my right to choose until I knew what information we'd be getting out of the man.

Owen pushed the door open and I caught sight of a bulky white man on the floor, half his body hidden by the foot of the pale blue bed. His hair was sandy brown and he had a tight swath of black cloth over his eyes, likely replacing the expensive goggles I noticed on the bed.

When he heard the door open, he stopped struggling and turned his head. I felt his distress but, bigger than that, his anger. He was so pissed that he'd been caught.

Owen walked quickly but softly around the foot of the bed, staying far enough away from the man that he couldn't be grabbed. I felt anger surge and I jolted forward, aiming to warn Owen. He saw something in the man that matched his violent feelings though, and he hopped back to avoid the two-legged kick.

"You missed," Owen said conversationally. The man grunted, and I felt his outrage again. His legs, which I noticed were bound together, kicked in Owen's direction again, but his aim was off by quite a bit.

"Ease up, Princess," Owen said. "I just have some questions for you."

The man spat this time and Owen glanced at the gooey mess that hit the carpet; his face stayed pleasant, but I could feel his disgust.

"You're being very rude. Breaking into my home with your friends— both dead, by the way," Owen lied easily. "Am I to assume you were here to kill me?"

The man stayed silent and Owen crouched down, reaching a hand out to lightly slap his face. Outrage again, amusement from Owen. I swallowed and leaned back against the doorjamb, thoroughly uncomfortable with the situation. Owen glanced up, gave me a casual smile, and then moved his hand down to grab the man's neck. With one arm, he hauled him into a sitting position and shoved him against the footboard of the bed hard enough that I heard his head thump there. The action was aggressive, but it wasn't backed up by any sort of violent intent. I'd seen men fight before, felt aggression swing out of them like fat, bloody fists toward my face. I knew what it felt like to rage at another human being and want to hurt them in whatever way you could.

Owen felt nothing of the sort; only disgust over the loogie on the carpet lingered ever so slightly.

"Shit," the man said, more out of frustration than pain.

"Who hired you?"

"Fuck off." The insult was casual, as if this were just a misunderstanding between friends.

Owen slammed him against the footboard again and the man kicked out, his anger suddenly boiling over.

"Jim. Jim, Jim," Owen said, his voice playful. The man tensed and shock exploded out from him. My brows shot up and I felt my entire body snap to attention as I got caught up in his panicked confusion.

"No," the man said, as if arguing. His voice was louder this time, failing to maintain his carefree façade.

"I'm not as stupid as you, Caruthers." Another panic bomb went off in the man's brain. "I have connections around here you couldn't even guess at. Before I take a job, I do my research. Are you here on Madeline's orders?"

"Shit," I breathed before I could stop myself. The tension singing through me clenched my muscles even harder, and I felt my stomach twist into knots. Madeline?

Madeline?

My conversation with Holly that evening came rushing back, specifically the part where she said Madeline had been planning something for tonight. Had Owen been what she meant to take care of that would free her up to come back to work? Was my date at odds with my favorite succubus?

Caruthers remained silent, but Owen pulled him back and smacked him into the bed again.

"Tell me the truth and your cute kids stay blissfully unaware of what their father does for a living."

"Dammit," Jim growled, struggling once again with his whole body. His fight was leaving him, though. He was no longer filled with angry bravado, but worry and fear. I was watching Owen's face and he realized it too, his earlier pride surfacing again.

"Stay the fuck away from my kids," Jim said after a few moments, his tone edging on a question.

"Done—assuming you tell me if Madeline hired you."

"Yes."

Owen's eyes met mine and I nodded.

"Good. Was it because I'm here to talk to her?" I caught a sharpened sliver of malice arcing through a puff of dishonesty as Owen spoke. Like the shock when we'd first met, it jammed sharply into my chest, and I winced.

"I don't—" Jim started. I was already shaking my head and Owen knocked Jim's head back again. "Dammit. Yes. It is."

"Good. Now. Is she expecting you to kill me?"

Jim hesitated, before sighing. "No. She wanted us to bring you back to her."

"Was it the wine you got to?"

"I don't know what you mean," Jim said. His tone claimed honesty, but I could feel the lie.

"I will hit you again," Owen said, not bothering to even glance my way for confirmation.

"Yes," Jim said, frustration making his voice gravelly. "Jesus. Your security is lousy. We were in and out while you were out picking up the skirt."

"Am I to assume I should dump every bottle?"

"Assume whatever, asshole," Jim said.

The doorbell rang and I jerked around, adrenaline flooding my veins. The sound startled Jim, too, and his surprise fluttered up against the edges of my shock, making me think of the bird I'd detected earlier.

"There's your ride, Jimmy. Sit tight."

"Goddammit," Caruthers bitched, struggling once more for good measure. Owen was up and approaching me before Jim's next attempted attack could be properly aimed; he only managed to knock himself over.

"Come on." His voice soft, Owen pressed his hand to the small of my back, leading me away from the door as he shut it.

"Who's here?"

"Clean-up crew."

"What are they cleaning up?"

"Well, they're not here to check for rings in the tub." Owen met my eyes, smiling to let me know he felt my question was adorably stupid. Insult made me bratty.

"Why didn't *you* pass out?" I asked, not really sure what I expected to gain by asking as if I suspected him of something. The conversation about the wine stuck in my craw, though, since I'd poured him a glass too. Had he gone Dread Pirate Roberts on me and just built up some crazy immunity to drugs?

"I don't drink."

"But," I started, turning to look up at him. I felt somehow helpless. "It was your wine."

"It wasn't, actually," Owen corrected. His casual tone made me feel even more powerless than I already was. When I felt the werewolf from more than halfway across the living room, the sudden electricity of his emotions nearly knocked me over. It chased out the irritation, the nervousness. For a second I was lost in a jumble of mental images that I couldn't quite clear up or understand. I didn't want to run and hide anymore, but my brain wasn't ready to just let go of the way the evening had gone wrong. The werewolf's desire had muscled in on the fear, tried to seduce it into surrendering its control over me.

"Whoa," I mumbled, leaning into Owen for support. Wine forgotten, I took an unsteady breath. Owen tried to keep a tight hold on me, but I veered away from him as we passed the couch. Making sure I was steady, he let me go and I dropped into the cushion's embrace. Closing my eyes, I walled myself up, shoving my shields into place as well as I could.

"Harvard," Owen said, his voice a greeting before it went serious. "One by the bottom of the stairs, one in the kitchen. Third's singing in the back room."

"Sway, Jolt." The tone sounded like an order, though I couldn't yet see to whom. "I've got the birdy." The werewolf's voice was painfully deep, giving me an impression of an imposingly broad barrel chest. Fighting through the crackle of lust and violence, I opened my eyes, turned to peer behind me. Just as I thought, there was a very large, stunning man looking down at Owen, nodding at the instructions he was being given. My head went fuzzy and I had trouble distinguishing words and voices. Squinting, I looked him over, trying to force my brain to work again.

He was dressed plainly enough in a bicep-baring forest green t-shirt and jeans. They were nice biceps, and I certainly understood the shirt, despite the weather outside. A blondes woman and a short, heavily muscled man split off from him. Silently, they moved toward the bodies Owen had mentioned. Doing my best to keep the werewolf's base emotions from invading my skull and taking over, I pushed to my feet.

I tottered at first, my body torn between collapsing as an escape and rushing them both. I wasn't sure if I wanted to hurt them or have my way with them, but that's what can happen when an empath stands too close to a werewolf. And really, as far as I'm concerned, being within a city block of a werewolf is too close.

Moving around the couch, I looked him over. He was at least a full head taller than Owen, and as soon as he noticed me his mouth split into a wide grin. It somehow made the crackling of his emotions worse; I felt like someone was slapping me with a bouquet of extra thorny roses.

"Hey sugar," he drawled. I gave him a small smile, having decided to take the flirty assault head-on, to make it clear he was getting nowhere. It didn't work with Mel, but you never get anything if you don't at least ask for it, right?

"How goes it, big boy?" I asked. He shifted his stance and I watched his arms flex, his spine straighten. Despite the lust hammering at me, I knew better than to assume he was hitting on me because of my cleavage or my pretty face. I could have been a sloppy, toothless, balding wretch and he would have tried to get in my pants the second it was clear I was a woman.

"You're a fine little thing," he said, making a show of looking me over from head to toe. I jerked a thumb at Owen.

"For tonight, I'm his fine little thing."

The wolf winked, nodding. "Gotcha." Turning back to Owen, he tipped his head slightly. "No disrespect meant."

Owen shrugged. "She's an attractive woman."

The subject closed, they moved on to payment, using code words that I didn't understand and didn't particularly care to. The woman emerged first, shouldering the unconscious man as she stepped out of the kitchen. Without a word to us, she hauled ass toward the front door, her hands holding the body in place. I watched in shock, thinking about how sometimes I was too tired to carry Chloe's cat, let alone an adult male human person strapped with weapons and body armor. Her partner looked equally as strained—that is to say, not at all—as he hefted the second man. He, too, silently crossed the room and left through the door.

The woman came back in shortly after, her face blank. Probing her slightly, I did my best to see what exactly she was feeling about this odd situation. She looked normal enough, wearing dark jeans and a billowy blouse. I considered that, even with the werewolf nearby, I couldn't detect her even slightly. When it dawned on me why, I noticed she was staring back at me. My eyebrows shot up and she gave me a half-smile.

I swallowed, realizing she'd caught on to my ability before I'd caught on to hers, and I stepped back, giving her an apologetic nod. I'd only formally met one other empath in my life and, while I hadn't been able to read him, he'd considered me an open book. I wondered if it was the same this time or if my shields had gotten any better than when I'd been young.

When her partner came back in, they whispered something to each other before addressing their attractive boss with only, "Sir?" When he waved a hand vaguely in their direction, they both turned and left through the front door. I had the fleeting thought, as she left, that it must be hell spending all that time with a werewolf. Either she was numb to it, or she knew tricks I really needed to learn.

"Should we deliver them back to Madeline?" the wolf asked. Owen crossed his arms and I turned my attention to his emotions. He was still unbothered by the situation. Thinking on the question, he shrugged a shoulder.

"Why not?"

They kept up their discussion and let myself go a bit, starting to feel a bit more comfortable now that the danger was outside. Granted, Owen had knocked the danger out and bound the men with plastic cuffs, but it still felt better having them out of the house.

The discussion going on in front of me was clipped and serious, and I zoned out without meaning to. I didn't realize my relaxation was letting the werewolf's emotions get to me until I found myself staring intently at Owen's bare forearm.

He was wearing a white shirt with tiny vertical stripes, and I sighed wistfully at the way the rolled fabric of the sleeves bunched around his arms. Moving my gaze upward, I caught a look at his jaw, the way the muscles there moved as he spoke. I could happily think about how nice it would be to run my tongue along his skin, how it would feel to give him a little nibble. My gaze took in his chin, his lips, swept down to his chest and of course, kept going south.

When I felt the blood flood my major erogenous zones, I lifted my arms, crossing them over my breasts. The werewolf made a low sound of appreciation and I turned my attention to him sharply. He was grinning at me.

Yes, it was wolfish.

"I think she likes you," he said, addressing Owen. A small smile touched Owen's lips but he didn't say anything in response. This was somehow even more embarrassing than if he'd pointed at my boobs and named my erect nipples.

"Um," I squeaked, taking a step back. Clearing my throat, I ran my gaze around the room. "I'll be … outside."

The wolf gave a knowing chuckle.

My cheeks were burning as I rushed through the French doors out into the sunroom, where our plates and the offending wine glasses sat forgotten. Realizing I could still feel the werewolf's lust in my brain, stuffing my psyche like cotton, I fled out the side door. The rain tickled my forehead, and I let out a quick breath, moving along the deck to the short steps that led down into the yard. The ground was cold against my bare feet, but I welcomed the discomfort.

After I felt I was a suitable distance from the werewolf's stupid lust energy, I took a deeper breath, surveying the yard.

It was large, both deep and wide. The stone fence was low at the back, allowing me a view of the Puget Sound. Tall trees dotted the grass, likely making for great shade when the sun was out. A pool that might have been Olympic-sized jumped with every raindrop off to my right, separated from a covered sitting area by an attractive stone walkway.

I followed the walk to the covered area, dropping into a plush lounge chair. Leaning back, I looked up, watching the rain spit at the clear glass. I glanced briefly at the house to see if I could spy Owen or the werewolf through the windows, but they were out of sight.

"Okay, then," I mumbled, letting myself relax in stages. I swung my legs over the lounge and rested my hands in my lap. I concentrated on breathing, on the cool air and on how this rainy yard was not sexy. There was nothing going on that should have made me feel either horny or angry.

Come on, hormones, back off, I insisted. With the better part of a large yard and a thin curtain of rain separating me from the wolf, I slowly started to feel like myself again.

OLIVIA R .BURTON

Ten

I might have nodded off, or it might have just been a very short time before Owen came outside. I opened my eyes to see him standing over me, watching me in silence. Wondering what he had to say for himself, or about my intense ogling inside, I considered him. He said nothing, just continued to stare down at me. I prodded with my empathy, opening myself up enough to search him. Nothing exceptional hit me, meaning he wasn't standing there unfavorably judging me. That was something, at least.

"This has certainly been the most interesting first date I've been on," I said after a moment.

"Has anyone else cooked you dinner, tossed you in a bathtub, and then exploited your abilities?"

"Yes, but it wasn't my empathic abilities they were using for their own gain."

Owen smiled.

"I'm sorry," he lied.

"No," I said, watching him. "You're not." He didn't feel he'd done anything wrong, so what did he have to apologize for?

He nodded. "Fair enough. But I'm not happy this all happened."

"That's the truth. Though you enjoyed the fight." I wagged a finger at him, then held my hand propped up on the armrest next to him.

"You're handy," he said.

"I can be," I responded, reaching up to his shirt. He tipped his head down to watch the action, but he still felt surprise when I grabbed the fabric over his belly and tugged. Immediately he put one foot forward to balance, but I brought my other hand up, grabbed closer to his collar and held on. Some of the residual lust of the evening was still percolating in my brain. I could feel the wetness of the rain on his shirt, but underneath his skin was warm. His hands spread out, grabbing the armrests of the chair for support as I forced him to bend over me. Pushing upward, I pulled him into a kiss.

I didn't bother starting slow. I bit his lip, shoving my mouth against his as I poked around his psyche. He was pleased, a little surprised, and more confused than I would have guessed. I liked the confusion. After a night of being confident, even in the face of armed strangers, the fact that I'd yanked him down for a kiss threw him off. I tugged on his shirt harder, letting my tongue press his. Keeping one hand on his chest to hold him in place, I slid my other hand down to his hip to work at the hem tucked into his pants.

Excitement flooded out of him, and I let it overtake me as I got my hand under his clothes to his skin. Feeling caught up in the moment, I shoved his shirt further out of his pants and ran my fingers over his fabulous abs to the button on his khakis.

He jerked away suddenly, his emotions a mix of glee and panic.

I yanked my hands back, holding them up like I was surrendering to the police.

"What?" I asked, looking around to see what danger he'd sensed that I hadn't. He stood over me, eyes a touch wide, and I met his gaze. "What is it?"

"Sorry," he said, and this time he was being truthful. "I just ..." He trailed off, his face going uncharacteristically sheepish. He tugged his shirt all the way out of his pants, letting it hang over his fly. "I have a gun holstered there."

I raised a brow. "By your dick?"

"It's small." An amused frown crossed his face before he clarified, "The gun."

I snorted, swinging my legs over the side of the low chair to sit up. This put me roughly eye-level with his, er, gun. He stared down at me, a peculiar expression on his face. After a moment, we both gave in to a tense laugh and I held my hand up to him. He took it, pulling me up and against his body. We watched each other for a moment, hands clasped. I left my free hand dangling by my side because, honestly, I wasn't sure what we were doing.

"So. Does this mean the date's over?" I asked quietly.

"I hadn't planned on kicking you out."

I made a tsk-tsk sound. "Well, I'd say putting a gun between me and your penis sends the wrong message, then."

He laughed, and it might have been the first fully genuine laugh I'd heard from him all night. We'd shared laughs, chuckles, maybe even a chortle or two. But this time there was surprise behind the sound, like he really hadn't expected the joke I'd made. It was as if every other time I'd quipped he'd seen it coming in some form or another, but liked it despite that. It made me feel proud for getting to hear it, getting to feel the fullness of it in my own belly. Shaking his head, he slid his free hand around to my back, tucking his fingers under my jacket to touch the skin along my spine.

"I wanted a back-up in case something else went wrong."

"Ah," I said, suddenly feeling a bit of the discomfort from earlier. Fighting it, I kept myself as jacked into his psyche as I could. He was an interesting man to be around. I hadn't seen him angry or scared, like he just didn't bother with certain feelings. I wished I'd been able to deal with the evening the same way.

Being aware of what he was feeling made me want to touch him, to undress him. I wanted to pull him against me, get inside of him and have him wrap around me. It was a male instinct, but I could dig it.

Slowly, I moved his shirt out of the way and touched his hip, then his back. The rain pattered the glass above us; it was definitely heavier now.

"Time to go inside," he said, his mouth close to mine.

"As euphemisms go, that one's pretty blatant."

Our next kiss was all teeth, both of us laughing.

"I want to have sex with you. How's that?" Moving his hand upward, he cradled my throat, pushing at my jaw with his thumb. When I obliged and leaned my head back, he ducked in and gave my neck a soft bite. My eyes had drifted closed and I felt my hands tense, fingertips pushing against his back. Moving his mouth to my ear, he mumbled, "Blatant enough?"

"Back in the house," I demanded, shoving at his body with mine. Happy with my response, he winked before turning, separating us except for our clasped hands. The rain was a shock to the system and I made a small sound of discontentment. I really didn't want to be standing in the cold rain right then. The sooner we got into the house and out of our clothes, the better.

Still a gentleman, despite the fact that I'd practically asked out loud, 'would you please put your penis in me?' he let me go first up the deck steps. He opened the sliding glass door for me, followed me in—making sure to lock it—and then followed me into the living room through the French doors. I turned to watch as he grabbed the doors, pulled them together and closed them, his hand sliding up to the lock at the top of the left one. As he slammed the bolt into place, I let go of my willpower.

I grabbed his arm, pulled it and ignored the slight resistance as he double-checked the lock. I snaked my other hand around to the front of him, yanking at the collar of his shirt to pull him against me. Obligingly, he curled his tongue against mine in a frantic kiss that shot lightning through my limbs. When I let out a soft sound, it seemed to release a dark impatience inside of him. It leapt up, clawing its way outward and into me. I wanted to tear at him, shred his clothes, pin him down and have my way with him.

His hands weren't gentle as they slid between us. I protested when he spread us apart. I think I actually growled when our lips separated and he shifted to grab at the fat buttons of my jacket. Abruptly, as he got the last button undone, he shoved his hands inside, squeezing my waist through the thin fabric of my camisole.

I threw myself at him, pressing into his groin with my own. Before I could kiss him again, he angled his head, nosing my chin aside. He bit me twice in rapid succession, hard enough that a tiny flutter of shock flapped in my chest. It chased out the aggression we'd shared and brought me back to my own emotions, making me worry about how fast I'd gotten caught up in his intense passion.

Determined to feel in control again, I cupped his face, turning his mouth to mine. I made the kiss aggressive, biting his bottom lip and sliding my hands down to grasp his shoulders. Twisting us both, I put his back to the couch, nudging him toward it. He took the time to pause and kick off his shoes, but moved with me, our hips matching each other like a dance. As soon as we were close enough, I grasped the bottom of his shirt, pulled away from him and yanked it up above his head.

Meeting his intense blue eyes under his tousled hair, I held the shirt in one hand, dangling it at my side. When he tried to tug at my hips, I placed my other palm on his chest and locked my elbow. His expression was dangerous as I held him at arm's length. Shifting my stance to lean back, as if trying to get the whole picture in one glance, I pushed away until only my fingertips touched him.

Taking my time, admiring his physique, I let out a small sound of appreciation. Giving him a smile to rival the one the werewolf had given me earlier, I leaned in, using my fingertips to propel him back onto the couch. Surprised by the action, he landed crooked, but I liked the way his body tensed as he did.

Pleased by the fact that I'd shocked him, even for a millisecond, I dropped his shirt to the ground and moved in close as he shifted to sit up. As much as his drive to take me was still scraping at my insides, I needed the space between us for just a little longer to get my head on straight.

Moving my gaze back to his, locking our eyes, I shifted my shoulders to slip my jacket off, trying to make the move as sexy as possible. I ignored the awkward thud of my phone in the pocket as it hit the floor. Extending his arms, he grasped the edges of my skirt, and his gaze dropped as he tucked his thumbs between the fabric and my skin.

Our eyes locked again as he slid his hands slowly up, over the backs of my knees, along my thighs, his hooked thumbs moving my skirt closer to my waist. I felt my breath start to come quicker, and despite my attempts to remain aloofly sexy and intense, I knew my cheeks had gone pink.

When I felt my narrow skirt lock up around the middle of my thighs, unwilling to go any further, I smiled. Frustration lashed out of him, smashing against me as he was forced to pause. Blinking at his stalled hands, he shifted to sit up straight and slid himself closer. I lifted a hand

and ran my fingers through his hair, curling them into a fist and tugging back a bit. Neck extended, head forcibly tilted, he bared his teeth in a tough smile. His hands were still on my thighs, his thumbs still hooked under my skirt as I pulled him back roughly and bent down. I gave the kiss bite, part of me wanting to see the mark my teeth would leave on his bottom lip.

As I pulled out of the kiss, I breathed against his lips. "The skirt's gonna have to come off."

"I agree," he murmured. Without waiting for me to stand up straight, he moved his hands possessively over my hips and my butt, searching out the zipper. I reached a hand back and stopped him, hooking my fingers into his as I stood up again. Arms wrapped around me, he watched my face until I loosened my grip on his hair. When I dropped my hand to his shoulder, he lowered his chin and moved his hands away. Leaning back into the couch, he looked up at me, curiosity rising in him just enough to fight the colossal desire thrashing about.

When I realized he was fighting his urges for my benefit, I relaxed slightly, doing my best to separate my emotions from his, making sure I wasn't losing him with my attempts at dominance. Sure, there are times when I can go for following the whim of my partner. It can be fun to let a man touch you the way he wants, undress you when he wants, and decide how far and how fast the sex will go.

I wasn't in the mood for that tonight. So, if Owen wasn't going to play my way, I would pack up my vagina and go home.

His steady gaze let me know he didn't mind. I bent my left knee slightly, knocking it against his leg, but he didn't move. I lifted a finger, making a swirling motion before I pointed toward his groin.

"You should pull that out before we go any further." His eyebrows wiggled lasciviously and I laughed, knowing I didn't need to clarify, but doing so anyway. "The gun."

Keeping our eyes locked, he moved his hands to his pants, unbuttoning and then unzipping with a certain level of flare that I approved of. Instead of showing me what lay under the zipper, though, he pushed to his feet, slid a hand behind my neck and pulled me into a quick, open-mouthed kiss. The tickle of his fingers on my skin was electric. There wasn't time for tongue before he rounded the couch and headed away.

"Hold that thought," he said without looking back. I watched him walk toward the back hall, calm as if he was grabbing a book I had asked to borrow. While I waited for him to unload his weapon, I unzipped the skirt and slid it off. I held it for a bit, suddenly lost in the realization that I'd missed a perfectly good opportunity to make a joke about packing heat. Shaking off my disappointment in myself, I tossed the skirt over the back of the chair to my right. I yanked my top off as well, draping it over the chair and then turning toward the hall, eager to watch him come to me.

He emerged, having removed his socks as well as the gun, his khakis and boxers hanging low on his narrow hips. I was able to enjoy a very nice view of the hipbones beneath his pale skin. I decided I would have to take the time to nibble down there later, but for now I just enjoyed watching him move. As he stepped around the couch, I twisted my upper body and pulled him so we were close. My eyes on his, a smile on my lips, I slowly began sliding my free hand down his naked chest, below the line of his boxers.

"That's all me," he mumbled against my lips. After letting him take my mouth once again, I moved my teeth along his jaw, scraping across his flesh.

"Good boy," I murmured back, licking his earlobe into my mouth. I bit down enough that I knew it would sting. Pulling back, dragging my teeth along his skin until we separated, I moved back to his mouth, kissing him again.

I felt full and fuzzy, distracted enough by his emotions overtaking mine in the moment that I simply shifted and adjusted to let him unhook my bra and slide it off. His fingers were gentle on my breasts at first, but when he began to pinch and tug, I let myself moan between his lips. I found that his tongue matched the pace of his fingers. He exhaled on the end of a kiss like he needed to eject me from his lungs, and I felt the tension in him constrict like metal about to snap. I let out a surprised little gasp when he twisted me suddenly, pressing my back to his chest.

One of his hands pinned me to him while the other moved down my belly, slipping into my underwear. When he quirked one finger against me, I gripped backward, digging my fingers into his thigh. I scratched him, rougher than I meant to, hard enough that I felt the pressure at the base of each nail.

I could feel him like a caged animal in my head. He was aroused and frustrated, the latter due entirely to the former. We'd been flirting and teasing each other for long enough that even I was ready to throw down, dispense with the pleasantries, and go at it like monkeys. I found that I liked the feeling of his impatience, that whatever he wanted to do to me, it wouldn't be slow and sweet.

"Okay," I said, pulling away from him.

I moved my hands to his, pulling him away from my flesh, though I had to fight him on it. When I turned to face him again, his eyes were too wide, his emotions barely contained. It was the first time he seemed unable to hide what he was really feeling in the way he looked at me.

"You look frustrated," I said, purposefully making it sound condescending. Before he could answer, I leaned in, grabbing handfuls of the fabric at his hips. I let my thumbnails scratch his skin and I followed my hands downward, dropping into a crouch. He didn't step out of them when they reached his ankles, and I didn't look up to see his expression. Deciding to indulge my earlier fantasy, I leaned in, licking a line up the left side of his hip and giving the skin a hard bite, getting as much of him between my teeth as I could manage. He groaned a little at the pain and disappointment sloshed against the eagerness within him, making me wonder if he would have preferred me licking just a little to the right.

Pushing to my feet again, I reached out to grab his hands. As I placed them on my hips, I pressed gently against him and moved up to whisper in his ear.

"One last thing and then I'm good to go."

The disappointment within him vaporized under an atomic bomb of excitement that clouded out over my skin and made me sizzle. He shoved at the fabric of my panties, dropping down with them. He paused, his shoulders level with my hips. I heard the quick sound of cloth rustling on the floor, but before I could catch sight of what he was doing, he came back up, his arms locked around my thighs. I gasped, letting out a sound that was half-panic as I felt the dam on his control break. He lifted me, shifted our weight and flung me onto the couch on my back.

He fell over me, shoved my right leg into the couch cushions and pushed my left thigh up, bending it until my knee was up by my ribs. Eyes intense, he moved his free hand forward, holding out a shiny package. It took me a second to figure out what he held; in all the foreplay, I had completely forgotten to ask about protection.

Silently, he watched me over the wrapper. I gave a small nod, took the condom out of his hand and tore it open. Before I had the chance to do anything further, he pulled it free of the wrapper and moved his hand into the darkness between us.

His free hand remained at the back of my knee, his fingers digging into the sides painfully, even as he finished with his delicate work below. Finally he shifted, leaned over me, his eyes intense even in the dark and flickering firelight. I expected him to kiss me, but when I reached up, he jerked back. Using his free hand, he grabbed my wrists. Making eye contact, he forced my hands back above my head, held them there long enough to make the point that he expected me to stay in that position.

As he shifted further up my body, I felt his other hand move in before his cock, feeling its way. Finally, as he ducked his head into my neck and gave my collarbone a surprisingly gentle kiss, I felt him slip inside. I shifted my arms, gripping the armrest of the couch, moving my right leg to ease the pressure of the position he'd left it in. Lifting my hips, I met his first thrust, tried to match his second, but he shifted his grip away from my thigh. His other hand stayed bracing him on the back of the couch, but he moved his hand to my belly and pressed gently.

Lifting his head so he could meet my gaze again, he gave me a condescending smile.

"I think you've done enough."

"Okay," I agreed breathily. I tipped my head back, kept my grip on the armrest, and breathed out. I felt Owen slide above me, shifting his stance and moving his other hand further up the couch. I watched his arm tense and felt the slow glide of his thrust. I sighed out with it, feeling my mouth fall open as he pulled back. When he seemed to have the pace he preferred, he lost himself in a rhythm.

Taking advantage of my empathy again, I reached into him and pulled his emotions into me. It quickly got dizzying. I had worked both of us into such a state that I wasn't sure it would take more than a few seconds for both of us to collapse into a spent heap.

His control was admirable, though, and as he moved faster against me, I lost the ability to separate who was feeling what. My spine was bowed, my fingers digging into the couch. I squeezed my thighs around his body, sucking in long, deep breaths edged by the sounds of pleasure. I opened my eyes to look at his face and found him watching me with an intensity that I wasn't sure I could handle. Rather than watch him watch me, I closed my eyes and pulled my hands forward, grasping his shoulders.

I was shoving my knee against his hand, not out of any desire for him to stop gripping me so tight, but just out of a need to do something. My body felt too loose, too open. I wanted to close around him, pull him against me and hold on. Abruptly, he let go of my knee and I felt his hand move between us, felt his fingers splay over my abdomen. When his thumb rubbed against my clitoris, I gasped out a shocked sound.

I couldn't help it; I thrashed, cried out again, slower this time. My arms spread out to grip the couch on either side of me. Lifting my legs, I squeezed into Owen's shoulders with my knees, forcing his hand out from between us.

I wrapped my legs around his back and pulled him into me. His hand sunk further into the cushions next to my shoulder, and I could feel his fingers leave the back of the couch. He planted his hand next to my other shoulder and as I began to fall back into my own mind, I got caught up in his orgasm.

It was like a spastic, joyful relief. Tension broke in his mind, along his body, and he stopped moving, pressing as hard against me as he could. He was breathing roughly into my shoulder, his mouth open. I could feel the wetness of his saliva, but I didn't mind. Trying my best to detach my emotions from his, I turned away from him, attempting to get my body to relax. I couldn't seem to unclench my legs and my hormones were not ready to risk losing the pleasurable waves still crashing through me.

I felt the strain in his arms as Owen pushed himself up, and I caught the somewhat goofy pride on his face when he met my eyes. I grinned dreamily, moving my arms above my head and shifting my hips. I kept my legs around him but eased my grip.

"You look like you just discovered damning government secrets."

"No word from Deep Throat, this time," he quipped. I snorted. Coming back to the thought I'd had earlier, I glanced around the room.

"Your landlord isn't going to mind—er—*this*, is she?"

"Doubtful. I'll buy her a new couch if she really insists."

As he moved his hand to the back cushions again, he pushed himself up enough to look around the room. We separated carefully and I stood, glancing around. I caught sight of my underwear, kneeled down to grab it and then watched Owen gesture to my camisole and bra. I grabbed them as I waved vaguely in the direction of the bathroom.

He made a gesture with his free hand that said, 'Please. Feel free.'

I took my time cleaning up and came back out into the living room feeling oddly chilly. Owen had pulled his boxers back on and gathered our clothes up. They were folded neatly on the coffee table, and he looked up from setting my skirt on top of my jacket as I came around the corner of the hallway.

"Well, that part of the date went very well," I observed, letting myself feel smug and self-satisfied.

"Better than being drugged by hooligans?"

"Hooligans?" I scoffed, pausing by the fireplace to hold my hands out to it.

"What word would you prefer I use?"

"Assholes."

He snorted, came across the room to meet me. Lifting his hands to his hips, he watched me warm myself against the fire.

"I need to tell you something but, before I do, I want you to know that I very much enjoyed your company tonight."

I shrugged a shoulder. "I get that from all the men who nail me to a couch."

"Really," he said and I wasn't sure he was reinforcing his statement or questioning mine. I waited in silence, dropped my hips down and sat on the warm stone, putting my back to the fake wood and its real fire. Owen's silence started to annoy me, so I frowned deliberately up at him.

"If you're pregnant, I am suing the shit out of the condom company," I said. He smirked, but I didn't feel the level of amusement I wanted. All I could feel from him was hesitation. "Jesus, just spit it out."

"I'm sort of seeing ... someone."

"Me?"

"Among others." He lifted a hand, gesticulating as if he could pluck the words out of the air. "I don't stay in one place for long. It's about convenience."

"Sexual convenience?"

"Occasionally."

"Okay." I wasn't sure how I felt but, thinking back on the evening, I'd accepted more incredible things about him. "Okay, then." I repeated. He dropped his hands to his sides.

"Okay then ... you're going to hit me in the gut and leave?"

"No. Okay then, as in ... okay then. It's just a date, just sex. You don't live here, and I never suggested that having sex meant you must only have sex with me." The heat at my back was starting to hurt, so I stood, putting my hands on his chest. I indulged myself by running my fingers over the lean muscles and met his eyes.

"As long as you're not lying to the others about whomever you're sexually conveniencing, I can't argue."

Eleven

It wasn't until we were on the car on the way back to my place that I started to think of the night in terms of everything that had happened and not just the naked parts. I glanced over at Owen, unsure whether I wanted to dislodge the fat contentment sitting in a cloud around him. Swallowing, I angled myself to face him as well as I could within the seatbelt.

"You mentioned Madeline, at one point," I said. A tiny bubble of annoyance popped from somewhere inside him. "Do you, by chance, mean a succubus who owns a coffee shop?"

The annoyance popped again, this time accompanied by a larger swell of displeasure. He turned toward me, his expression still pleasant despite what I felt from him. Blinking, he turned to look out the front window again. He took his time and I let him stay silent. He'd indicated that talking about his job was mostly off-limits; I considered that he might just ignore my questions entirely. I wasn't sure I could let that stand, even though I knew it might ruin my chances of ever getting him naked again.

"Are you two friends?" he asked, finally. I shook my head, realized he probably couldn't see it in his peripheral vision in the dark car.

"Not exactly. You might have noticed her shop is below my office and—if you've been in—that she makes a kick-ass chocolate cake. I love chocolate cake." He smiled, nodded.

"Well. I have business with her, let's leave it at that."

I swallowed again, lifting my hand to rub my nails against my lips as I considered. Talking over my fingers, I pitched my voice casually, even though I was worried my persistence might make annoy him.

"I don't really know if I can leave it at that. She's a nice…um. Woman. She spends most of her time at the café, and while we're not best buds, I am kind of fond of her." I let the sentiment hang in the air and dropped my hand into my lap before I continued; I knew he could tell what I was about to ask. "Are you here to, you know, *solve* her?"

We paused at a stop sign and he turned to face me; there was no one around in my neighborhood this late, so we didn't get any honks for staying still.

"I wasn't hired for that, specifically. But depending on how things turn out, I can't promise I won't have to do so eventually."

I bit my lip and we stared at each other. After everything tonight, I felt that this was the most awkward it had been between us so far. That included when I'd woken up in a bathtub and then confronted him while he was holding a gun.

"Can I ask what you were hired for?"

He sighed, and I felt like a kid who'd asked for a pony one too many times. He stayed quiet but his emotions were burbling, making he think he was considering my question instead of simply being aggravated by it. Turning back to the task at hand, he pulled away from the stop sign. We both said nothing as we drove the rest of the way to my house. We pulled into my driveway, where he shut off the car and turned to me.

"Do you watch the news, or read about it?"

"Not really. I catch the weird stories, but not usually the everyday stuff."

"You should look into some of the everyday stuff that's been happening in the last week. Specifically," he said, very seriously, "strange deaths in the area." He looked toward my house then, breaking eye contact so that he missed my reaction to his words. The body at the grocery store jumped to mind, and I remembered that I had nearly run into Madeline right after finding it.

Without going into what I'd seen and felt, I nodded. "I'll do that."

He smiled and I felt my seatbelt unbuckle. I glanced down and watched his hand follow the buckle across my lap, stopping on my thigh. I let out a breath, and then, catching his soft smile, I leaned in to kiss him. He kept one hand on my leg, the other pushing into my hair. He squeezed my thigh as I pulled away.

"My Tuesday is full, but I'll call you Wednesday."

"I may have more questions," I said.

"If they're not, 'will you please remove your pants?' I may not answer them."

"Then I'll start with your pants and work my way up."

"I like that about you."

I laughed and pulled back, grabbing my bag from the back seat. We didn't say goodbye, but I did glance back and give a small wave as I let myself into my house.

My bed was bouncing and it wasn't because of the sexy dream I was having. At least, I don't think dream-me was reacting to having sex with a faceless dream man by yipping, "Gwen! Wake up! Wake up, Gwen! Get up! Time to wake up!" in Chloe's voice.

I grunted, shoving a hand at whatever kept poking me in the ear, felt my palm get caught and tickled. I let out a whine and kicked out, but found that my leg was trapped and couldn't go much further. I just grunted again and turned my face into the pillow. The whole bed shuddered and a slim arm wrapped around my hip, pulling me close. I opened my eyes to find Chloe grinning at me, her eyes bright.

I just grumbled and closed my eyes.

"Tell me about your date! Did you get lucky?"

"Mmhmm," I grumbled, hoping she would take it and run. I had no idea what time it was but the fact that I was conscious enough to wonder anything at all was incredibly disappointing. Chloe leaned closer and I could smell mouthwash on her breath. I got a bit self-conscious about my own morning breath, but decided that she had put herself in the line of fire.

"So, you got lucky and then what? Where did he take you? And then," she said, her voice going low, "where did you two go to dinner?"

I cracked an eye open a slit and caught her cheesy wink as she used the arm trapped partially under her body to shoot me with a finger-gun. It reminded me of when I'd run into Mel in the elevator, which made me smile. Chloe took that to mean I was awake enough to jostle some more.

"Come on! Speak, girl! I'll give you a cookie!"

Pathetically, that was all it took. I took a deep breath and rolled onto my back, hoping it would help make me conscious enough to eat a cookie without choking to death. Chloe was quiet as I stretched my body away from unconsciousness, her arm staying draped over me.

"Where's my cookie?" I demanded after a bit.

"I'll buy you one later. Now spill."

I smirked. "Did that last night."

"Nice," she said. I gave in, still blinking excessively in an attempt to get my eyes to work correctly. They didn't want to stay open.

"He cooked for me," I began through a yawn, "and gave me a tour of the house he's staying at. Apparently he has a very wealthy friend in the area who lets him use the place. It was beautiful, great view. I drank half a glass of wine, got dizzy, and then woke up in a bathtub." Chloe blinked at me as I spoke, her body going tense as wariness swarmed in. "Turns out he's here on business with our missing café owner, who sent thugs to the house to rough him up, and I just happened to be in the way."

Chloe sat up, watching me seriously. Something was bubbling up inside her; I couldn't quite place it, but I was completely sure it wasn't something I had ever seen in her before. Feeling strangely vulnerable lying down, I pushed upward, pulling my knees against my chest. Chloe watched me until I realized she was waiting for me to finish.

"He took care of them, which was …" I shook my head, not wanting to talk about that. "Well, neither one of us got hurt, but the intruders can't say the same. Which is probably best for me as I don't know why they would've left me alive after doing whatever they were ordered to do with him."

"You said he's here doing business with Madeline?"

"Not exactly *with* her. Did you get my text?"

"That's why I'm here. You were drunk on hormones and it was two in the morning when you sent it. Full of typos. Unless you really did get paid and were hoping for 'well talk in the morning.' I don't know much about wells, though, except that apparently Timmy can't stop flinging himself down them. So come on, Lassie. Speak: tell me what's up with Madeline."

"He wouldn't tell me why he's here, but he gave me some cryptic suggestion that I should look into deaths in the area in the last week. I wanted you to remind me, maybe see if your search skills are better than mine."

"Deaths like heart attacks?" Chloe asked, her expression dour. I shook my head, though I should have nodded in agreement. She was probably right, it just hadn't occurred to me until after she'd suggested it.

"Just deaths in the area. He didn't say anything else. Do you think Madeline's killing people?"

"Unlikely," Chloe said offhandedly, pulling out her phone as if she'd just gotten a message she wanted to check. She rolled her thumb across the screen three times and then set the phone down, looking up at me again. "She's been around for long enough to know better. But he's here for a reason and the fact that two bodies have shown up since Friday is pretty scary."

"One on my lawn," I said, thinking back to what I'd sensed in my half-asleep haze. There had been three sets of emotions when I'd first hopped out of the bed, and only one had been human. "Does Madeline live around here?"

Chloe shook her head, but it wasn't an answer. She wasn't entirely listening to me, a faraway look on her face. I swallowed hard, wondering if she was going to go all serious on me like she had when I'd been attacked by a demon the year before.

We sat in silence for about a minute before her phone played the opening sax riff from the *Night Court* theme song. I frowned at the sound, wondering why she'd picked that when I'd never heard her mention the show once, and she grabbed the phone, reading the screen intently. After a moment, she nodded.

"Four deaths match a succubus M.O. in the area. The two you found, one downtown that the police chalked up to a mugging Saturday and one at a train station Tuesday."

"How—" She didn't let me finish.

"Is your boyfriend here to kill her?"

"No, but I'm certain he wouldn't hesitate if it came to that."

Chloe nodded, pushing off the side of the bed. She opened my closet and started pulling stuff out. The emotion I'd felt in her earlier was like hot coffee to my senses: it was warm and bitter, but comforting. She was feeling very protective of me, though not just the way one friend is with another who's considering buying an unflattering top. If it came to it, she would throw down over my safety. She'd done so before.

"Come on, get dressed. You don't have any early appointments today, so I think we should go to The Internets and—"

"The mugging Saturday. Where was it?"

"Just, like, downtown," Chloe said, peeking out of my closet. "I could get the exact address if you need it."

"I don't— No. I don't know. I was just curious. This whole situation is just really weird."

"Very weird," Chloe agreed, going back to picking through my clothes. Before we could discuss it any further, my phone rang, buzzing across my nightstand. I grabbed it, my first thought that it might be Owen calling for an early morning booty call.

"Hello?"

"Gwen, it's Stanley. I have a favor to ask you."

I blinked, not sure if my level of confusion was to be blamed on not being awake or at the rapid change in topic.

"Stan? Hi. What time is it?" I pulled the phone back, saw that Chloe had woken me up at the ungodly hour of 7:23 a.m. Pressing the phone to my ear, I amended, "Never mind. What did you need?"

"I got a disturbing call from my neighbor this morning. Apparently Norma sent flowers to my house. I don't know how she got my address, but I can't get hold of my agent to find out."

"Wow, I'm sorry. Are you still in Seattle?" He'd mentioned he was leaving, but my date with Owen had shoved all talk of his plans right out of my mind.

"I'm not supposed to be. I was going to take a car to the train station-"

"I would have driven you," I interrupted. Stan let out a soft laugh.

"You're not a morning person, I know. I was about to leave when Maria called. She's been feeding my cat and watering my plants, and she said the flowers were left on the porch, addressed to me from Norma. They—" He cut off. Chloe had stepped out of my closet, holding a blue shirt and dark grey slacks and watching me. After a brief silence, he continued.

"The card said that she wanted us to enjoy the flowers together, that things would be better once we were out of Seattle. I don't know what that means, but I'm getting sort of worried. I've already notified the police but I don't particularly want to go home. Unfortunately, when I called down to extend my stay here, the desk said that I had a package, also from Norma, here at the desk."

"Jeez," I hissed, torn between being impressed and horrified at the woman's determination. Stan was quiet for a moment before sighing.

"Would you mind if I stayed in your guest room until this is sorted out? I don't think it should be more than a day or two."

"Of course. It's yours as long as you need it."

"Thank you so much, Gwen. I'll get a cab and—"

"No cabs. Chloe and I will pick you up."

"Are you sure?"

"Of course. Have your stuff ready, stay in your room. Door-to-door service."

Stan thanked me again, gave me the room number, and double-checked to make sure I knew my way there. I pinned his question on how frazzled he was, not blaming him for forgetting that I'd dropped him off at the hotel just twenty-four hours ago. After we said our goodbyes, I hung up and turned to Chloe.

"Change of plans. We're rescuing Stanley Sneedley from a stalker."

"Never a dull moment with you," Chloe said, tossing me the clothes she'd picked out.

Twelve

"Are you sure this isn't a problem? Should I just find another hotel?"

"Stan, it's fine," I assured him. He was feeling guilty, and it was kicking me in the back of the skull. Thinking back to our conversation Sunday night, I perked up slightly.

"You said you bake?"

"Occasionally, yeah. Why?" It took him less than a second to get it. "Oh." He started laughing, which made Chloe giggle like a schoolgirl. She was giddier than the situation called for. Frowning her way, I reached a hand over and smacked my knuckles lightly against her thigh. This made her snort.

"I doubt you even have baking supplies, Gwen. Stan, we'll leave you Gwen's car in case you want to go to a store and get supplies."

"I'm sure I'll be fine," Stan insisted.

"You haven't seen her kitchen cabinets."

"Ah ..." Stan seemed to reconsider. "You're probably right. Are you two off to work after this?"

"Yep," Chloe said. We'd decided on the way not to mention Madeline or the deaths in the area. Stan knowing about my empathy was a far cry from what we were dealing with, and I felt it best to leave it that way.

"Well, if I'll have the house to myself, I'll just get some writing done."

Chloe made a small squealing sound and I rolled my eyes. Luckily, we were pulling into my driveway and she wouldn't be having fits of fangirl glee for much longer. Stan only had two bags, which hadn't surprised me. Once we were all inside, I made my way straight into my office.

"I'll get you the spare key to the house and one for my car, in case you want to go out. I have food, though." Chloe and Stan were silent, but I felt the twin spikes of cynicism from both of them that basically said, 'Yeah. Sure.'

I pouted a little as I dug into the accordion folder in which I kept my extra keys. When I got out to the living room, I found Chloe leaning in toward Sonny's cage, telling him how pretty he was. He was ringing his bells at her and showing off. I leaned into the guest room off the living area and watched Stan as he dug around in his computer bag.

"Here," I said, holding out the keys. He glanced up at me and smiled.

"Oh, thanks. Is there an outlet behind the desk?" he asked. I nodded, unsure what to say. We had gone from no contact for a decade to temporary roommates. When I only stood there staring and holding out the keys, he switched his focus from his laptop to me and smiled.

"You two go to work. I'll be fine here."

"Okay. Well." I set the keys on the nightstand and then backed up awkwardly, giving a small wave. I didn't have a problem having him in my space, but it was going to take some getting used to, especially considering the circumstances. "I'll see you tonight."

Fleeing, I headed out to the living room, caught Chloe's failed attempt at hiding a smile and grumbled at her.

"Shut up."

With Stan's issues bumping up against our own, we didn't make it to The Internets until just after their lunch rush. My first appointment had been a fairly well-adjusted young woman who came in sporadically to talk about mild personal issues; unlike some of my other clients, she didn't leave me drained or paranoid.

The first thing I saw as we entered the café was Mel, leaning over the new waitress, his face too close to hers. I took in the scene with confusion. Unlike most women, she seemed severely unhappy with his advances; it was like watching him hit on me. Chloe made her way straight to the counter, asking to talk to Holly in private. As I watched the waitress pull away from Mel, shaking her head, I aimed squarely for the two of them and made my way over.

"Really, I have a boyfriend," she lied. "I'm sorry. Please—"

"Jeez, Mel, leave her alone."

The girl turned to me, relief flooding her face. She swallowed thickly and nodded, though I could tell it was an unintentional reaction to my rescue, not an agreement that I had a point. Mel looked up at me, his face lacking all traces of the confidence I was used to. His blue eyes were wider than usual, his five o'clock shadow looking thicker on one side. The shirt he was wearing was open one button too far and it made him look sleazy rather than sexy.

Suddenly, I wasn't sure who I felt more sorry for.

"Did you need help?" the waitress asked desperately. I glanced down, saw that she'd gotten a nametag: Jenny. I shook my head at her and then jerked a thumb behind me, toward the front of the restaurant.

"No, but I think Holly does. I have to talk to this idiot."

"Hey," Mel said, though his protest was mild. She was already ducking away from him, rushing toward the cash register. I followed her progress as she hustled and saw Holly gesturing Chloe into the kitchen. When I turned back to Mel, I found him in my face.

I jolted and swore, annoyed by his proximity, and not just because he's Mel. It was different, though, than what I normally felt near him. When I pressed a hand against his chest, he took it as an invitation, grabbing my hips and pulling my body against his, pressing his crotch to my belly.

Baffled that being so close to him still wasn't physically painful, I stared up at his normally pretty face. His emotions were strange; not just milder, but also of a different type than I was used to. We were inches away from each other and I didn't feel like hitting him or shoving him. I still wanted him gone, but the revulsion was unfamiliar, more a gooey disgust and not so much a personal reaction based on some genetic mix-up that had given me magical powers.

"You're still all screwed up," I mumbled from inches away. The false confidence he was projecting across his face crumbled, and he pushed away from me.

"Look, I know you're always saying you don't want to sleep with me, but this line you're taking about my mojo being screwed up is just rude. I'm fine," he insisted. The emotion rolling out of him was akin to an A-student who'd gotten their first D in a class they were convinced they'd passed with flying colors. I felt one side of my mouth tug up in an amused grin. When his expression scrunched into a full pout, I let out a snort.

"When was the last time you got laid?"

"What?" he demanded; it was a stall tactic, I could tell. "Last night!"

Knowing he was lying, I just crossed my arms, lifting a brow and giving him a cynical stare. He sighed, his arms coming up in a frustrated flail.

"Tuesday, okay? It was Tuesday night. But everything is *fine*."

"Is that why you couldn't shave straight this morning?"

"What?" he asked, hands coming to rub along his jaw. Watching him stand there so out of sorts made me laugh. Mel blinked down at me before his eyes went wide, his expression filling with embarrassed outrage. He lifted a finger and shoved it against my chest, just above my left breast. I felt the impact, but it wasn't hard enough to do any damage.

"I'm not mated," he said, horror singing through his voice as if I'd accused him of tossing a basket of happy kittens over a cliff. I had no idea what he was talking about, or why he'd used a phrase to describe animals coupling as if it was sacred and all-important. "You—I'm leaving. There are plenty of better places to pick up women." Pushing past me, he stalked toward the front, slamming the door open as he rushed through. I shook my head, still confused but chuckling over his behavior. It had been a year since I'd met Mel and nearly every moment he spent trying to annoy me had been torture. Now he seemed mildly annoying at worst, and I wasn't sure if I would ever get used to not hating him on sight.

I moved to the front of the counter and gestured to the kitchen, asking Jenny if she minded me going back.

"Thanks for that," she said in lieu of answering. Gesturing toward the front door, she continued. "I've heard he's a nice guy, but he was just giving me the willies." To demonstrate, she gave a full-body shudder. I just nodded.

"Yeah, me too."

At my admission, she smiled, sighed with relief. It took her a second to realize I'd asked a question, and she gasped.

"Oh, right! Sorry. Holly said to let you back there, so … yeah, just come around the counter." She moved like a timid mouse toward the far wall, lifted the bar and waited for me. I wandered over, nodded at her.

"Thanks."

I found Holly sitting on an exposed shelf, among Tetra Pak boxes of soy and almond milks, cans of chocolate powder, and sacks of flour. I took the time to look around the back room of The Internets, marveling at the industrial-sized cooking equipment. So many delicious cakes had been baked in this room, I thought. I kind of wanted to drop to my knees like I'd entered a holy place.

Holly was leaning over her thick thighs, elbows resting on her knees. She looked tired, and I was guessing she hadn't been able to sit down since before the lunch rush.

Chloe was leaning against one of the counters, one ankle crossed over the other, her phone in her hand. She glanced at me, gave me a cursory smile, and then turned back to Holly.

"And you're sure she was here Monday through Thursday last week? She didn't call out until Friday?" Chloe asked.

"Definitely. We had a *Who* night Tuesday and she was dressed as a Silent," Holly explained. Chloe let out a sound of appreciation. "I left at midnight but I know she was there the whole evening before that. The only time I didn't see her was—well. When she was …" Holly's cheeks went rosy pink as she trailed off, and I felt discomfort splash out from her. It rolled along my skin like syrup.

"When she was what?" Chloe asked.

"She and some guy went into the back office for a while at around ten, but they were only in there for, like, fifteen minutes. I mean, it may have been up to twenty-five minutes, but probably not." She was lying about the 'probably not.'

My eyebrows flew up and I felt the embarrassment from Holly jump into me. Chloe was unbothered.

"Oh, that's not a big deal." She shrugged a shoulder, tucked her phone into her pocket again. "As long as it wasn't in the kitchen, I think it's fine. Health codes being what they are." Sensing that Holly was still uncomfortable essentially ratting out her boss for screwing a customer right on shift, Chloe pushed away from the counter. She waggled her brows and gave Holly an easy, lascivious smile.

"I mean who doesn't dream of getting paid to have a quickie in the afternoon, you know?" When Holly let out a quick bark of a laugh, Chloe jerked a thumb at me. "This one's always trying to bed the PI who works upstairs from us."

"Am not!" I argued.

Holly's brows went up and she turned to me. Her embarrassment burned away under a smile and a stab of curiosity. "Mel?"

"I'm not always trying—"

"You should!" Holly brows jolted, mimicking Chloe's, and she pushed to her feet. She gestured at me, more at ease than she'd been just a few seconds earlier. "He's a good lay."

"You slept with *Mel?*"

"Oh yeah. Couple months ago."

I just stood there, jaw dropped open, shaking my head.

"He's so …" I gave a shudder that matched Jenny's from earlier. "*Mel.*" Spitting his name out, I made a vomiting sound. Chloe laughed next to me.

"Oh, come on. You know that one day, you two will go at each other in the supply closet, come out all disheveled and bow-legged."

"We don't even have a supply closet!" I countered. Chloe rolled her eyes.

"The records room, then. The counter in there is probably big enough for him to—" Before the action she was miming with her hands could get too dirty, I stomped my foot, interrupting her.

"Are we done here?" I demanded. Holly laughed, clapping her hands together at my discomfort. I had a feeling she thought I was joking about not wanting to sleep with Mel. Most straight women just don't seem to understand where I'm coming from.

"Yeah, we're good." Chloe turned back to Holly, lifting her chin, her brows.

"You take a break soon, okay? You look beat."

"I'm not used to all the long days. I'll be fine once I see the paycheck."

"Well, I'm sure Mad will be back soon."

Chloe waited until we were upstairs in my office before she caught me up.

"Madeline was downstairs all day Tuesday, so she couldn't have killed the man at the train station. Otherwise, it's up in the air. I don't buy that she did any of this, but I can't get ahold of her and Holly couldn't really provide an alibi for the other three murders."

"And you're sure they're murders?" I asked, heading into the records room to get tea started. Chloe followed me as far as the doorway and then leaned on the jamb.

"Train guy was absolutely killed by something, and if I was your boyfriend my first—"

"If you were my boyfriend?" I asked, lost for a second as my brain replayed the image of Chloe thrusting her hips and moving her hands as if doing impure things to a phantom sexual conquest.

"Yeah, you know who I mean. Tall, foxy white guy?" Chloe asked, teasing. "Here to see a woman about a corpse?"

"I know," I lied, shaking the thought of getting intimate with Chloe out of my head. She was cute and all, but it would never work.

"Right, if I was Owen, my first guess would be succubus just based on how he died. According to his family, he was in great shape when they dropped him off at Union Station but he was a mess by the time he got here."

"Union Station?" I asked, grabbing a mug from the cabinet.

"Down in Portland. They found him up here, slumped in his seat looking disheveled and sick and, you know, dead."

"I'm getting to know dead better than I ever wanted to," I said with a wince. "But, again, how do they know he didn't just have a heart attack like the others?"

"They're chalking it up to undiagnosed cancer. His insides were, like I said, a mess. There's no real way to just explain something like this, but the police will note the death down as natural causes and move on."

I shook my head. "I don't understand. A healthy man stepped onto a train in Portland and got hauled off in Seattle dead of cancer? That doesn't just happen, does it?"

"No, which is how we know it's hinky. Okay." Chloe shifted, standing as if she had to give an important presentation to a bunch of stuffed-shirted businessmen. "Lots of creatures feed on people, right? Some are like Dirk and it's pretty obvious what happened when you find a corpse with no blood, covered in bite marks. Others feed like Madeline, on the … I don't know." Chloe waved her hand as if she couldn't explain it but her emotions said otherwise; there was an edge of a lie behind her words. "Essence of a person. That still takes its toll on the body."

"Madeline causes cancer?" I squeaked, horrified that I'd been in her presences nearly every day for over a year.

"No, though if she really pressed she sort of could. But like I said, she knows what she's doing. Holly said she was in the back room with some guy, right? She was feeding. It's probably why she has so many customers. Ladies, men, anyone she can get her hands on, if there's sex to be had, she's gonna suck it down. Ah." Chloe snorted as she realized how she'd phrased things, and I felt the smirk she gave me. "No pun intended."

"But—okay, you lost me. What's going on with the heart attacks and who's got cancer?"

"No one's got—okay, follow along. A succubus can cause an emotion in someone else and, if the person chooses to act on it, the succubus can slurp up the aftermath and chow down. If the person chooses not to act on it, though, the succubus can still feed, but the victim fights it. The essence— the soul," her voice went hard and this time excitement sparked briefly, "takes the hit. Madeline's owned The Internets for years, in this same building. She wouldn't still be around if she'd spent the last decade killing people. She just, you know." Chloe winked, sidled close like she'd seen something in me she really liked. "Sets her feelers out, tests if someone's willing and if they are, she gets her kicks."

I gave Chloe a quick once-over and then caught her gaze, making it clear I wasn't willing. "And if they're not?"

"Then she leaves them be and the person goes on about their day wondering why they really want to get laid."

"I already got laid," I pointed out, convinced Chloe was about to get her feelers on me. She grinned and winked, grabbing my mug off the counter and moving to pour the freshly boiling water in over the teabag. She was quiet as she tipped the sugar dispenser over the cup quickly, letting barely a pinch drop in. I realized she'd stolen my tea for herself. "How do you know all this?"

"How do I know anything?" she asked, glancing at me. I shook my head, at a loss. Her expression pinched briefly with pity and she shook her head. "I ask questions. Madeline and I have had many a chat."

"In the back room?" I asked, my tone accusatory. Chloe shook her head.

"Not allowed."

"Not ... allowed?"

Chloe blinked and I felt embarrassment and regret spike out of her as she realized what she'd said. We both heard the outer door open; Chloe twisted without another word and left to greet my next appointment.

"Hey Camilla. You want some tea? We've got the water ready!"

OLIVIA R .BURTON

Thirteen

Since Stan had my car, Chloe was driving me home after Camilla left. Because nothing else seemed as pressing or interesting as our current problems with a rogue succubus and my gun-toting lover, I piped up as soon as I was buckled in.

"If we're so sure Madeline's innocent, I'll just give Owen a call and let him know." Chloe made a sound that seemed to agree with me, but I could feel the doubt in her. "What?

"He believes she's killing people and she's sent men to his house to, ah, have a chat with him." Her tone indicated she was convinced the chat would have involved fists and feet, or maybe guns and knives. "I don't think he's going to just back off if you tell him you think she's innocent."

"But you think it too. And you seem to know what you're talking about. You could tell him all about your history and how you've talked with Madeline. You said she's been at this a while, that you trust her. I bet he'd believe someone with your experience."

Chloe's face was carefully blank, but my suggestion that she tell him about her past brought up a surge of emotions in such a mix that I couldn't entirely get a handle on them. Reaching my hand over, I touched her arm.

"What's wrong?" She was quiet for a moment, opening her mouth twice as if she couldn't decide how to answer. Finally, she glanced at me, her expression settling on discomfort. The soup of emotions boiled off until she was left with amusement and cynicism.

"He walked into our office, what, twelve hours ago, and you want me to sit down and have a chat with him about growing up around trolls and empaths?" She raised her voice slightly, as if parodying herself. "'Hi! I'm Chloe Warren! I want to talk to you about the succubus you're here to kill and why I think she's keen.' You think he's going to back off just because I say so?"

"I don't know," I said, feeling stupid for suggesting it. "I don't know what else to do. I like Madeline, I don't want her to get arrested or something, as long as we think she's not guilty. And that's what we think, right? That's where we landed?"

"That's where I landed. You don't sound like you've made the leap yet."

"I'm kind of trapped between a rock and a hard place here. I just met the guy, but he saved my life from men *Madeline sent*, and you're telling me that the two bodies I've stumbled on in the last week probably died from a succubus. She's the only one I know, and Owen seems capable. He seems like he knows what he's talking about."

"I think you're just thinking about his rock-hard place," Chloe said, shaking her head. "I've saved your life too. And you've known me way longer. Don't assume you know him just because he fed you and gave it to you good."

I sighed, not liking that she had a point. Despite Chloe getting squirrely sometimes when her personal life comes up, she's someone I trust more than nearly anyone else.

"I didn't say you shouldn't try," Chloe said after a while. We were pulling into my neighborhood and I realized I'd lost track of time as I sat in the passenger seat pouting. "Give him a call later tonight, tell him what we found out. Let him make his own decision. It seems like Madeline's pretty capable, too. If she can send muscle after your boyfriend, she's probably in good shape. It's not your job to save her."

"Yeah, you're right." We pulled up into my driveway and Chloe patted my shoulder.

"Now cheer up. Maybe you'll get inside and find that Stan baked you a dozen cakes."

I perked up at the idea, though I knew how unlikely it was.

I opened my door to light and warmth and the smell of food. I froze in place, confused by the sensations, as they were paired with the sight of my living room. I'm often too impatient to prepare and cook real food. My microwave gets more use than any other appliance except my fridge.

Around the bend of the kitchen was my small dining table, at which sat Stan, Sonny snoozing on his shoulder. Now that I was closer, I could hear that the music he was listening to was low-key, something in French pumping out of his laptop. I had never bothered to take any language in school, so I probably wouldn't have understood anything other than 'Oui' or 'croissant.' Possibly 'tiramisu,' assuming that was French at all.

Stan had stuffed a pillow between his narrow butt and my kitchen chair to lift him to an ergonomically correct typing level. On the stove next to me, a pot of stew bubbled intermittently next to a covered pan that smelled amazing. My oven was on low, but I didn't bother checking what was inside.

Stan hadn't noticed my arrival and I found the sight of him at my table too sweet for words. Some vindictive part of my brain reminded the rest of me that this was what I had given up coming home to every night. I had lost nightly home-cooked meals and a sweet, loving husband because I had decided to take the coward's way out. Ignoring that part of my stupid brain, I moved forward quietly and stood behind Stan to watch his work.

He was typing at a pace I couldn't have hoped to match even after several cups of coffee. Occasionally he'd back up a few words, delete, rewrite, and then move on. I read over the story he was crafting but realized I didn't understand it so far in. The word count had just crossed forty-two thousand and kept steadily climbing. Standing, I did my best to bring him out of his writing trance gently. I cleared my throat and stepped to the side.

His fingers continued for two more sentences before one hand paused and the other stopped dead after mashing the shortcut keys to save his work. Turning to me, he blinked twice and then smiled. I tipped my head, grinning as the comprehension slowly filled his bespectacled blue eyes.

"Oh. Hi. I—how long have you been here?"

"Not long. I just wanted to let you know I'm home; you can continue."

Sonny had awoken, moving to puff out his feathers and stretch himself completely conscious. Absently, Stan lifted a finger to poke into Sonny's neck and rub. It was almost too cute for me to bear.

"I think I'm okay for now. I should check the food, too. I turned it down to warm ... Well, I think it was recently." His brow creased in distress and he slid the chair back, getting to his feet and moving around me to the stove. I turned to watch him and nearly whimpered when he lifted the lid on the covered pot. Spicy scents hit me, and my stomach growled, trying to keep the threatening hunger at bay. The hunger wasn't intimidated; it attacked.

"What is that, oh my god, gimme," I demanded. Stan glanced at me, a small smile on his face. When I reached out to grab a piece of the sausage out of the pan, he caught my hand gently, shaking his head.

"It'll be better together, I promise. Can you put Sonny away while I set up?"

Despite what my feelings for him had been just a few seconds earlier, I fought off a burst of loathing. Separating me from food never ends well. He just watched me with his sweet face, still holding my hand. Unable to argue with that expression, I sighed, moved my hand out of his and tucked it under Sonny. My traitorous bird danced to the side, trying to avoid my finger, wanting to stay in the curve of Stan's neck.

"Come on, Sonny," I insisted. Stan twisted to see Sonny's face, murmuring something to him quietly. Apparently the bird agreed with his suggestion and relented, stepping onto my finger. I brought him to my mouth, giving his beak a gentle kiss and petting him with my other hand.

That seemed to subdue his distaste for me.

Before heading back into the tempting kitchen, I hit the bedroom to put on comfortable clothes. By the time I got back to the dining area, Stan had moved my pots and pans to the sink, made up two plates, and poured two glasses of white wine.

"I love you," I said. Each plate held one of my brightly colored bowls, a mound of mixed veggies and sausage, and a giant hunk of steaming garlic bread. I could probably eighty-six the vegetables without having to eat them if I really wanted. I'd been pretty good at doing so as a child, though my father had caught me nearly every time.

Stan smiled as he slid between the wall and one of the dining chairs, but kept his eyes on the plates, making sure he didn't accidentally dump stew all over. I took the seat across from him and dove into the food without considering I was being rude. He ate more daintily than me, his posture perfect. Somewhere around the fourth time I crammed food carelessly into my mouth and whacked my teeth with my fork or spoon, I nodded over at him and made the effort to sit up like a human.

"This is good," I announced, my fork paused in front of my lips. For some reason, I felt the need to point at the food with my other hand. You know, just in case he thought I was talking about something else. His face lit up.

"Thank you. It's mostly vegetables."

I felt myself scowl but I kept eating. He laughed when I didn't argue or balk. After another bite, I stabbed at one of the sausage chunks and lifted it toward the light.

"This isn't meat," I said, realizing it shouldn't have surprised me. He shrugged a shoulder but didn't elaborate. Deciding it was delicious either way, I ate it and then set the fork down, grabbing a napkin. Wiping my face, I waited until I had swallowed and grabbed for the wine.

"How did you teach Sonny Morse code?" Stan asked. I frowned over the rim of the glass and then shook my head after I swallowed.

"Huh?"

"He knows his name, your name, and hello. I figured you taught him."

"I don't know what you're talking about." I squinted at my ex and then twisted to stare around the corner, through the kitchen and across the living room. Sonny was standing next to his dish, picking at his own food. I turned back to Stan, confused.

"He rings his bells in patterns that spell, 'hello.' I thought it was a fluke but when I said hi back, he spelled his name. You didn't know?"

"I don't know Morse code," I said, baffled.

"Maybe his previous owner taught him?"

"I got him as a baby from a pet store. I don't think so." I was getting an idea of who might have taught him, though. I glanced uncomfortably toward my fridge, back to Stan and then immediately back to the fridge. Stan followed my gaze and a bubble of surprise popped in his psyche.

"Oh yes, I wanted to ask you about that," he said. Before he had finished speaking, I was on my feet, moving between the dining set and the fridge. The magnets had been moved around.

The candy thief had struck again.

Across the bottom of my fridge, some of the words and phrases it had previously laid out had been moved to form several new sentences. Like the first time I'd discovered my magnetic poetry crowding my fridge, I wondered how there were magnets of words that could not have come in any of my sets. Our names, for example.

I kneeled to read them and Stan stood behind me, bending at the waist.

Hi, Stan! Big Fan! :D

Gwen, you forgot your payment.

I lifted my gaze long enough to catch Stan push his glasses up his nose, before he pointed to what I was looking at.

"Did you write that?"

"No," I said with a sigh. Stan leaned to the side to meet my eyes, watching me for a moment before shifting and holding out a hand to help me up. Unlike Owen, he didn't pull me toward him, but he did make sure I was steady before letting go. I shook my head, unsure how to explain the fridge to Stan. He waited patiently but did glance back at the table as if worried the food might go bad in the ninety seconds we stood idly by. Realizing I was still hungry and the food was still delicious, I jerked my head in a gesture that we should continue eating.

"I have a sort of … pest problem," I explained, moving to take my seat again. Before saying or eating any more, I grabbed the wine and drank it all.

"A few months ago, I bumped up against … Shit," I said, shaking my head. Stan folded his hands together, nudged the plate out of the way, and gave me his full attention. I took another bite of food, trying to decide what to tell him. Finally, I decided to wing it.

"You know how I have a power." I used the fork to point at my head, referring to my empathy. "And that I'm not the only one. There are other people out there who have abilities, a lot of them more powerful than me. A few months ago, I somehow crossed the path of something that got into my home and left me all sorts of notes. It also ate all my— Dammit!" Realizing that my sugar stash was probably decimated again, I dropped the fork and jumped to my feet. Stan felt a stab of pity when I smacked my knee against the table in my rush to get up. The pity only grew as he watched me hobble toward the cabinet where I kept most of my sweets.

Surprisingly, they were left mostly intact. Only one box of Twinkies had been emptied, the wrappers left in a sticky pile on top of a blue scrap of paper. Gratitude spelled out in familiar handwriting mocked me: *Thanks!*

I turned to stuff the box and wrappers into the recycling bin I kept under the sink, but I left the note on the counter. I stared at it for a moment, before turning and finding Stan watching me with a look of concern on his face. He was genuinely worried about my state of mind.

"Uh," I murmured, before flexing my sore knee and moving back toward him. "Sorry. You probably didn't expect all this when we ran into each other at The Internets on Friday, right?"

He gave a nervous laugh before shaking his head and grabbing for the wine. He took a sip, reconsidered, and then finished the whole glass. I nodded at him.

"You're probably gonna need that. The short of it … No." I shook my head. "I don't think it works without the whole story."

I explained the candy thief as we ate, detailing everything from the morning I'd woken up to a house barren of sugar and a fridge full of prophetic notes spelled out in magnetic poetry. I told him about the sticky notes, which were usually helpful, occasionally rude, and always confusing. By the end, Stan knew all the salient details of my experience with a child-nabbing demon, an old friend of Mel's who'd become a vampire, and the candy thief that had helped keep me alive during the whole ordeal.

While I hadn't at first appreciated the notes that showed up without explanation, and while I still didn't appreciate the fact that every note seemed to be given in exchange for my sweet snacks, I had gotten used to it happening. Stan hadn't had the time or experience to get used to it, though.

"So this thing just shows up and rearranges your things and you don't object?"

"Oh, I object. I just can't do anything about it. Plus, may I repeat, it seems to want me safe and sound. That's the most important part, I think. And hey, apparently it's a big fan of you. That's … something. Your fans are pretty cool, right?"

Stan was staring at me askance, his expression skeptical, his psyche stuffed with nerves. I reached a hand across the table to rub his fingers.

"There's nothing to worry about. It's just weird. It's like having mice, but the mice don't just eat your food, they also leave you notes."

"Always the same sort of notes?"

"Yeah, you know. Well, and sometimes just silly ones. And …" I trailed off, realizing that I'd gotten lax when it came to my foreshadowing fridge. "It sometimes tells the future."

"What?" Stan's voice went wry, and I felt cynicism bump up against my curiosity. I pushed to my feet, leaving my empty plate and glass as I closed in on the fridge and looked it over.

Taking my time, I scanned the front of the fridge, seeing things that I had missed, or just forgotten about since November. The appliance explained where my keys had been when I'd misplaced them two weeks ago

(*Second drawer on the left*), as well as warning me not to get dressed in the dark (*Red shoe is not black shoe*) that had been valid the second week in April. Chloe hadn't let me live that down for a while.

As I parsed every sentence the thief had set out for me, I started to really wonder why I didn't pay more attention to what it was trying to tell me. Most of the lines were nonsense until I looked at them after the predictions had come to pass, but maybe if I took the time to really memorize every one I could be ahead of the game.

As I got to the bottom and really considered how much work it would take to memorize everything from, 'Don't go in that exam room alone,' to 'It's the silver knife you gotta watch out for.' I felt my shoulders slump.

"There's probably something here I need to pay attention to, but I'm just not sure what."

"It's a refrigerator, Gwen," Stan said from my right. I blinked and glanced over, realizing he was rinsing off our dishes and loading them into the dishwasher. I shook my head.

"It's not that simple, okay? I know it sounds weird, but you see this one?" I pointed at the one at the very start. "Right after I found these, I nearly slipped and broke my neck on some spilled water. I still don't know what a lot of these mean. But if I'd been paying attention, I could have avoided a very embarrassing shoe incident in April."

Stan looked skeptical, but I felt like I was on my way to convincing him. He nodded once and set the dish he'd been rinsing into the dishwasher, then turned off the water. Rounding the open door of the washer, he stepped up close and looked over the words with me. I watched his face as he read down the list, wondering which phrase was causing which expression. When he had finished, he cleared his throat delicately and then tapped one toward the top.

"Werewolf puppies?"

"That's one I don't understand. The only werewolf I know doesn't have puppies. He's a grown man not interested in settling—" My conversation with Mel that afternoon jumped to mind. "Uh. Settling down." Mel slept with everything that moved, but as far as I was aware he didn't have any illegitimate kids running around. He'd been acting strangely, though, and had mentioned being mated as if it was a bad thing. I wondered if the fridge knew something about his relationship status he didn't. Was Mel pregnant? Was that a thing? I'd have to ask Chloe.

"And this one?"

"She missed the convention because your boyfriend didn't," I said, reading the one he'd tapped. Even though I'd skimmed it just minutes before on my own, saying it out loud made some thought in the back of my mind tingle like it was waking up. I'd been single for most of the last decade, dating sporadically but never seriously. It had been since high school that I'd really bothered calling anyone my boyfriend.

And yet, Chloe had referred to Owen as such several times that day alone.

The thought wriggling in the folds of my mind tried its best to make itself known, but I just couldn't quite grasp it. I shook my head and turned to Stan, wondering what the candy thief had meant and why I couldn't make it out.

"Is everything okay?"

"I'm not sure," I admitted. "These all make sense eventually. Not at first, not until the thing I'm supposed to know happens, but they're here for a reason. This one ..." I bit my lip and shook my head again, before moving past Stan and heading into the living room.

"Gwen?"

Waving my hand in the air as if to placate him, I grabbed my bag off the chair by the door and dug around until I found my phone. Chloe answered before the phone had even fully rung once.

"Hey," she started. I interrupted.

"Where was the body found on Saturday?"

"The—what?" I'd thrown her off.

"Saturday. You said one of the people who died was found on Saturday, downtown. *Where* downtown?"

"I'd have to look at the address again, but I think—"

"Was it by the convention? Anywhere in that area?"

Chloe was quiet for a few moments and I started tapping my foot impatiently. I'd spent nearly the entire day at the convention with Stan, but more importantly so had Owen.

"It was," Chloe said finally. "Why?"

"And you said the guy on the train was from Portland?"

"Yes. Why?" she repeated, her tone wary.

"Because Owen was at the convention and Norma wasn't."

"Norma, Stan's stalker?" Chloe asked, sounding lost. I turned to find Stan had followed me into the living room and was standing by my other chair, watching me with concern naked on his face. I nodded, even though Chloe couldn't see it.

"I think Madeline's innocent."

"Good," Chloe said, before I heard a knock at my door. She hung up and I realized I could feel her just outside. I dropped my phone onto my bag on the chair and went to open the door. Chloe stepped in, waved briefly at Stan, and then turned to face me. "Because we're going to see her."

"We're what?" I asked, shutting the door. Chloe turned and marched down the hall toward my bedroom without answering. I looked to Stan as if he'd be able to offer an explanation, but he was just as confused as I was.

Giving in, I followed Chloe down the hall and found her in my bedroom, digging through my closet. I felt Stan follow me in but I didn't mention it.

"Chloe, what are you doing?"

"Get dressed. We're going to see Madeline. What's this about Norma?" Her eyes flicked past me to Stan. "He should come with us if the stalker's involved."

"Come with you where? Who's Madeline?"

"She's a succubus. She owns The Internets, the restaurant downstairs from our office?" Chloe made it a question, as if Stan might not remember going in and buying me a hot chocolate. "She's invited us over to discuss murder."

"I don't—" Stan started. I shook my head and waved my hand his way.

"You can stay, don't worry. Chloe, he doesn't need—"

"You're the one who thinks this Norma chick is killing people. Madeline's being blamed for something Stan's stalker is doing and maybe he can help."

"I don't—" Stan started again, his voice high.

"I'm not dragging him into—" I got a face full of t-shirt as Chloe tossed clothes my way. When I uncovered my head, I found Chloe had moved past me to speak to Stan.

"No one's going to hurt you," Chloe explained, matter-of-factly. "Gwen, get dressed. I'll explain what's going on."

"Chloe—"

"Get dressed or I'm dragging you there in stained sweats and no bra," Chloe said, wrapping her arm around Stan's shoulders to lead him out into the hallway. I huffed out a breath but considered that I didn't really have a choice in the matter. Resigned to the direction my evening had taken, I dropped the clothes on the bed and moved into the closet to grab a bra.

OLIVIA R .BURTON

Fourteen

Stan had been remarkably calm under the circumstances, but I knew him well enough to understand that it wasn't necessarily a good thing. Finally, as Chloe led us toward Greenlake, she tucked Norma's last letter into the folder, switching her attention to her phone. She typed some text in, pointed to a light up ahead and ordered me to take a left. I obliged, glancing in the rearview mirror at Stan. He was staring out the window, his expression thoughtful but tense. Chloe took a breath to speak, but Stan got there first.

"Is this some sort of party? One of those murder mysteries where everyone has an identity and we all guess at the end of the—" He stuttered. "Of the role-play who's the killer? This is a game?"

"No, this is all real," Chloe said, her tone bordering on rude. Stan's posture changed slightly and I felt a slice of insult wedge into him. He turned to face the back of her head, his brows drawing in. "This is kind of a defining moment in your life, Sneedley. Suck it up and go with it, because I'm not going to pick your skinny ass off the floor if you faint when we get inside. Up here, third house on the left."

"Chloe!" I snapped, irritated that she'd done a complete one-eighty from the way she'd been treating him before. She met my gaze, but before I could chastise her further, I felt Stan's mood sway away from nervous and baffled. He turned to frown at the back of her headrest, cynicism chasing away the very last of his nerves. When neither Stan nor I launched into a lecture about her behavior, Chloe winked and then pointed. I hadn't even put the car in park before she was out of it and crossing the small yard to the front door.

"You'll be fine," I assured Stan as he unbuckled his seatbelt. "Chloe is surprisingly great to have around in a crisis."

"This entire situation sounds ridiculous."

"Wait until you get inside and meet the succubus."

"I'm sure she's very nice," Stan said, his tone polite but unable to hide the fact that he thought I was making the whole thing up.

"This one isn't how you'd picture."

"I'm sure she's very nice," Stan repeated.

Madeline's house looked to be about a hundred years old, though the white-edged windows and sky blue paint looked modern. It had a bright red front door and a porch that jutted out no further than your average teenager's under-bite. Chloe had walked in like she owned the place but left the door cracked. Stan and I glanced at each other and I shrugged before stepping in ahead of him.

It was like stepping into a soup of sex and sexual frustration.

The air was thick with arousal and desire. Everyone was clothed, but I was betting that if I'd walked up to any one of the men standing around the living room and rubbed myself roughly along his body, I would have discovered an enthusiastic erection. In that moment, I liked the idea more than I could properly articulate.

I found myself staring at a man who would not have caught my eye in any other situation. He was wide at the shoulders, with a narrow waist, thick thighs, and a skeletal nose. His eyebrows were too thin for his Neanderthal brow and his lips were unappealingly thick. In any other place, I wouldn't have given him a second glance.

In Madeline's living room he could not have been more attractive.

I felt Stan step inside, pressing himself to my back slightly to the left of matching up our hips exactly. I could hear his breath over my left ear, and it was coming a little fast. The feeling I'd had coming in, the worry I'd been holding onto about Stan, crept back into my brain. He was unprepared for this, and standing here thinking about bedding a perfect stranger in front of my ex-husband suddenly didn't seem so appealing.

I took a deep breath, which pressed me a little harder against Stan; he lifted his hands to my waist, held on, and leaned his lips a bit closer to my ear. As I was able to separate my actual emotions from those in the room, I felt myself let out a nervous giggle. Stan's hands were sliding forward around my waist, and he'd shifted to press himself more symmetrically against me. Unless I was mistaken, I wasn't the only one thinking about getting naked and rolling around with someone else on the floor of Madeline's living room.

Chloe turned to look me over and her eyes were a little heavy, her lips damp. I thought in that moment that she was about to cross the room and make a me-sandwich with Stan. I couldn't decide if I would have objected.

"Um," I squeaked, before trying to step forward. Stan held me in place and I let out another sound; it came out of my throat as more of a moan than I think I'd intended. Closing my eyes, I tried to picture what I was feeling more precisely.

My emotions were there, under the others. I could see lust above all else, growing out of Madeline to tangle like a living vine through the mess of fear, anger, panic, and a breezy, familiar amusement. I grabbed onto the fear, which was easier than I expected it to be. Both Stan and I were feeling it, though it was nearly strangled by the lust. Opening my eyes, I looked down, letting the fear take over and make my skin cold. My heart started beating a little harder and I grasped Stan's hands with my own, catching sight of goose bumps along my arms. Somehow, touching his skin seemed to magnify the fear I could feel from him, as if I could pull it into myself and suffer in his place. Gently, I pulled Stan's hands away from my belly and looked up to meet Chloe's eyes.

I stepped out of the circle of Stan's arms and turned to the side so I could look between Chloe and my ex. They had similar expressions on their faces, and I was betting that I hadn't seen either look at me this way before. Even Stan, back in the good old days, had never been quite as direct as this.

Doing the only thing that felt true to me in that moment, I took a very deep breath and screamed. It was a release of tension, an announcement of discomfort, a demand for order, and an expression of the fear I'd focused on so heavily.

Stan jumped back, tripping over the slight bump of doorjamb and toppling. Chloe's body tensed, her eyes going alert immediately. Madeline gave a small smile and shifted in her seat. As my breath gave out, taking the scream down with it, I pointed at her and spoke.

My voice was strangled and raw, but I managed to demand, "Stop."

Her smile widened as she laughed. The tension in the room faded slightly but I still forced myself to step even further away from Stan. Despite holding onto the fear and seeing through the layer of lust she was using to coat my skin, I was still having trouble remembering that this was the absolute wrong time to lie on the porch with him and stick my hand down his pants.

Chloe sighed, taking a step back from Madeline as well, shaking her head. Her own lust was receding behind a wave of annoyance. She glared at the succubus, shook her head harder like she was trying to dislodge a fly from her nose, and then her gaze wandered to the guard at the back of the room. They eyed each other for a minute—ignoring the fact that Madeline stood and all but cut off their line of sight—and then Chloe snapped herself out of it.

"Cool it, Mad. We're not here to hurt you. Or fuck you." When nothing changed immediately, Chloe hopped forward, shot a fist out and punched Madeline in her shoulder just hard enough to knock the taller woman slightly off-balance. The lust in the room dissipated a little more, but I held onto my blanket of fear. Madeline straightened up, gave Chloe a mischievous little smile, and then took a very deep breath. Everyone else in the room seemed to exhale with relief.

As I've said before, Madeline isn't a very attractive woman. She's tall, but it doesn't work for her like with most women. Her limbs are ungainly, somehow looking out of proportion and unevenly muscled. She carries her weight in her front, pairing a saggy belly with wide hips above thighs that would be the star of any cellulite-themed tabloid. The yellow shirt she wore was too tight around her middle, really showing off the flab she carried just below her modest bust.

Her skin is clear but ruddy around her nose and cheeks, as if she's always just finished scrubbing too hard with a scalding washcloth. The hair on her arms is too dark and thick, though that particular trick of genetics had given her stunning lashes. Even after considering all that, one would still look on her face and be surprised at how unattractive it is. Buck teeth, small eyes, thin lips, and no chin were the least of her facial problems. She has a turkey neck, round cheeks and big ears.

Despite her appearance, and the fact that I'm straight, it would not have taken much in the seconds before to get me naked and into her bed.

"Sorry about that," Madeline said, her voice just a touch too squeaky; she always sounds like she's coming off a helium high. "It's sort of a security measure. These guys," she waved vaguely to the guard on her right, "are used to it and have been trained to resist, but outsiders walking in without an invitation? No chance." When she turned back to Chloe they shared a look I didn't understand, but I could feel frustrated, regretful embarrassment in Chloe.

The guy to whom she referred cleared his throat and I looked him over. Like the others in the room, he was impressively thick. Some of the guys looked more doughy than beefy, but they all gave me food-type thoughts; that is, they made me want to put them in my mouth.

Wincing over the residual lust—and if I wasn't mistaken, Madeline's hunger—still clouding my mind, I stepped outside to extend a helping hand down to Stan. He had fallen in such a way that the cut of his pants and the position of his legs hid any sign of whether or not he was still turned on. (I tried not to look, I swear.) Regardless, he refused to touch me, rolling over and pushing himself up and away from me. I dropped my hand when he didn't take it, doing my best not to feel insulted. His eyes darted between Madeline and me before he cleared his throat.

"Miss?" he asked, addressing her. "Can I ask that you refrain from using your powers on me?"

Madeline's lip quirked and I could tell she was confused about Stan's politeness, but charmed by it anyway.

"I will—assuming your friends here can vouch for you? While I haven't met the man I'm hiding from, I do know he's an attractive blond." Madeline turned to Chloe, lifted a brow. Chloe nodded.

"Vouched. This is Gwen's ex. Harmless as an infant."

"Stanley Sneedley. Ma'am," he said, unbothered by Chloe's assessment of him. Rubbing his palms on his thighs, he took a few awkward steps widely around me through the living room. Holding out his right hand, he met her gaze and waited patiently. As Madeline took his hand, an emotion passed through her, and I tensed, concerned for a split second that she was going to break her word and pull him into an embrace.

Something in his face changed her mind, though, and she let go of his hand and gestured behind her.

"Let's have coffee and we'll talk. I promise," she put her hand over her heart, "I'll thin out the sex mojo until you've gone."

We sat around Madeline's minuscule table while she moved about her small kitchen, pulling out supplies. She hummed something quietly as she put three different types of creamer, lumps of sugar, and mugs out on a tray. I spent the time building up my shields, knowing it wouldn't stop her from making me horny, but feeling more secure for it anyway. I also spent some time inspecting the bins she had in the corner: trash and recycling filled with wrappers from sugary, fattening snacks.

It answered my question about how a creature that fed on emotions had managed to get such a flabby mid-section.

Madeline set the tray down in the center of the table, which only left us a finger's width of table to work with. Chloe ignored the coffee and the tray full of various dairy creamer options but Stan cleared his throat and began politely pouring coffee into each cup. He didn't meet my eyes but I noticed a light flush along his neck and ears. As Stan picked up the first creamer and busied himself reading the ingredients, possibly just as a distraction, Madeline sat. There was no more room at the table, but she had an extra dining chair against the back wall. Chloe turned her own chair away from Stan and me to face Madeline.

"How are you all feeling?" Madeline asked.

"Better," Chloe said.

"I still kind of want to shove Stan to the floor and take his pants off," I admitted. He jerked away from me so quickly that his knee slammed against the leg of the table, making him grunt in pain. Tiny coffee tsunamis hit all three mugs, overtaking their sides. Chloe just gestured vaguely toward me.

"Ditto me to Gwen."

"Really?" I asked, a bit shocked. Chloe looked at me just long enough to give a shrug and a nod and then turned back to Mad.

"So, what's the scoop? Why is someone after you?"

"There's another succubus in town, one I don't know, and she's killing people. I've got eyes and ears looking for her, but she's pretty elusive. She showed up Tuesday, left a nasty corpse at the train station, and now seems to be hopping around the city."

"We think we know who she is, and we think she's here for him." Chloe jerked a thumb at Stan, who had moved subtly in his seat to face away from me, cradling his knee gently. I let him be nervous, pretending I hadn't noticed.

"Oh?" Madeline asked, shifting to cross her thick legs. She had to tuck her foot against the cabinet to keep the position, but she leaned forward and rested her forearms across her knee.

"Yeah, name's Norma, but I haven't done much looking for her yet. I wanted to make sure it's okay with you before I do."

I frowned at Chloe's wording, wondering why she was pitching it so comfortably, as if she'd be the one hunting Norma down and putting a stop to her antics.

"Well, she's not kin, I can assure you. Speaking of, I've sent Callum away, just in case this ..." Madeline sighed, shook her head. Her lip curled as she continued. "*Investigator* gets any ideas."

Uncomfortable looking directly at her, I turned my attention to the spilled coffee. It had bled to the edge of the tray, soaking the doily she'd laid under the pot. I glanced around the kitchen looking for napkins as Chloe continued.

"Have you seen him?"

"Nope. He and I have a history, though. He killed my mother."

We all froze, Stan and I looking back toward Madeline slowly, as if scared she was about go off on any one of us. She watched us blankly for a moment before laughing softly and shaking her head.

"It was years ago and she was old enough that she deserved it." Madeline met Chloe's eyes and waved her hand by the wiry hair tufted out near her ear, as if that explained it. "You know. Regardless, I'm not terribly comfortable having him in my city, let alone having him suspicious of my activities. After mother's death... Well, that has no bearing." She turned her attention to me directly and I felt a sadness creep in that hadn't been there just a moment before. "I'm sorry you got caught in the middle, before."

"I ..." Trailing off, I shrugged, unsure what to say. "It's okay."

"No, I didn't do my research. Well, I did, but not quite enough. I knew where he would be staying, but not that he had a date. The men I sent knew, though, which is doubly my fault. I should have specified that only he was to be addressed."

Stan turned to me and I felt my ears mirror the pink in his. Swallowing, I shook my head.

"It was sort of last minute, and I didn't get hurt."

"You could have, and that wasn't my intention. In fact, no one should have gotten hurt, but I admit I panicked. After hearing about the death at the train station and being alerted that—" She met my eyes, quiet for a second as if considering exactly what to say. "What do you call him?"

"Owen," Chloe answered for me, nervous energy crackling through her in one quick line. Madeline's eyes darted to her for a moment before she continued.

"Once I'd heard Owen had come into town, that he'd shown up at my café even, I rushed into a plan without thinking."

"Have you alerted him that you're not at fault for the deaths?" Chloe asked. Madeline sat back in her chair, uncrossed her legs and shifted into a decidedly un-feminine, open-kneed position. To avoid my eyes trailing to the crotch of her khakis, I rolled my gaze to the ceiling, became fascinated with the stucco.

"I've attempted to send messengers, but none of them have come back to me. He's frustratingly good at his job. One of the best since ..." Madeline's eyes trailed to Chloe, her lids going heavy as her lip quirked. I felt Chloe's panic again and I took a deep breath, instantly worried Madeline's hunger was taking over and one of us was about to throw ourselves into her open arms. In the end, she just kept speaking as if nothing had happened.

"That's why I've asked you guys to be here. I wanted to apologize to you, explain the situation, and ask that you get a message to him." I could tell her eyes had turned back to me when her power leaked out to cloud about, soft and warm. I felt my nipples go hard, and it made me squeak.

"Stop, please," I admonished, moving my gaze back to her face. To her credit, she blushed a bit, her spine straightening.

"Sorry. Habit." I felt the lust she'd pushed onto me recede and I fidgeted in my own seat. Stan scooted his chair away from me and Chloe glanced at him minutely, fighting a smile.

"I usually feed pretty consistently at work, a little here and there to keep myself sustained. But I've had only the guards around me and I've been keeping up a pretty thick cloud of—well, you felt it. I'm feeling a bit frazzled and drained. I think, if you hadn't screamed and distracted me, someone in this room would have gotten lucky." She gave a wide-eyed waggle of her eyebrows and Chloe snorted out a laugh.

Stan swallowed thickly, his body language making it clear he was convinced he would have been the one crying, 'Jackpot!'

"I'll try to get the message across that you're not at fault here, but if we can't?"

"Then I'd stay away from Owen. If one of us has to go, I'm going to make sure it's him."

"Understandable," Chloe said, but there was a hint of displeasure behind it that her voice didn't convey. She glanced at the puddle of coffee and then to Stan and me individually. Her gaze back on Madeline, she spoke.

"Gwen and I actually found her second victim."

"Really?"

"Friday morning at the QFC by work."

Madeline took a second to consider, a wisp of curiosity curling through the room. "And you think it's this one she's after?"

Stan shifted uncomfortably in his seat when she gestured to him. "They think it's a fan of mine."

"A stalker," Chloe said. "Not a fan. You were at the café that morning, come to think of it. Can't be a coincidence. Did you talk to anyone? Did anyone say anything weird to you while you were in line or anything? You may already know what Norma looks like."

"She wouldn't come into my place," Madeline said, shaking her head. Her voice went hard. "I don't mark much as territory, but no other succubus will enter that building without my permission."

"I didn't speak to anyone suspicious in any case," Stan explained. "I got there early, figuring I'd get some breakfast before coming up to see Gwen. I actually got into a nice discussion with a young woman about books—not mine—after I ate. I'd been there at least an hour when you showed up." He glanced at me but couldn't seem to keep his eyes on mine.

"If she was following you, it's likely she waited some before giving up. It's rare for one of us to be so timid in going after prey," Madeline said, drumming her fingers on her knee. "Then again, the fact that she's killing so recklessly means she's abnormal. Perhaps it's her time." Madeline didn't elaborate, but I thought back to her comment about her mother's age.

"We'll do our best to let Owen know what's going on." Chloe said after a few moments. "He's not going to stop looking for a perpetrator, but we'll try to make sure he's after her and not you."

"Unpleasant, if necessary. I'd prefer to take care of her." A crease formed between her brows. "She should be taken out by one of her own, if possible. I dislike humans being brought in to punish those they don't understand."

Guilt rolled off Chloe's skin, but she stamped it out quickly. I frowned at the back of her neck and then glanced over to Stan. He didn't seem to notice anything outside of his knee, as fascinated by it as I had been by the ceiling. Madeline pushed to her feet.

"I can see you're not interested in the coffee, so I'll let you go. The sooner you get word to Owen, the better."

She reached out to take Chloe's hand, and something passed out of her as skin touched skin. Chloe squinted at her, a small smile touching her lips.

"I'm not a burger, Mad," Chloe said, her voice gentle. Madeline let out a laugh and pulled her hand away.

"Right you are. See yourselves out, then." Winking at Chloe, she turned and headed out of the kitchen. "Too tempting," she murmured as she rounded the corner.

Fifteen

Out in the car again, Stan let out a heavy breath, and I felt a spasm of stale panic rumble through his body. I'd let him have the front seat, as his legs were longer than mine and I felt bad that he'd been so uncomfortable inside. Chloe spoke up as we left Greenlake.

"Did your fridge have any other words of wisdom? Maybe an address where we can find Norma?"

"No address. It was pretty much all the same stuff as usual, though the candy thief wanted us to know it's a fan of Stan's books."

"Sugar addiction aside, it has good taste."

"Watch it," I warned. Chloe laughed and reached back to pat my knee. She let her hand linger a bit too long and, in the wake of Madeline's influence, I found I kind of liked it.

"It also said something about your payment, Gwen," Stan pointed out. Chloe pulled her hand up to place it back on the steering wheel and I rolled my gaze to Stan.

"My what?"

"It said you forgot your payment. Does this creature require currency in exchange for these notes it leaves?"

"Just Twinkies and it takes those whether I want it to or not. If it's going to start demanding cash as payment for—" I cut off, realization clicking into place. "Work, head to work."

"What's at work?" Chloe asked.

"My payment. When Laurel and Hardy—they left me something after we helped them with the kids. It was a little blue box and I locked it in my drawer at work. That has to be what this asshole means. It can't be about a client or an insurance check. It has to be whatever the fairies gave me."

"You don't know?" Chloe asked.

"It wasn't really … a good time. To check."

Chloe glanced at me in the rearview mirror and I felt her disapproval, even though she said nothing. It was mere minutes until we pulled up to our office building, getting a lucky spot just as it became available right in front. Chloe unbuckled her seatbelt and then lifted her skinny hips to get her wallet out from her pocket. I didn't admire said skinny hips as they hovered to allow her fingers to slip into the tight pockets of her jeans, no sir-ree bob. She pulled out a twenty and handed it to Stan.

"Get a sugar-free mocha while we run upstairs. It'll make you feel better."

Stan blinked down at the bill in his hand, but didn't refuse it. I got out, pulled his door open, and then reached across to unbuckle his seatbelt when he just sat there. His ears got pink again and I felt a rope of lust that wasn't entirely him reach out and grab me. I pretended I felt nothing and stepped back so he could get out of the car without touching me. Chloe used her key fob to lock her car doors after they were all shut, and we headed up to the doors. Stan moved into the bustling warmth of the café while we unlocked the far doors and headed into darkness.

Chloe bolted up the stairs like a pro, and I grumbled, wishing she'd sprung for the elevator down the hall. On a sigh, I followed her up, trying to match her pace. I found myself checking out the aforementioned narrow posterior more than I really felt was appropriate. Thinking back on how Chloe had said she'd considered taking out Madeline's lust on me, I slowed. At the top of the stairs, Chloe turned to watch me and I found myself unable to meet her eyes.

When she realized what was going through my mind, she fell into a fit of giggles. As I pushed open the stairwell door on our floor, she slapped my ass. I turned and did my best to glare. I think my eyes were a little more come-hither than go-thither, but she didn't take it as an invitation to shove me against the door and stick her tongue down my throat.

"So where's this payment?" she asked.

"Um," I said, trying to sort through my emotions. I was sitting at the bottom of a waterfall of lust, confusion, nervousness, and worry. I hoped Stan was able to at least distract himself with the free magazines or Wi-Fi at The Internets. Finally, I pointed at my office.

"I stuck the box in the file cabinet, at the very back. I didn't really know what else to do with it."

"Cool," Chloe said, walking with a slight skip into my office. I heard the drawer slide open, heard the folders scrape as she moved them. After a second, she came back with the familiar blue box that I'd received from a pair of fairies who had asked me to help them find some missing children. Well, they'd actually asked me to find the demon that had kidnapped the kids, but I hadn't been much help when it had come to the demon. The kids I'd been able to help, with the aid of Chloe, Mel, and a witch named Merrin. The demon had nearly made me electrocute myself and had fed me to a vampire for fun.

Unworried about the Tiffany-blue box being some sort of trap or trick, Chloe leaned against her desk, tugged at the ribbon, and tucked it into her pocket. She wiggled the tiny lid off the box and peered inside. On a delighted, "ooh," she reached in and pulled out a tiny plastic magnifying glass. The handle was so small it disappeared between her thumb and index finger; the lens—a cheap, cloudy-clear plastic—was barely larger than a fat man's thumbnail. I could have gotten the stupid thing out of any cereal box. I squinted at it.

"That's it?"

"Yep!" Her response didn't match the cynicism of my question. When she didn't elaborate, I gestured at nothing with my right hand.

"What am I supposed to do with it?"

She held it up to her eye like it could actually help her read small print or fry an ant. "Clearly you use it to find something."

Chloe handed me the toy before closing the blue box and setting it on her desk. She watched me inspect it and laughed, a cloud of affection leaking out of her; it was tinged with something a little more than platonic tenderness. I tucked the magnifying lens into my pocket, crossed my arms and looked her over.

"Are you mentally undressing me?"

"Yeah."

"Well. This is certainly different."

"Eh," Chloe shrugged and pushed away from the desk. She flipped the lights off as she got to the doorway and then stood there, holding the door open for me. I didn't move from my spot, half-convinced she would grab my ass again.

"I just have a lot of energy to burn off." She waggled her brows and jerked her chin toward the stairwell. "Come on. If I'm not getting lucky, I'm dropping you off at home and you and Stan can work this off yourselves."

"I think sex with you would be less awkward."

"Well, then let's have at it, babe!" Chloe stepped into the room, started to shut the door. I laughed and shook my head.

"I don't ... usually see you that way. I mean, right now I do, but it feels like cheating."

"On Owen?"

"No." I said, shaking my head. "That's not exclusive. I just mean, we're friends—we're best friends. Having sex on the office couch because we've been whammied by a succubus ... It seems wrong. It's not quite drunk driving, but we shouldn't be behind the wheel."

"You'd rather drive a stick. I gotcha." When I barked out a laugh, Chloe pulled the door open again and waved a hand at chest level between the office and the hallway. "Let's go, then."

We found Stan sitting alone in the corner of The Internets, a small to-go cup in his hands. His eyes were fixed on a dark-haired couple four tables away. The girl was small with scraggly hair and pretty, hazel eyes. I couldn't see her full face over the shoulder of the man hunched awkwardly across her table, but she looked angular, androgynous. Her brows were drawn down and the annoyance within her felt familiar somehow, but I couldn't place it. She wasn't human but I didn't know what she was.

The annoyance was almost liquid, a thick blob at the forefront of her gooey psyche. Other emotions—all her other emotions, it seemed—were there, too. It was like someone had dumped an entire fruit salad into a gelatin mold that hadn't quite finished setting. Her emotions were sweet, little bits of candied fruit, and her annoyance particularly reminded me of a chunk of pear. Pity was a slightly smaller chunk of pineapple floating just behind the annoyance-pear.

The closer I paid attention, the more I noticed the man wasn't human either, but he was painfully, embarrassingly desperate. The girl's pity made perfect sense in an instant.

"Mel's here again," I mumbled, confused. Chloe followed my gaze and nodded, stepping toward them. I shook my head, grabbed her arm. "You get Stan. I want to make fun of Mel some more."

Chloe rolled her eyes over a smile and moved toward my ex. We followed similar trajectories until a few tables away, when Chloe broke off and headed for Stan. The fruit salad jiggled madly, an apple slice of panic pushing against the edges like it was trying to escape. I frowned at the girl, watched as she shoved her chair back and darted away, disappearing around the corner toward the bathrooms. She was bony under her baggy clothes, and I tried to decide if that was normal for whatever type of creature she was, or if she'd been forced to live on the streets like a homeless youth. It was proof that just because you had powers didn't mean you could get through life as successfully as Madeline or Mel.

Feeling a little sorry that she was suffering the double whammy of vagrancy and now being hit on by Mel, I wondered if she was the cause of his desperation. Was she turning him down out of some street-kid code of not getting yourself stabbed and left in a ditch? Usually, Mel didn't give off the stab-and-ditch vibe, but lately that wasn't the case.

If this was what being mated meant, I could understand why Mel had seemed so terrified of the prospect.

I got closer, twitching as I stepped into his storm cloud of anguish, which was edged with a dark lining of pain. Frustration sparked out of him, nicking my skin but only just hot enough to irritate. When I stepped up next to him, Mel turned his attention away from the bathroom hallway and watched me in silence for a moment.

He was clean-shaven this time, but his shirt was buttoned all the way up to the very top, with the exception of a button between his pecs. Chloe and Stan closed in, but Mel didn't turn to them immediately.

"You ready?" Chloe asked. Mel perked up, but it felt hollow.

"You know I am, baby, let's do this," he said, still sitting down.

"What?" Chloe asked, just as confused by the waver in his come-on as I was. Mel's emotions dipped a little more toward sadness.

"Nothing. Never mind. I should go."

"No luck with the girl?" Chloe asked, pitching her voice the way you'd talk to a sad child.

"The ... She was... No. She has a boyfriend. Probably. I think." Shoulders hunched, he looked up at Stan and I felt a stab of jealousy shoot out of him and into my gut. "You three all going home *together*?" Mel asked.

"Not exactly," Chloe said. Stan had turned his attention to the bathroom hall, curiosity and a bit of worry dominating his thoughts. His lust seemed to have mostly washed away with the drink he'd ordered, and it made me a bit sad. I found myself surprised by my reaction; the sadness then turned to shame when I realized a tiny part of me had considered using Stan to our mutual advantage and ridding ourselves of the leftover lust energy.

A bit disgusted with myself, considering our history, I looked Mel up and down, mulled over tossing him a bit of pity sex to quell the urge. As I actually took the time to inspect him, though, I realized that it was somehow even less appealing than usual. While his emotions were no longer torturous in a physically painful way, I could not actually convince myself that I wanted to sleep with him. The idea sat somewhere on the Scale of Unappealing Things between necrophilia and having sex with a beloved family pet.

Fighting off the urge to vomit as I remembered that he was, in fact, occasionally dog-shaped. I took a step back.

"Can we go?"

"Yes, please," Chloe agreed. Even she seemed put off by Mel, and she's usually his biggest fan. Stan looked between us, obviously confused, and then reached out a hand to Mel. They shook as Stan did what he did best and acted politely, despite the fact that Chloe and I were sharing mutual expressions of nausea.

"I'm Stanley. I guess we're leaving, but it was nice to meet you."

"You too, Stanley. Enjoy your night." On a bitter pout, Mel got to his feet, stepped around us and headed dejectedly toward the door. I noticed Stan wiped his hand on his pants when Mel had stepped outside. Maybe Stan wasn't immune to whatever Mel was putting out, after all.

I'd been lying in bed awake for somewhere around an hour, and it was starting to get tiring. Not the type of tiring that put me to sleep, apparently, but tiring nonetheless.

Chloe had dropped Stan and me off, promising us we'd both feel better after we slept. Stan had gone straight to the kitchen, taking his restlessness out on the dishes he hadn't gotten to do before we dragged him out of the house. I'd cooed at Sonny some before jumping in the shower for some me time.

It hadn't helped one bit.

Whatever Madeline had crammed into my brain wanted another warm body. It wanted biting and kissing, hair pulling and back scratching. I was acutely aware at ten-past midnight that Stan was sleeping peacefully down the hall, an attractive prey. I could feel my foot hanging off the side of the bed, jerking arrhythmically as I considered the faint feeling of calm coming from my sleeping ex.

I was about thirty seconds from calling Chloe and asking to belatedly take her up on her offer when I realized I had another option. Owen had given me a card with his mobile phone number scribbled on it. My body froze in place at this realization, the gleeful shock momentarily paralyzing me. I swear I didn't squeak like a mouse as I tangled and then untangled myself from the sheets in my rush to get my purse from the front room. Stan's emotions stayed nearly flatlined as I pounded down the hall, grabbed my purse and hustled back to my room.

I shut my door and then moved into the bathroom and closed that door, too. Leaning back on the edge of the counter, I felt my foot start its tapping again as I dialed Owen's number. He answered on the first ring, which surprised me. I think part of me thought he'd be sound asleep.

"Yes." His voice was calm, no-nonsense and wide-awake.

"Hey. It's Gwen."

"Hello," he said, a smile creeping in. "You're up late."

"Are you up—I mean, did I wake you?"

"No, you didn't wake me. And I'm not up, but I could be," he said. I gave a breathy laugh.

"Well, I can't sleep. I was hoping you could help me with something."

"Something serious?"

"Sex," I said before my brain could explain to my mouth how we should all work together to make this not only not awkward, but possibly also not desperate or tacky. Owen's silence made me think that he was just as shocked at what I'd said as my brain was. After a few moments, in which something rattled like a grocery store basket full of canned food, he sighed out and spoke.

"Really?" Instead of the confusion I'd expected, I could hear that he was pleased.

"Yeah. I was going to be diplomatic, maybe make up a story about there being a bat in my attic and how you should bring a tennis racket and help me take it out but we're both consenting adults. So … Do you consent?"

"Absolutely." There was a predatory tone in his voice that made my insides sizzle.

"I have company but I could probably be at your place in forty-five? Are you there?"

"In forty-five?" He paused and I heard something heavy slap onto a concrete floor on his end. "Yeah, I will be."

"Perfect," I said. Without thinking, I hung up and rushed for the bedroom. My haste was dangerous and I nearly brained myself yanking the open bathroom door. It didn't occur to me until I'd already changed out of my pajama pants that hanging up like I'd done had probably been pretty rude.

OLIVIA R .BURTON

Sixteen

I perhaps drove a bit too fast on the way to Owen's place, but I didn't see any cops, and if they saw me they didn't seem to care. I parked in the driveway next to his sedan, reminded myself that it would be uncouth to stick my hand down his pants before saying hello, and knocked. It took him a minute to open the door, but the smell of him freshly showered wafted out as he did.

I was pretty sure that, had I been a man, that alone would have shrunk my underpants two sizes. It was like being in high school again, all hormonal and barely in control of myself. With a mildly embarrassed smile, I stood in place, giving a little wave. Leaning in to kiss my cheek, he wrapped his arm around my back and tugged me over the threshold.

Doing my best to control the urges inside me, I stayed facing the living room, hands clasped over the handle of my bag in front of my hips. Owen stepped around me toward the kitchen, and I noticed his left hand looked like it had been scraped up and cleaned.

"What happened?"

"Walked into a door. Do you want something to drink?" Catching my frown, he smiled. "No wine, I promise."

"Were you fighting?"

"No drink, then?" he asked, pausing at the entrance to the kitchen. Realizing he was refusing to answer, I found a bit of irritation had erupted into the lust clouding my brain. That was probably for the best, though, considering I have no willpower when it comes to sex or food. We stared at each other for a few moments, before he tipped his head. "Are you really that worried about me?"

"I ... guess." I wasn't sure. He looked fine, and nursing him back to health wasn't exactly why I'd driven thirty-five minutes north in the middle of the night. When I continued to stare dully, he smiled at me, turned to face me completely, and stepped forward. That was enough of an invitation for my hormones, apparently—they took over.

I dropped my bag on the floor and practically flew the short distance between us. I leaned up into him and found his mouth open and ready for me. The kiss was desperate, and he made a small sound of surprise when I began to do exactly what I'd told myself not to and grabbed the waistline of his pants. Amusement flooded out of him and I found myself smiling when he spoke.

"No gun this time."

"Smart man," I purred as I tugged at the button of his jeans with one hand, the other already moving his zipper downward. Evidently he hadn't been sure before that moment that I'd really come over just to have sex; I felt a bump of confusion before lust and desire took him over. He moved his hands to my shirt, pulling it up, his rough knuckles pressing against my underarms when I didn't immediately let him undress me. As I finally got his button undone, he shifted, jerking away from me except for his hands on my shirt.

I opened my eyes to snarl at the delay, and his face was mischievous. I wanted sweaty, fast sex and he was playing games. He pulled at my shirt again and danced his hips out of the way when I reached for his pants. At my annoyed sigh, he laughed.

"You got to be in control last time. I think it's my turn."

I blinked at him, not sure if I disliked the idea or if I was just objecting because my hormones worried that might slow things down. Finally, I sighed as though the concept bored me and pulled my arms up. Stepping forward, he pressed the open front of his pants against my belly, blocking my access in case I decided to cheat. He tugged my shirt up halfway and pushed the collar back over my hair, leaving my arms trapped up in the air. I felt my bangs feather downward as the shirt moved back far enough to leave my face free. He cupped my cheeks and leaned in for a kiss that was far gentler than I wanted in that moment.

I felt silly standing there with my arms above my head, but he moved to slide his palms up the sides of my arms, making sure to keep our hips pressed together. He pulled away from the kiss after a few more seconds and moved to nibble along my jaw, cupping his fingers around my elbows before moving to gently hold my wrists.

"Why the booty call?" he asked, very close to my ear. I sighed out, completely unable to understand what he'd said for a few seconds. He waited patiently for my brain to catch up and then moved on to kissing my neck as I mumbled out a response.

"Saw a succubus today. Feeling amorous."

His lust slammed to a halt like a car crash. Pieces of it broke away, flying off into the atmosphere, coating my skin and making me feel warm. Annoyance and suspicion replaced the lust, immediately cooling the warm spots on my skin. My eyes fluttered open and I watched him lean his upper half away from mine, letting me go. His expression was pleasant enough, but he was no longer interested in kissing or undressing me.

We stared at each other for a moment, before I glowered and tugged my shirt completely off, lowering my arms.

"What?" I asked. He lifted a brow.

"You saw Madeline?"

"Yeah, she called to …" Realizing that he had every right to be suspicious of me in that moment, I took a deep breath. "Oh shit."

He watched me patiently, making no move toward or away from me. I shook my head.

"I forgot."

"What did you forget?" he asked, a touch too calmly. Had I not been pressed against him, I would have been unable to catch the nearly imperceptible threat behind the words. It sobered me somewhat that he could be so worried about what Madeline might throw his way that just mentioning her name made him suspicious of me. I stepped back, stuffing down the tiny impulses still begging me to pull his pants off and finish the discussion later. I considered putting my shirt on, and then decided it didn't matter.

"Shit," I said again, feeling a laugh slip in. "Madeline called to apologize for sending her guys here and putting me in danger. She also said to get a message to you."

"Did she?" The question was rhetorical, his suspicion growing around us both. It was a tingle in the air, like you might feel right before lightning strikes next to your feet.

"She's not the one killing people. But there is another succubus in town who is. Her name's Norma Laby and, coincidentally, she's stalking my ex-husband."

Owen's face changed minutely from curious to calculating. I felt that spike of annoyance again, but it wasn't directed at me. His lip quirked after a bit and he nodded.

"That explains a lot about my day," he finally said. I raised a brow, watching him, before he shook his head. "And what does Madeline want me to do with this information?"

"For starters, she'd like you to reconsider killing her." The fingers on his left hand twitched slightly and his expression went thoughtful. "Chloe said that she was going to look into it," I added.

"Oh?" he asked, a narrow, fingernail-sized sliver of amusement seeping through. "And what is *she* going to do if she finds something helpful?"

I frowned. "I'm not sure, to be honest. There's a lot about that girl I don't really know, and I can't predict what she's going to be doing at any moment. She hit on me earlier."

"Really? And you weren't up for it?"

"S'why I'm here. We're friends and it seemed … I mean, I wouldn't look at her and want to have sex with her on most days, so to do it because my brain had been influenced seemed wrong."

"But you're okay with showing up at my place in the middle of the night to use me for sex?" He gave me a smug half-smile, and I noted that the desire I'd so affectively chased away earlier was coming around again. I shrugged a shoulder.

"You and I have already been the beast with two backs. We've—quite enthusiastically, I'd say—discussed doing it all again."

When he continued to stare at me with that half-smile still on his pretty face, I straightened my posture, lifted my chin slightly.

"It's just good sense," I said, affecting an air of arrogance. If I had a pipe, I would've tucked it between my lips and checked my pocket watch. The other half of Owen's smile returned, and he gave a slow nod, as if considering an important proposition.

"Well, if it's just good sense, then we should get to it."

"Just like that?"

"If I think of anything else I need to ask, I'll let you know," he said, stepping closer. He slid his hands around my hips, cupping my ass and pulling me against him. Every ounce of lust that had receded to percolate in the back of my head rushed forward, making me feel thick and warm all over. Leaning up to kiss him, I linked my fingers across the back of his neck and helped hoist myself into his arms. I wrapped my legs around his hips as he moved toward the back bedroom, and kissed a line from his lips to his ear.

"Please hold all questions until after the presentation," I said, before tugging his earlobe between my teeth.

I woke topless, sprawled facedown across a bed that wasn't my own. My cheek was wet against the sheet, my groggy gaze aimed right at a pair of sleep pants I didn't recognize. I squinted, rolled slightly to look up across a naked belly, and found Owen standing over me, shirtless. I took in the attractive sight of the line of pale hair peeking out from his pants before I tore my attention upward to a mug of something warm in his hand.

Noticing where my attention had been, he smiled, affection hitting me as he tipped his head to mirror the position of mine. I gave a half smile, yawned hugely and rolled completely over. The blanket only followed enough to cover one breast, but I was both too tired and feeling too good to care. Owen's eyes flicked to my exposed nipple as he spoke.

"You sleep like a toddler on crack."

I pouted and pulled the blanket up to cover myself, which made him laugh. He sat on the bed next to me, gestured with the cup.

"Not that I think you need it after all the thrashing you did last night, but I brought you coffee."

"I'm not really into coffee."

"It's half flavored cream and nearly a quarter sugar."

"Gimme," I demanded, pushing myself into a sitting position. I pulled my knees to my chest to hold the sheet in place and reached for the mug. He smiled as I took a tentative sip and then held his other hand out to me. My phone was in it.

"Your phone was nearly as busy as we were last night."

"Eh?" I grunted, frowning down at it. Resting the cup on my knee, still holding the handle, I grabbed the phone and unlocked it. "Holy crap."

I had eleven missed calls from a local number I didn't recognize and six voicemails from the same number. Fighting off a brief bout of panic while I reminded myself that Stan and my family all had area codes outside Seattle, I decided to leave the voicemails until later. It had been four hours since the last one had come through, and I had a handsome, shirtless man attending to me in bed.

As I took another sip of the saccharine coffee, which I was fairly sure no one but me would've been able to stomach, it occurred to me that I hadn't really mentioned my sweet tooth to Owen. Or, if I had, I didn't remember making clear the exact depth of sweetness I preferred.

"This is suspiciously good."

"Ah, well." Owen dropped a hand onto my foot through the blanket and I felt a hint of sheepishness slide through his perfect emotional wall. "I kind of have a confession."

"Mmm?" I asked vaguely, taking another giant gulp. The sugar had mostly settled to the bottom, which meant I was getting to the syrupy good part.

"The Sneed con wasn't the first time I saw you."

Lifting a brow, I tipped back the cup all the way, waiting as the last of the toothsome globules slid onto my tongue. The motion dropped the sheet further down my chest, but I just gestured for Owen to continue as I set the cup down.

"Saturday morning I was at The Internets, just seeing if I could catch Madeline. I saw you come in, sleepy and out of sorts. You ordered tea and the woman working the counter told the barista to add in a few extra pumps of sweetener. You were cute, so I noticed."

"Oh, Holly," I said, feeling a sudden spike of affection for her; I was going to have to start tipping better. "You should have come over and said hi."

"I did later," he protested. "At the café, though, you looked half-asleep and I was there on business. It was only after the fifth person asked where

Madeline was that Holly got frustrated. She vented on the one of the others behind the counter that, if she had to answer that question the whole weekend, she was going to make a giant sign with some very rude words on it. I left when I realized Madeline wasn't coming in. It's why I got to the con so late."

"Well, it's a good thing you thought I was cute or I wouldn't have had anywhere to go in my time of need." I reached out to press a hand to his cheek, wishing he was near enough to kiss. When he didn't move closer, I dropped my hand. "Something wrong?"

"Not with you. We both have to go soon, though. I let you sleep—and drool, it seems—" I wiped at my mouth self-consciously. "For as long as I could, but according to the beeping alarm on your phone, you're only an hour out from your first appointment."

"Oh shit," I said, shoving at the covers and hopping to my feet. I was thirty minutes from home, unprepared to go into work, and at least twenty minutes out from home to work. After the post-coital clean up I'd had the sense to pull on underpants, but that was it. Where my other clothes had gone was a mystery. Before I could rush by in search of them, Owen grabbed my arm and pulled me toward him, spreading his knees so I slipped between them. Since he was sitting down, this put my naked breasts at just about his eye level. I frowned down at him, but it was half-hearted.

"I have to go."

"At least kiss me goodbye before you tear out of here topless."

"What if I said I have notoriously bad morning breath?"

"I'd point out that you just smell like sugar and coffee, now." He didn't give me another chance to argue, but I wouldn't have anyway. He slid a hand up the side of my body, his thumb probably—okay, very likely— deliberately grazing my nipple before he cupped the back of my neck and pulled me down into a kiss.

Good god, nothing sounded better right then than climbing into his lap and making what was probably epic bed-head even worse. His hair looked great, but there was no way mine wasn't a mess after both sex and cracked-out-toddler sleep.

My skin tingled everywhere but, instead of grabbing on and straddling him until he moved those talented lips to the rest of me, I kept my arms down by my side. He broke the kiss and I stood up straight, putting his face between my breasts again. His gaze staying on mine, he jerked his chin toward the other side of the room.

"Your clothes are on the dresser. You kind of just threw them off haphazardly last night and I tried to straighten up in here. I almost couldn't find your left sock, and your bra ended up behind the nightstand."

"Pretty sure that was your fault, buddy."

"Oh," he said, feigning deep thought. "Maybe it was."

"Now let go of me so I can get dressed. I'm going to be late enough as it is."

"Only to work, I hope."

"Unless you bought joke condoms, yes. Just to work."

He lifted his hands away from my skin, holding them out like I was about to frisk him for weapons. Believe me, I considered it; good sense won, though, and I moved across the room, yanked on my clothes as fast as I could, snagged my phone from the bed and then leaned down to give Owen a kiss on the cheek. He stayed seated on the bed, watching me calmly, his emotions a low pulse of contentment and mild arousal.

"I'll call in a few hours and we can talk more about the succubus problems."

"Sounds good," he said, getting to his feet. I didn't give him a chance to see me out as I sprinted out of the bedroom and across the living room. I grabbed my bag off the table next to the couch, where it looked like Owen had rummaged through it to get my screaming phone, and ran out the door.

OLIVIA R .BURTON

Seventeen

Rather than take the time to get home and then back to the office, I'd called Chloe on the way, asking that she bring me the extra clothes I kept at her place. I tore into the building with twenty minutes to change, brush my hair, and give my patient's file a quick look-see. As I pushed open the door to the office, Chloe jerked a thumb at the hall behind her desk, not saying a word. I hustled around the desk, down the hall past the records room and into our private bathroom that I paid good rent money for. Chloe had left my clothes on the little IKEA cabinet where we kept toilet paper and soap. Set out deliberately on top of my pants were a brush and a travel kit. I opened the kit and found a toothbrush, toothpaste, face wipes and a little mini-stick of deodorant.

I made a mental note to give her a big, sloppy kiss of thanks at some point, and got to making myself decent. By the time I was done, you could barely tell I'd spent the night having sex and drooling buckets on someone else's pillow.

"I take it you—oh!" Chloe's brows shot up in surprise when I leaned in, grabbed her face and kissed her on the mouth. I made a show of it, with a big, "mwah!" sound and a pinch of her cheek as I pulled back.

"I thought you just wanted to be friends," she said, smiling up at me from her seat. I shrugged and leaned a hip against her desk.

"I just would not have made it home and then here in time. I left a message on Stan's cell, but he wasn't awake I guess. Hopefully he won't be insulted that left him there alone all night."

"He'll probably make himself a sensible breakfast and spend the day writing. That should distract him from everything that's going on."

I nodded, turned and moved into my office. Chloe followed me in, sitting in the chair across the desk from me as I booted up my computer.

"So where were you last night that you couldn't change clothes or clean up?"

"Owen's," I said, ignoring the teasing in her tone.

"Really?"

"Yeah, Madeline left me all fired up and Stan wasn't going to be of any help, so I drove out to Edmonds." I sat down, logged into the computer, and then looked back to Chloe. "Totally worth it."

"I bet," she said with a laugh. We sat in silence for a bit as I opened the files I needed, scanned them and then glanced at the clock.

"Only two today, right?"

"Yeah, Georgia and then Carlos later."

"Good. I'm going to actually talk to Owen later about the succubus issue. I was able to pass on Madeline's request and tell him about Norma, but then we were a little too busy to really do...anything that wasn't sex, actually."

"Gotcha," she said. After a second, she continued, "What did he say about Norma?"

"Not much. He said that Madeline not being at fault explained the day he'd had yesterday and that was about it. Oh!" I said, remembering my voicemail-laden phone. I looked around for my bag, realized I'd left it in the bathroom, and bolted to my feet.

I gave a wave at Georgia as she stepped in and, instead of asking me where I was hustling off to, Chloe went right into business mode. When I returned from the bathroom with my purse, Chloe was handing Georgia her credit card back, sticking the tablet computer we used for payment into the drawer. She scooted back, grabbed a receipt off the copier as it printed, and then handed it over.

I realized my curious voicemails would have to wait.

"Do you know this number?"

I handed Chloe my phone as we took the elevator down to the main level, following the hall to the front of the building. She read it, nodded and gave the phone back.

"That's Mel's cell."

"It is?" I asked, confused. Why had Mel called me so many times the night before and left six messages? Knowing we had several hours until my second appointment and knowing that I was completely starving, I'd coaxed Chloe into heading out for lunch. Despite the fact that I would have been completely fine with eating several cakes and cookies at The Internets, Chloe tugged me the opposite way, toward the same Thai place I'd taken Owen.

I scrolled through the list of voicemails, chose the earliest one and hit play.

"Gwen. It's Mel. I'm doing it. I'm gonna go, I'm gonna do it. I just thought you should know, since you never got to experience my hot body. I thought you should know

that, now that I'm mated, it's over. You haven't got a chance."

"That was weird," I said, as the message finished. His voice had sounded resolute, but hollow, like he'd made a decision he wasn't particularly happy about.

"Hmm?" Chloe asked, peering left and right as we crossed the street.

"Mel left me a bunch of messages." I hit play on the next.

"Me again. You should know, though, if you really feel you need to have sex with me before I go off and have babies, I could make it happen. Call me."

The next was even briefer and just as confusing. *"Or text me. You can text me. You could email me if you want."*

By the fourth message, which had arrived only fifteen minutes after the third, Mel's speech was slightly slurred.

"I forgot to give you my email. But texting would be quicker." He'd hung up without giving me any email address.

Time-stamped ten minutes later, another slurred mess asked, *"Did you email me? I haven't seen it. Let me check my other ac—hic—counts."*

I paused before the last message as we got seated, asked for a pot of green tea and then held the phone to my ear. This one rambled so long I wasn't sure how it had gotten through.

"Gwen. Look. I know it's a whole thing with us. With you and me and you pretending you don't like me but you like me. You like me, right? We're cool. You'd do me a solid, right? I'd make it fun! For you, I mean. I could have fun, too. But we should get naked and have sex and just see where it goes. Do you know how long it's been since I had sex? It's been, like, a week. A week! You don't. That's not. A week!" His voice cracked, and paired with the slurring, the message started to make me very uncomfortable. *"A week, Gwen. That is so long. My penis is lonely! Even the pretty girl wasn't interested. She said she could rock my world but wouldn't! She wouldn't! Why wouldn't she? There's a smiley face on my dick and no one wants to see it!"*

On that note, he started weeping. I skipped forward a few seconds, but it was just more weeping through the end.

Feeling like I'd just witnessed someone strangling a puppy, I set the phone down. On second thought, I slid the phone away from me, staring at it like it was radioactive. Chloe just sat across the table from me, chin in her hands, watching.

"So? What was up?"

"You ... just listen. It's ... horrifying."

Chloe grabbed the phone, leaned back and listened to each voicemail in succession. Her face matched her emotions as they changed several times, from amusement, to confusion, to sadness and finally to a level of discomfort that didn't quite reach mine, but was close.

"Jeez," she said, setting the phone down. Like me, she pushed it away as if scared it was going to make her listen to the messages again.

"Is that what all werewolves get like when they—he called it being mated?"

"I hope not. It's supposed to be pleasant; love, basically. That doesn't sound like love, doesn't sound like it would make someone a great parent."

"You lost me."

"Oh, ah." Something piped up from the back of Chloe's psyche, but her face remained pleasant. The odd mix of nostalgia and lust died down quickly enough that I didn't address it. "Basically, werewolves are sterile until they find The One. If Mel's fallen in love, he's liable to start making babies. Not by himself, obviously."

"Yuck," I grumbled. Chloe laughed.

"Why yuck? You love babies."

"But baby Mels running around? That would be terrible. They'd be just as obnoxious, but they'd also smell like diapers."

"Diapers," Chloe snorted, shaking her head. Deciding I didn't want to hear anything else about this subject, I shook my head and got to the business of deciding what I wanted to eat.

After lunch, Chloe excused herself and I dialed Owen's number. He didn't answer, so I left a message, making sure to keep it brief; listening to Mel ramble on had made me a bit gun-shy of voicemails. Surprisingly, he called back as I was hanging up.

"Oh, hey, I just left you a message," I said in lieu of hello.

"Sorry, I couldn't get to the phone."

"No problem. What are you doing?"

"Working."

"Ah, well." I bit my lip, a bit startled by his tone. "Should I call back later?"

"No, I have a few minutes to talk."

"Then I'll make it fast. Have you found anything else about Norma, where she might be?"

"Only that there was another murder," he explained. "Guy in West Seattle stepped out to get the paper early this morning and his wife found him a half hour later around back, just dead. Their car was missing, as well."

"Jeez."

"Yeah." His tone was final, irritated.

When I didn't respond, he spoke again, and I got the impression he was making an effort to lighten the mood.

"It's been a while since I've had this much trouble with a creature. Norma seems to be just human and just sane enough to blend in, but crazy enough that she follows no discernible pattern. It happens with older succubi, but I can't get any sort of handle on what she looks like so I don't know if it's her age or if she's just off her rocker. I've been all over the city trying to find some way to identify her, let alone find her."

"Sounds like a lot of legwork."

"Yeah, but it keeps me pretty." This time, I could hear a smile in his voice. Liking this tone better than the hard edge with which he'd started the conversation, I chuckled. As I shifted in my chair to prop my leg up on the filing cabinet, my brain clicked onto a solution.

Owen spoke, stopping me from swearing at myself for not thinking of it sooner. "As soon as I deal with her, though, I'll let you know. We can have a celebratory dinner."

"I think I can help you!"

"Like I helped you last night?" His voice oozed sex and I bit my lip through a laugh.

"Yes but, before that, I think I can legitimately help find Norma."

"Oh?" I liked that he didn't sound cynical or condescending. Chloe would have. Chloe would have given me a look like you'd give a five-year-old who claims he's going to teach himself to fly.

"I got a thing from some fairies last year, this little toy magnifying lens. Chloe said it looks like it might be able to find something? Would that help?"

"If you've got what I think you do, yes, very much. I can come pick you up now. Are you—"

"I can't now. I have a client to see in a bit, but after that, I'm wide open."

"Hmm." I could tell he didn't like the delay, but he didn't argue or ask me to cancel the appointment.

"Look, pick me up at my house in two and a half hours and we'll go find her. I want to change before we go anywhere. I want a full shower."

"Oh?" he asked, his tone softening. "You didn't make it home this morning?"

"I can't *imagine* why," I said. Owen gave a short laugh and I heard a door shut behind him.

"Okay, four o'clock. If you're ready any sooner, let me know. I'll be there."

"Looking forward to it."

As we closed the office for the evening, Chloe asked if Owen had made any headway with our murderous succubus.

"No, nothing yet. He says he's running around the city trying to find a witness but he hasn't had any luck. But I have that payment from Laurel and Hardy. I think I can use it to find her, right? Or I can give it to him to use?"

"I wouldn't give it to him. It would be just like a fairy to make sure it won't work correctly if it changes hands."

"Well, then I can use it. I think?" I said, frowning at the floor as I realized I had no idea what to do with a magical toy. Chloe hooked her arm into mine as I took a step toward the elevator, and steered me to the staircase.

"I haven't used one but Owen might know how. He's been at this a while, it sounds like. I'm sure he's handled payment from fairies before."

"He kills them, he doesn't work with them."

"You don't think monsters want other monsters dead?"

"Ah." I breathed out a confused sound, shook my head. "I hadn't thought of that."

"Well, ask him at least. Otherwise, I'd treat it like a Magic 8 Ball: just start asking it questions, see what happens."

We were out on the street, separating to head to our cars, when Chloe turned back to me.

"Have you heard anything else from Mel?"

"No, thank god. The crazy bastard's probably—hopefully—found his future wife and is crying on her shoulder. I don't want any more weepy messages."

"I hope so. Poor guy sounded so sad."

"Yeah. It was pretty gross."

Chloe snorted at my insensitivity and headed off toward her car with a wave. I glanced up at the front of the building toward where I thought Mel's office window was and wondered if he'd made it into work that morning. Thinking better of it, I dropped my gaze back to the ground and moved quickly toward my car. If he was up there and he caught sight of me, he might jump out the fourth-story window just to come beg me to have sex with him again.

I'm not the heroine in a preternatural romance novel; I don't need this shit.

I made it home in record time and pushed open the door, yelling to Stan that I was home. Sonny screeched at me from his cage, incredibly loud, startling me so I bumped into the door and dropped my bag.

"Sonny!" I snapped, more out of shock than anger. Hanging from the side bars of the cage, he grabbed one of his bell ropes and jangled it before screeching at me again. I kicked the bag into the living room, shut the door, and then peered into the cage. Sonny had plenty of dry food, but there was no fruit in his dish and it looked like the remnants of the last feeding were a day old, at least.

"Aww, baby, did Stan forget to give you snacks?" Sonny rang the bells again, moving to the door of the cage and holding on for dear life. I opened the door and let him crawl up my arm. This did not appease him. He screeched again, making me yelp and clap my hand over my ear. A conure screech is no joke, let me tell you.

"Stan? Are you here?" Sonny and I moved first into the kitchen so I could give the bird a chunk of apple and shut him up. He took the sliver I gave him but then immediately dropped it, screeching again.

"Hey, mister!" I said, wrapping my hand around his delicate little body and pulling him close so I could look into his face. His leg wiggled at first, before he cocked his head to look at me with one eye. "Stop yelling! What's wrong?"

He yelled again.

"Sonny!" I put a finger on the top of his beak, hoping it would be clearer, but he just struggled slightly in my hands. Wondering why Stan hadn't come out to ask about the ruckus, I took Sonny to the guest room and found it empty.

Stan's laptop was on the desk, off and closed, next to his mobile phone; his suitcase and toiletry bag were still packed, lined up in an orderly fashion on the dresser. The bed was unmade, which was a red alert in and of itself. I couldn't feel his emotions in or around the house, but my brain refused to accept that as an answer.

"Stan?" I asked again, knowing it wouldn't do any good. Dread was pooling in my belly, but I tried to ignore it. Surely nothing was wrong. It was Stan, after all. The universe wouldn't mess with the sweetest man ever.

Er, not after it had thrown me his way. Making him put up with my bullshit was already more bad karma than he deserved.

Tucking Sonny onto my shoulder, I moved through the house at lightning speed, checking every room. Stan wasn't in either bathroom, any of the three bedrooms, or the laundry room. I even ran out the back door and checked the shed out of desperation. Sonny stayed perched on my shoulder silently as we searched.

When I got inside again I realized the back door had been unlocked when I'd gone through just minutes before.

"Dammit," I snapped. "Dammit, dammit!" Sonny went into his cage quietly, either sensing my distress or smug that he'd gotten his point across to the dumb human. I did give him a handful of fresh fruit to snack on and turned on the TV for him. As I bolted to the back of the house, I dialed Chloe, setting the phone on my bathroom counter as I stripped.

"Hel—"

"Chloe, Stan's gone," I yelled at the speaker. "I think Norma got him. He didn't answer his phone all day, probably because it's here." Owen's words from our phone call came back to me. She'd killed someone in West Seattle, and stolen their car. I was betting it had happened closer than I'd assumed when he'd mentioned it. "Shit! Shit, shit! She killed another neighbor, took Stan in a stolen car. I'd bet my life on it."

"Oh my god," she said, and I heard a voice in the background. Chloe put her hand over the phone, but came back shortly after. "I'll be there as soon as I can. You looked around for a note? Maybe he just went for a walk."

"He would have let me know, and there's no note. The back door was unlocked, too, which he would *not* have left. Sonny hasn't had any treats all day and I know that doesn't sound like—"

"I understand. I'm on my way."

Chloe hung up as I tossed my phone onto my bed and hit my closet. I had time to shower but it seemed frivolous under the circumstances.

I was dressed in jeans, sneakers, and a light tee when Chloe pushed open my door. She had changed too, into an outfit similar to mine but topped with a light jacket. There was a black line of nylon around her left thigh, and when she came closer I realized she'd strapped a knife there.

She didn't give me a chance to ask about any of it.

"Where's the toy?"

"I have it, but I told Owen I wouldn't use it until he got here."

"Right," Chloe said, turning and scanning the room. As she started toward the guest room, she spoke again. "How long?"

"I called him right after I got out of the shower and he said fifteen minutes. I'm assuming—"

My front door opened and Owen stepped in, dressed similarly to Chloe and me. His jacket could have been the twin to hers: a slick, thin, black windbreaker unzipped to his sternum. He gave me a comforting smile. When the sunny glare from the open door disappeared, I noticed that he had gone a few steps further than Chloe: he had a knife strapped to each thigh, and the cuff of his left pant leg fell funny on one side.

"Ready?" he asked. Unlike Chloe, whose emotions were a mix of anger and a thin swirl of worry, Owen seemed at peace with the situation. I blinked at him, unsure what to say, as Chloe stepped out. She jerked her chin at him in greeting and then gestured to me.

"She's got the Find but neither one of us have ever used one."

"It's not complicated. Can I see it?" They both turned to me and I looked between them. I suddenly felt like the clumsy sidekick in a spy movie. Was I the Tom Arnold of my own life?

Trying to decide if I wanted to glower or simply accept my comedy-relief fate, I dug into my pocket and pulled the little toy out. I handed it to Owen; he held it up, looking it over and then giving it back. He spoke as he moved to the shelf in the corner of my living room.

"Yeah, I've seen one like this before. These assholes must shop at the same party store, or something." Plucking a DVD from the bunch, he popped it open and slid the cover art out before closing it, the DVD still inside. He was gentle at handling the case and made sure to leave the art on the shelf where it wouldn't get stepped on or ruined. Handing me the DVD, he jerked a thumb toward the door. Chloe nodded, and they both moved to leave. I looked down at the plastic I held in both hands, feeling useless. Owen left without another word, but Chloe stood framed by the dying light in my doorway gave me a small smile.

"Come on."

Unsure what other option I had, I moved toward her, doing my best not to glower. I knew they were both trying to help and that I should've been glad for competent friends instead of jealous of them. But I just kept thinking that I didn't have a knife or a snazzy windbreaker; I had a toy magnifying glass and a *Ghost Rider* DVD that lacked a cover. My mood only got worse when I stepped outside and found that Owen had, in fact, managed to procure a windowless van.

OLIVIA R .BURTON

Eighteen

"You stay in the van."

"What?" I demanded. Chloe leaned back in the side door and pointed threateningly my way, not elaborating on her order. Owen had already climbed out and come around to the passenger side, but he said nothing. It was probably wise on his part, since Chloe looked pretty damn serious.

The Find, it turned out, was basically a magical GPS. Per Owen's instructions, I'd aimed the little lens at the side of the DVD case and then politely asked if it would take me to Norma. My initial instinct had been to ask it to find Stan, and Owen had made the point that Stan would likely be with Norma. I'd argued but he'd made the very valid, if frustrating, point that if he wasn't and we found him taking a long stroll, we would've wasted our one shot at the succubus.

The DVD was unharmed, Owen assured me, even though the magic in the lens had temporarily tattooed the side of the case with a moving map, a little dot jumping and wiggling to indicate our position. When I'd asked why fairies had enchanted something to turn a DVD into a map, Owen had explained that anything flat and monochrome would do; the case had just been the first thing he'd seen.

The map was spastic, changing course whenever it felt like it, but Owen had been able to decipher its message and get us to a warehouse in Tacoma. The last villainous creature I'd confronted had dragged me to his house, a nice Queen Anne two-story. As evil lairs go, this warehouse seemed to be a step down. Or possibly a step up?

It'd been a while since I read *How to Be a Villain,* and I couldn't quite remember what one exactly wanted in an evil lair.

When Chloe had stared me down sufficiently, I dropped my head and sighed. As soon as she was out of the van, though, I turned to glare at them both through the passenger's side window. Owen stepped up next to the van to smile at me. Getting the message, I rolled down the window and tried not to sound like a toddler as I whined his way.

"Why do I have to stay here? If Stan's in there, I could—"

He pulled a gun out from under his coat and held it pointing skyward while his gaze stayed steady on mine. Chloe started doing some stretches, pulling her knees to her chest one by one, twisting to the side, looking athletic and competent all the while. I frowned at the gun and then looked back to his face. When he had my attention he leaned in, gun still held away, and kissed me quickly on the lips. Still close to my mouth, he smiled and spouted my own line back at me:

"I like the amount of holes you have, thank you very much."

I grunted in irritation.

"Why does Chloe get to go?" I asked, wondering why she was suddenly ready to Rambo it up.

"Yeah," Owen said, lowering the gun to the ground and turning so he could see us both. The expression he aimed at Chloe was a challenge, his emotions speaking of mischief, like he expected her to squirm. "Why *does* Chloe get to go?"

In answer, she drew her own handgun out of her jacket and held it with both hands, aimed down at the ground. Her expression was stern as she met my eyes. I sighed and nodded.

"Fine. Go rescue Stan. Make sure he's alive to write another day."

Owen gave me a wink, and then they both turned and took off rapidly toward the warehouse. I was now alone in the van, without even a fancy computer or some earpiece chatter to keep me busy. I couldn't quip at them or ask what was going on. I had to be content with sitting silently, watching the warehouse and hoping that Stan, Chloe, and Owen all came out unharmed.

I rolled up the window, sighed, crossed my arms, and tried not to pout. Chloe seemingly had no business running into a situation like this, but she'd proven herself to be a great shot back when we'd squared off against a demon and a vampire. She'd saved my butt—and Mel's, but bringing that up just gets you a view of said butt as he flexes it and invites you to touch—in record time, and come out completely unscathed. I didn't know much about her history but I knew she was pretty good with a gun.

I just had to trust that she and Owen could get Stan out and not get shot up in the process.

Uncrossing my arms, I lifted my hips, twisting to pull my phone out of my pocket. I checked some of my social network feeds, discovered they were pretty stagnant at that time of the evening, and went on to a puzzle game. I got bored quickly, though, and found myself settling into another pout, this one more epic than the last.

It didn't occur to me that I was looking at Mel's SUV until I'd been staring at it for a minute or two. I hadn't really noticed it as we pulled up, because there were several giant vans and trucks parked around the area. But as far as I could tell, that was definitely Mel's car. No one else had quite such an ostentatious ride, especially not here.

Still staring at the giant, gleaming black SUV parked down the lane, I unlocked my phone, glancing at it long enough to find Mel's number in the received list and call it. He answered on the fourth ring, still weeping from the day before. I could practically hear the snot on his face.

"Gwen, she left me. I came here to tell her I love her and she just left. I'm alone again. It hurts to be without her. I can't fight it anymore. I just want to be near her, to look at her."

"Mel, where are you?"

He answered me by snorting wetly and letting out a sob. I made a face, but pressed on with my questioning.

"Are you in Tacoma?"

"Why doesn't she love me? She's all I think about. I can't even get another woman to look at me, and she just ... Gwen, why?"

"Snap out of it! Are you—"

He gasped, cutting me off. "I just heard someone come in. Maybe ... two people? Why does she keep bringing other men around? My love!" He wailed like Romeo drunkenly calling to his Juliet, and hung up. I stared down at the phone, not sure if I was more disgusted or annoyed. Either way, I damn well wasn't sitting in the van anymore.

I tucked my phone into my pocket as I slid out the van door to the ground. Looking around to make sure there wasn't a crying werewolf or wayward succubus around, I shut the door as silently as I could and then started walking toward Mel's SUV. I wasn't exactly nervous, but I was aware that Chloe and Owen had guns and that I didn't know anything about guns other than that they could put holes in people. The warehouse was across a narrow road from where I was, but bullets went through walls and across roads, right?

Why did the bullet cross the road? To embed itself into my sternum, my nerves insisted.

I got to the SUV and peered in through the driver's side window. The back windows were all heavily tinted, but the front three were clear as day. The vehicle looked familiar, but Mel didn't keep too many distinguishing items inside, last I remembered. Maybe that nice stereo was standard and this car had nothing to do with Mel. Maybe I was just being silly, working out something to distract me from Stan's peril.

Trying the door on a whim, I made a happy sound when I found it was open. I climbed inside, scaled the massive, center console, and tried the glove box. It was locked. No registration clues, it seemed, but when I looked into the back of the car, I realized it had to belong to Mel.

The whole back—flat without its last two rows of seats—was made up like a fancy hotel bed. There was even a shiny gold box tucked behind the driver's seat, with little foil-wrapped chocolates inside.

"Don't mind if I do," I said to myself, reaching down to grab two (make that four—ah, five). I sat in the passenger seat of Mel's car, staring out the front window at the side of the warehouse, pondering what this could mean. The only possible explanation I could come up with was that Mel was mated to the succubus.

I was three chocolates into my haul before I realized that, should Chloe come back to find me missing, I was going to be in big trouble. I could worry about the implications of having Owen kill Mel's future wife from the safety of the van, and I wouldn't have to worry about getting yelled at by Chloe if she found me gone.

"Gwen!"

I heard my name as I dropped out of Mel's car and guilt flooded in. Chloe is childless, so her angry voice isn't exactly a mom-voice, but it's a pretty good approximation. Like being punched in the gut with, versus without, brass knuckles: they both get the job done but one is just a bit more effective.

"Sorry!" I yelled, closing the SUV door and running toward the van. Chloe's head snapped around, and her eyes were murderous. I noticed very clearly, in that moment, that she still had her gun out, pointed at the ground. She glanced about before gesturing to me with her empty hand.

"Let's go!"

I felt my shoulders hunch. I hadn't snuck out to go do drugs in a park; I'd just done a little inspection of a friend's car. As soon as she could reach me, Chloe grabbed my arm and dragged me toward the open side door of the van. When I got close enough, I saw Stan propped against the inside wall, bound and gagged. His expression behind the swath of tan cloth was mild, his emotions a babbling brook of confusion, disappointment, and faint distress.

"What—"

"Get in, we're getting him safe before she comes back."

"Before—"

"Get *in!*" Chloe snapped, shoving at me. She shut the side door on me before I was completely through, and I had to yank my ankle away from its guillotine-like slam. Righting myself, I looked over to find Owen in the driver's seat and Chloe buckling herself in where I'd been. When we'd started moving, Chloe turned to look me over. She was not pleased with me.

"What were you doing? We told you to stay in the van!"

"I was just looking at—"

"Your holes! Don't you remember what he said about your holes and how you don't want any more of them?"

"Yes!" I insisted. Chloe took a deep breath and shook her head. I'd never seen her this anxious before, and that included when she'd been thrown through the air like a softball by an angry demon. "I'm sorry."

The van hit a bump and I nearly toppled, catching myself with my left arm on Stan's outstretched leg. I glanced over, and something pulled my eyes to his crotch. Despite the fact that absolutely no lust, desire, or arousal was present in his psyche, he had an erection. It wasn't just a passing thought, either; his penis was committed to the cause.

"What were you doing?" Chloe asked, actually expecting an answer this time.

"Ah," I cleared my throat, tore my eyes away from Stan's pants, and then turned to her. Stan remained quiet next to me and I wondered if I should un-gag him. "Mel's car is—was there. I wanted to see if he was in it."

"Mel's car?" Chloe asked.

"Yeah, I think he might've been here for Norma."

"Mel the werewolf?" Owen asked, taking a turn less gently than I would have liked. I slid a bit, felt my shoulder squish against the wall of the van, and realized I was still palming two candies. I tucked them into my back pocket and then crawled to Stan, sitting on my heels next to him.

"Yes, the werewolf," Chloe said, turning to point at a street sign. "Turn—"

"I got it, I know where we're going."

Suspicion sliced out of Chloe toward Owen, but her expression remained blank, leaving him unaware of it. When she didn't ask him to clarify, I continued.

"Yeah, it was his car. I tried calling him but he was just crying some more and—"

Owen let out a laugh that startled us all. It was a bark of noise, an explosion of humor that tapered off into an uncoordinated guffaw. Chloe frowned at him but she was starting to feel pretty amused herself.

"What am I missing?"

"You're saying Mel got whammied," Chloe explained. "If we don't get it fixed soon, it could get very bad."

"I'm saying what?"

Owen continued to chuckle and Chloe shook her head as she sighed, but they didn't answer. Deciding that could wait, I looked back to Stan. He turned to meet my eyes and I cocked my head as I frowned at him. His psyche was still dominated by the same emotional cloud, but something in there was off. I leaned close like I was going to kiss him, but he just watched me, his eyes crossing a bit. Owen spoke as I inspected Stan's strange emotions.

"When a succubus feeds for keeps it either kills its prey—in the case of humans—or leaves its mark. A werewolf has enough energy to feed a succubus a few times over, so if they're fed upon deeply enough, they get sort of stained."

I was listening, mostly, but still watching Stan. He was gagged, so he said nothing, just watching me curiously. There was something there I couldn't place, but it wasn't him. It was jerky and unpleasant and made me feel like I had grabbed a handful of tiny bugs, which were trying to escape the prison I'd made for them of my palm. I pulled back and realized I recognized that undercurrent.

"Do humans get stained?" I asked, still watching Stan. He lifted a brow and tipped his head as if he was fully invested in the conversation, unbothered by not being able to chime in.

Chloe looked between the two of us and then at Stan. "Is he already marked?"

"I'm not sure what it is but I recognize it from Mel. There's something here that's not Stan. Mel's emotions are defective, like they're shorting out. This ... jumpy feeling is there, too, but with Mel, it's worse. It's different."

"Norma," Owen said. I nodded but scrunched my face up into a scowl as Stan's emotions perked up. He tried to speak through the gag and I reached around the back of his head to untie it. When he was free he spoke.

"Is Norma around? Are we going to see her? I'd like to see her."

"Uh," I said, glancing at Chloe. "Sure. We're gonna go see her."

"Oh good. She was so interesting. Our conversation was ... We had such ..." He trailed off, and I felt the distress around him bubble harder. "That is, I really wanted to contribute, to talk to her, but I didn't have much to say. She wanted to know about you, about our marriage. She wanted to know why I smelled of you when I left your office. I think she was jealous, but I don't know why. You're nothing compared to her."

I let his comment go, deciding that I couldn't take it personally. Sure, I had cheated on him, but Norma probably wanted to give him cancer and leave him dead in the street. Surely he didn't really think my betrayal was worse? This had to be the doing of Norma's succubus mojo.

"Did you tell her?" I asked, pushing past my guilt. Stan shook his head, his brow creasing.

"I didn't ... There wasn't much to say. I told her we were divorced, about how it ended. I couldn't concentrate on you, though, on our history. I was distracted by her breasts."

Owen laughed again from the front and even Chloe fought off a snort. I frowned down at Stan.

"By her breasts?" I asked. He nodded rapidly, but the distress around him was getting overwhelming, making me feel like I'd gotten water up my nose and I couldn't breathe well enough to get it out.

"Yes, I couldn't stop staring. Or, if she wasn't facing me, I looked at her behind. Both are very attractive and she's so interesting that I know it shouldn't matter, but I can't stop thinking about how much I want to put my hands—"

"Okay!" I squeaked, pushing forward to tie the gag around his mouth again. He frowned up at me and tried to talk over the cloth, but I couldn't understand him, thankfully. Two or three jumbled words into being gagged, he stopped speaking and I felt the cloud of his feelings shift back to a mild confusion. Not being able to talk seemed to comfort him. All of it was on another level, though, as if he was acting without his own permission.

"That's why we gagged him. He wouldn't stop describing the things he was thinking about her body," Chloe explained. Her cheeks were a bit pink, but her discomfort level was low. "He got kinda graphic."

"Well, this is horrifying," I mumbled, trying to ignore the embarrassment flooding through me. Stan and I had been pretty graphic as hormonal teens, but it was one thing to remember the two of us goofy in love. It was entirely another to know that my prim and proper ex-husband had no choice but to want to get jiggy with some succubus.

We went silent as we drove, Chloe shifting to look forward at the road. I did my best to stay steady on the slick metal of the van, spreading myself out across from Stan, watching him. He met my eyes and his expression was blank, his emotions continuing to burble in the same distinct and very not-Stan way.

"I'm sorry you got whammied," I mumbled over to him.

"It's almost over," Owen said, as the van slowed to a stop. I pushed further up on my knees and tried to see if I recognized where we were. All I saw were houses and vague neighborhood shapes. It wasn't until Chloe got out and pulled the side door open that I realized we were at Madeline's.

OLIVIA R .BURTON

Nineteen

Owen hefted Stan over his shoulder, which upped the rumble of distress in Stan's psyche, and turned to wait for me. As soon as Chloe and I were out, Owen twisted effortlessly and headed up the walkway to Madeline's porch, knocking once on the door. Chloe hooked her arm into mine, not needing psychic powers to sense what I was thinking. I watched the door open, saw Owen slip in and met the eyes of the muscle-bound meathead I'd been eyeing last time. He was expressionless and, at that distance, I felt a little grossed out at the thoughts I'd been having about him before.

"Everything is gonna be fine," Chloe said as we headed up to the house. "Madeline will be able to fix Stan, get Norma's influence out of his head."

"Won't that just put her influence in?"

"No, she knows what she's doing. It's a succubus thing."

I glanced at her unhappily but didn't bother asking how she knew. Chloe was talking to everyone, lately, and had likely been doing research in her downtime. While I'd been pawing at Owen and cringing at Mel, she'd probably been borrowing books from the library or Googling answers and getting exactly what she needed on the first try. I never found what I wanted unless it was dessert-related, but I couldn't honestly use that as a reason for why I didn't know what was going on.

Madeline was standing over Stan as he sat slightly askew on the couch. Owen was standing to the side, hands linked behind his back as he watched Madeline inspect my ex. She tipped her head and an airy feeling of interest blew out of her, sweeping away as mild surprise whooshed in. Without the cloud of desire she'd laid out for us the last time, her emotions felt more familiar. When she crouched in front of Stan, I felt the twitchy thing in his psyche tense.

As she reached out and put a hand to his chest, something in him exploded in a panicked mess.

"Hey!" I cried, jerking forward before I knew what I was doing. Chloe pulled me back, stepping between Madeline and me and shaking her head. The muscle around the room regarded me with vague interest but didn't make a move. I peered over Chloe's shoulder and watched Madeline as she moved her hand to the back of Stan's head, her touch gentle. Stan's legs twitched and I felt that panic inside him grow. Whatever was crawling around in his brain was not happy with whatever Madeline was planning.

Abruptly, Madeline stood and turned to face Owen.

"I'll need a few hours with him, but after that he'll be back to normal." Stan struggled a bit against his bonds, although his expression stayed bland. I sighed, watching his body shudder and seize, despite the fact that he seemed unaware of it. I wanted to go curl up around him, to pull his head into my lap and pet his hair. I wanted to protect him from pain, to be the woman I should've been for him ten years ago. I felt Chloe's sadness match mine, and when I turned minutely to meet her eyes I realized she was feeling sad for me, not Stan. For once, it made me feel a bit angry that she would regard me as anything but a screw-up.

Owen and Madeline had been talking while I was watching Stan, and I forced myself to tune in.

"Can you find her through him?" Owen asked.

"Not without letting him go to her. I can untie him, give him a car and follow whatever meandering path leads him there, or I can get her mark off of him. The longer the mark stays, though, the harder it gets to remove. Or, if you do things the hard way, the harder he takes it when she dies. His essence will rebuild, if given the time, but if he's still bound to her and she dies … it won't be pretty."

"Then get on with it," Owen said, crossing his arms. "We may have another way to locate her."

"Another victim?"

"Yeah, but he's already pretty far gone from the sound of it."

"Beyond saving?"

Owen twisted to look to Chloe and me, expecting us to answer Madeline's question.

"You mean Mel?" I asked. Madeline's brows shot up and the laugh that shot through her lips hit me like a warm blast of wind.

"Norma got to our werewolf?" she asked

"Yeah, he's all—ha ha—moony over her, crying about how he can't get laid, but he can't stop thinking about her," Chloe explained.

Madeline started laughing again, but this time it was a wheezing, delighted sound. I found myself pulled into it, wanting to go to her and share the experience. I walked right into Chloe as I took a step forward, and she turned as if confused at what I was doing. When Madeline straightened up there were tears in her eyes and she put a hand out to Owen's arm as if she couldn't stand without the help. Owen glanced at her hand on his arm and I felt a slice of irritation arc out of him, but he said nothing.

When she was able, Madeline explained what was so funny.

"Werewolves sleep with everything that moves, right?" We all nodded. "But when a succubus gets hold of one, we naturally want them to ourselves—regardless of what emotion we feed upon. Something with as much energy as a wolf is a gift, essentially, and one you don't want to share. The mark we put on them royally fucks with their confidence and sense of well-being. It's worse if we feed on something other than sex, but sex is bad enough."

Madeline took a step back and moved her hand off Owen's arm to hold it up, palm out toward us.

"I'm not saying it's right, and I haven't done it since I was young, but when you screw with a werewolf's confidence, they—it's like putting an emotional chastity belt on. No one is going to touch them with a ten-foot pole. Part of it is the mark, of course, making people uncomfortable to just be around them, but that confidence—" She laughed again, shook her head as if to apologize. "That being gone? You might as well dunk the wolf in cat piss and dress it in old ham." She collapsed into a fit of giggles again and I found myself drawn in.

"Mad, you're getting Gwen," Chloe said quietly, tightening the grip I hadn't realized she had on my arm.

"What?" she asked. Chloe shoved a shoulder into me, knocking me back when I tried, once again, to walk closer. "Oh, shit." Straightening up, Madeline shook her head, took a jumpy breath and then let it out slowly.

I felt the desire I'd had fade away.

"What happened?" I asked. Chloe shook her head, and Owen continued to stand like a sentry, a small smile on his face.

"You're not shielded, and that's dangerous for an empath around me, especially in my current state," Madeline explained. Waving a hand at me, she stepped back toward Stan. "Go, find her. Use Mel—" She fought off more laughter. "And let me know if you need help. I will be indisposed for a while, though, so if you need me before I'm done … well, you'll have to wait."

"He's going to be okay?" I asked, gesturing to Stan. Madeline nodded, using her sleeve to wipe her face.

"He'll be better than okay."

"Madeline," Owen said, his tone a warning. She rolled her gaze to him and I felt the change in atmosphere immediately. Whatever history they shared had just been pulled to the forefront. Owen remained still, his face blank, his emotions tinged with a sort of malice I realized I had felt in him before, though I'd felt it in much smaller doses. Anger whipped out of her, a tornado that I was convinced might tug my hair out at the roots. Chloe's disinterest was a buffer between their standoff and me and I was thankful she couldn't seem to sense that Owen and Madeline both felt like they might go at each other's throats any second.

Swallowing thickly, Madeline nodded, her anger dying down. "You're right. I won't go too far."

"What is going too far?" I demanded. Owen and Madeline turned to me and spoke in unison.

"Rape."

"Come on, Gwen," Chloe said firmly, hooking her arm around mine and pulling me toward the door. I fought against her, desperate to get to Stan and get him out of there. Chloe was stronger, though, and managed to cut me off at every pass, keeping me in her grip. When we got outside, she put herself between the door and me.

"Stop," she ordered.

"But—"

"He'll be fine. I trust Madeline not to make Stan do anything he wouldn't do outside of this situation."

"He—"

"Will be fine. We need to find Norma."

"And thanks to you being distracted, that's going to be more of a pain in the ass than I'd hoped," Owen announced as he closed the front door and moved down the two steps to our level.

"I was distracted?"

"The Find," Chloe clarified.

Shaking my head, I took a step back, feeling suddenly, colossally overwhelmed. There were too many worries and too many questions. I felt out of my depth and lost.

"Just give me a minute to think, okay?"

Chloe and Owen exchanged glances and I turned away from them, shoving my hands into my hair. I took a giant gulp of air and moved my hands in front of my eyes. Pressing my fingers to my eyeballs hard enough that I saw colors, I tried my best to make sense of the situation.

Days ago everything had been normal. I'd been working and feeling good. Chloe had been trying to get me to eat healthier and I'd been doing just the opposite. That was par for the course for us and I rather enjoyed the give and take, where she gave me vegetables and I took them and dipped them in some fatty dressing and then mostly just slurped at the dressing.

Then Stan had shown up, talking about having a stalker. That stalker had turned out to be a succubus who'd, in turn, been hunted by a man that I was now having sex with. The sex part, that made perfect sense, but the situations leading up to the sex still had my brain in knots: succubi, stalkers, werewolves on crying jags, ex-husband roommates, and a partridge in a pear tree.

So, what was the solution to all these problems? What was I trying to get out of this situation? Where did I want to be this time tomorrow? These were the tough questions I asked myself while standing on a Seattle sidewalk with my face in my hands.

"Okay," I said through my fingers, still facing away from my friends. "It seems like Norma is basically everybody's problem."

I turned, dropped my hands to my side and tried to ignore the feelings poking at me from both Chloe and Owen. They both figured me for a dummy. Pointing at them, I continued.

"You two shut up. You have knives and guns and succubus experience and I have an ex-husband who's been mind-raped and a tiny plastic magnifying lens that apparently just does whatever the hell it feels like doing, despite what I ask it to do." Owen opened his mouth to speak and I pointed at him. "I said shut up."

The arrogance in him flashed to surprise and I felt my own stab of smugness at that.

"Look, I know you two are the big damn heroes and I'm just the goofy sidekick. I'm okay with that, you know? I get it. What I'm not okay with is feeling like everything is happening around me and I'm just stuck in life's van, unable to help or participate. I can't do anything for Stan and that makes me feel like shit, but I can help with Norma, right? You can help me figure out how to stop her. We can figure out how I can be useful. I don't want a gun or a knife and I'm not going to pretend I can do some flippy ninja shit and kick her ass, but I want to feel useful. I want to help. I want to make what Stan is going through in there better by being able to tell him that we stopped Norma. I want to make sure he knows no one else is ever going to mess with him like this again."

I paused to give myself a moment to overcome the stinging at the back of my throat as I realized I'd unintentionally jumped back in time ten years to when I'd been the one ruining Stan's life. Swallowing thickly, I pressed on, tried to bring my rambling speech to a logical end.

"We can all work together and you can shove your 'staying in the van' right up your ass. Asses. You both get a van to shove up each of your asses."

Taking a deep breath, I crossed my arms over my chest, stared them both down and waited for them to nod or speak or give me some indication they knew what I was talking about, because I feared that even I didn't know at that point. It was about thirty seconds before Chloe turned to Owen and spoke.

"We only have the one van, so I nominate your ass."

"I'd rather not pay the damage fees on that one, thanks. But, whadd'ya say we get Gwen some ice cream?" Owen's voice went slow, like a parent placating a tantrum-throwing toddler. "And come up with a plan that doesn't involve a foreign object or my rectum?"

I looked between them, torn between giving another angry speech and taking them up on the ice cream offer. Luckily for them, I'm a sucker for ice cream.

I'm not sure if it was a bad joke on their part, but Chloe made me stay in the van while she ran into the ice cream shop to bring me back my sweet treat. They probably suspected I was too worked up to conduct myself responsibly in public, and the only reason I didn't throw another tantrum was that they were probably right.

"I take it this isn't a typical week for you?" Owen asked. I turned away from watching Chloe through the store window and considered staying silent and refusing to answer. His expression was sweet, though, and he was feeling a bit worried about me.

"Not at all. I don't hunt monsters like you and I don't own a gun like Chloe. I'm just a therapist."

"Stan will be fine. He's in good hands. Hands that won't touch him in his bathing suit area, I promise."

Despite myself, I laughed, shook my head.

"I believe you. But …" I splayed my hands in front of me, waving them spastically as if I could work off the anxiety I felt over the situation. "He's such a good man and he doesn't deserve anything like this. I just—I can't let him get screwed over again."

"Again?" Owen asked, tipping his head. He reached across the gap between us and grabbed my hand. I let him pull it closer, holding it so both our arms were stretched. I glanced back and found Chloe had paid the lady behind the counter and was nodding at something she was saying. When she scooped up the cup of ice cream (with bonus chocolate-and-sprinkles-covered waffle cone on top), I turned back to Owen.

"I'll explain later." He nodded and squeezed my hand, and I wondered how a guy who seemed like such a decent fellow had gotten into such a dangerous line of work, and why he enjoyed it so much.

When Chloe was back in the van and the ice cream was in my hands, I gestured vaguely with the cup. Owen switched the van into gear and pulled into traffic. Without pretense, I bit off the pointy end of the cone and felt a happy little sigh run through my body at the taste of sugar on top of sugar on top of waffle cone.

"So, what's our plan?" I asked, still crunching on the cone. Chloe, who'd taken a seat on the bare floor just behind the gap between our bucket seats, rolled her eyes good-naturedly at my open-mouthed chewing.

"You're going to call Mel and offer to have sex with him."

I nearly choked on my cone.

"Excuse me?" I said when I was able to swallow and breathe normally. Chloe knocked her knuckle against my pocket where my phone was tucked.

"Mel's got Norma on his mind, but he's still Mel. He still wants to have sex and it sounds like Norma's not interested. If we can get him to come to us, we should be able to use him to find Norma."

"And why am I the one who has to call him?" I asked, soothing myself with a giant scoop of chocolate ice cream, caramel swirl, marshmallow bits, and gummy bears. I loved Chloe so much in that moment. Even her telling me I had to offer sex to Mel couldn't overcome the happy that was this fattening cup of deliciousness.

"Because you're the new-car smell," Chloe answered, getting to her knees.

I grunted around the ice cream, trying to make it sound like I was asking for clarification. Watching the scenery, I realized Owen was taking us back to my place.

"He's never slept with you before. He's fallen pretty hard for Norma, but he won't be able to resist you offering sex," Chloe explained, grabbing a napkin from my lap and reaching out to dab at my chin. I fought the urge to growl at her and pull my ice cream away. She probably wasn't going to take it, even though it was vegan, but that didn't mean I wanted to risk it.

"Not only are you pine fresh but you're a challenge," Owen said, giving me a look that sat firmly on the fence between affection and disgust. I ignored him; as long as he wasn't trying to steal my sugar, I had no beef with how he saw me in that moment. "Un-Mated werewolves can't resist new—ah." He cut himself off, and I had the sense that he'd been about to use a very rude word.

"New partners," he said finally.

Chloe eyed him but didn't say anything. I crammed another spoonful of ice cream into my mouth and chewed on a rock-hard gummy bear. Thinking about what they were proposing, I realized it was all just a means to an end. I didn't actually have to have sex with Mel; I just had to claim I would to get him to come to us.

"You're sure he won't just turn me down?"

Chloe let out a bark of laughter and shook her head.

"No, no, I don't think he will. Unless he's with Norma in that moment, I don't think we have to worry about that."

Twenty

Chloe unlocked my front door and let me walk in ahead of her. I'd somehow managed to get ice cream on my hands, and she hadn't let me touch anything between the front seat of the van and the house. I was okay with this, as it meant I could use both hands to eat ice cream. I was down to my last frozen marshmallow and chunk of soggy waffle cone.

I kept walking straight through the living room to finish my ice cream over the kitchen sink. I dumped the cup and plastic spoon when I was done and washed my hands. Once clean, I licked at my lips and realized I'd probably gotten ice cream on my face, too. My belief is that food is to be enjoyed, and if you're not eating like a five-year-old, you're not doing it justice. This does not often serve me well in my professional or social life, but ... well, my reasoning begins and ends with, 'ice cream.'

After dabbing at my mouth with wet paper towels, I stepped back into the living room and found Owen standing just inside the door, watching Chloe. She'd gone to Sonny's cage and was cooing to him, which he seemed to appreciate. As she stuck a finger through the bars of his cage to scratch his cheek, Owen turned to look at me.

"The sooner you call Mel, the sooner this is over."

I frowned his way and dug my phone out. Keeping my eyes on him, I unlocked the phone and had a thought.

"Did you guys buy me ice cream to butter me up for this?"

"And to stop you from babbling about shoving vans up people's asses," Owen said, grinning like an evil mastermind. I scowled, but couldn't argue.

"Make it convincing," Chloe said. I frowned at her and then down at my phone. I really, really did not want to tell Mel I would have sex with him. Even just as part of a plan, it seemed like a terrible idea. What if he carried this fake confession with him for the rest of his life and never let me alone about it?

"Ugh. What if he records this and plays it back as blackmail some day?"

"Just call him."

"But—"

Chloe darted forward and pinched my arm. I yelped and jumped to the side, grumbling. Owen shook his head at us like we were misbehaving puppies, but said nothing.

"Fine!" I said, giving her my best snarl. She wrinkled her nose at me.

"You're adorable," she cooed in the same tone she'd used on Sonny. Then her voice went hard. "Now dial."

Fearing another attack, I stepped away from Chloe as I opened my recent calls list and hit Mel's number. Shoving my free hand through my hair, I sighed and waited. Mel answered late, probably just before the voicemail would've picked up.

"Gwen?"

"Mel, hi," I said, unsure how to start the conversation. I had a flashback to my call the night before with Owen and figured I could probably play it the same. "How are you?"

"I'm lonely. She's gone again." His tone was tragic, sending my plan of being flirty and casual right out the window. How was I supposed to flirt with someone who sounded like their favorite uncle had just been trampled by rhinos?

"Nor—" Realizing he'd never actually told us his lady friend's name, I cut myself off. "What's her name?"

"Norma." As he sighed out wistfully, I turned to face Chloe and Owen, gave them an enthusiastic thumbs-up. They just frowned at me and I realized they had no idea I'd just confirmed that Mel was, in fact, just what we needed to track Norma. Or maybe they'd already been so sure, they thought I was an idiot for doubting them.

When Mel didn't keep speaking, I pressed on.

"So, I have a proposition for you. If you're up for it. If you want to, I mean. You don't have—" Chloe pinched me again and I whined at her, pulling away. Mel didn't notice. "What I was saying is, is, uh. I think you and I should…" I trailed off, my mouth working silently. It was possibly going to be physically painful to say that I wanted to have sex with Mel, I just knew it.

Chloe glared at me, lifting her hand and making a pinching motion with her fingers. Apparently it would be physically painful not to say it, too.

"Have sex with me, Mel," I blurted. Owen let out a quiet snort, pressing a hand to his lips to cover it.

"Have sex with you?" Mel asked, bewildered.

"Yes. You should come to my house and we will have—some." I had a hard time saying it again. I stuttered, feeling my lip curl in disgust. "Some—some sex. We'll—we'll do it. Together."

Owen's whole upper body was shaking with laughter, palm holding in most of the laughter, though snorts pushed through here and there. Chloe shook her head, controlling her laughter but not her emotions. Suddenly the amusement in the room was strangling. I found I was smiling, despite the fact that I was not proud of what I'd just done.

"You—really?" Mel asked. When I didn't answer immediately, I heard the phone shift and then the sound of him blowing his nose.

Astoundingly sexy, this one.

"Yeah. Yes. *Really*. I actually want you to do me. This is *not* a ruse," I caught myself claiming before I cleared my throat and continued. "I promise. This is real and it's … happening."

"But you hate me." He had a point, but I'm a quick thinker.

"That just means better sex, doesn't it? Hate? Hate sex is what we should have!" I announced, sending Owen into another snorting fit.

"Really?" Mel asked again, a sniffle chasing his confusion over the phone line.

"For God's sake, Mel, do you want to put your penis in me or not?" I snapped. I didn't have it in me to keep begging him. On any other day, I would have gotten out just the word 'let's,' and he would have magically appeared next to me, sans underpants. He made a stuttering sound but didn't answer, which made me even more impatient.

"This is a limited-time offer. Come on. Chop, chop!" I felt so greasy in that moment, I needed to be done. Even if we never caught Norma and Stan had to go into Witness Protection in order for me to be done ordering Mel to nail me, in that moment I was okay with that.

Mel made a small sound that could have been a sob or could've been an insulted gasp. I stayed silent, waiting for him to decide. Maybe Chloe was wrong and he was too far gone in Norma's trap. Maybe we'd have to go to him, tie him up, bring him to Madeline and she'd have to get into his brain meats and unscramble what was there to get to Norma.

That had to be a thing, right? This couldn't be our only plan. *I* could not be our only plan.

"Let me shower, I'll come right over. I can't believe this, Gwen. I—"

"Don't shower. Just come over."

"I'm kind of—"

"We'll shower together. Just get over here."

"I—okay. I'll be there as soon as I can."

"Great."

Unable to listen to the pathetic whine in his voice anymore, I hung up, shoved the phone at Chloe and then stepped away, indulging in a full-body shudder. When the shudder wasn't enough, I let out a long, wavering cry, trying to overcome the slimy feeling across my skin. Owen had managed to control his laughter, but his eyes were gleaming a bit, and Chloe was giggling, shaking her head. I pointed at both of them in turn.

"I hate you both. That. Felt. Awful."

"At least you don't actually have to sleep with him," Chloe reminded me. "Unless you want to." I ignored that.

"But he's going to *think* I want to, now. Forever. He will always hear my voice in the back of his head, suggesting we get naked!"

"You weren't exactly convincing," Owen pointed out.

"Hey," I snapped, stepping toward him. I shouldn't have been insulted; I hadn't meant a word of what I'd said to Mel. But did Owen not understand the sacrifice I'd just made? Insulting me in my hour of selflessness was just rude. He held up his hands in surrender.

"I'm just saying. I've heard you when you really want sex, and honey, that wasn't it. He's just desperate."

"Well," I amended. "I guess you have a point."

"He'll probably still come to the door with no pants on, though." Chloe pointed out. I whipped around to glare at her.

"Not funny!" I said. Behind me, Sonny rang his bells, and I turned back to him. "Don't you start!"

All the back and forth was making me sick, so I moved to flop onto the couch. Chloe followed and dropped down next to me, handing me my phone. I eyed it as if it was radioactive but reluctantly took it. I gestured to the chair between Owen and Sonny's cage.

"Sit, make yourself comfy."

He glanced around the room as if looking for traps, then perched at the end of the seat, leaning his elbows on his knees. I snorted.

"We're not going to hurt you."

"Yes, but as soon as he's here, I want to go. I'm behind schedule on this and I'd like to get it done as quickly as possible."

"Well, hopefully this plan works better than your last one."

"The problem wasn't the plan," Owen said and I felt a spark of irritation pop off him. His voice remained calm, his face neutral. "You were concentrating on Stan, so it led us to him."

"So it's my fault?"

"Yep," Chloe said, patting my knee. "You're just lucky he was actually in danger and we didn't just get taken for a ride."

"And we can't use the thing again?"

"Nope, one time only."

I moaned, not sure if I felt guilty or not. If I'd concentrated on Norma, we'd have her, but not Stan. I actually preferred knowing Stan was safe. It was selfish and gross to consider his life more important than those of the strangers I had likely put in danger by leaving Norma out in the world, but I could probably blame that on human nature.

"Well," I said. "How do we get him to take us to her?"

"We ask."

"That can't be it."

Owen laughed, nodded. "Like Madeline said, it may take him some time, but he'll find her."

"Then you kill her?" I asked, unsure how I felt about that, despite all that had happened. I'd been around two corpses the last week. A third, however deserved death might be, didn't sound appealing.

"At this point, yes," Owen said. I bit my lip.

"And you're just cool with that?"

"She's a nutter, G," Chloe explained. I turned to her. "There isn't really a place to put creatures like her when they can't control themselves. Madeline's a functional member of society—probably not just human society, either. She may be dangerous, but she controls herself. Norma is killing at random, drawing too much attention."

"We're not going to torture her," Owen added as if that should make everything better. "We're just going to kill her."

"We?" I demanded.

"You don't have to go if you don't want." Owen smiled, and there was something sinister about it. "The wolf and I can go alone."

"No," I mumbled, shaking my head. "I got Mel into this. I'll … What can I do?"

"You can be bait," Owen said conversationally.

"Oh, come on."

"We'll get you more ice cream," Chloe offered.

"I don't …" I trailed off, realizing I couldn't lie and say I didn't want more ice cream. That would be crazy. But bait? I had to be bait? Suddenly, their plan from before didn't seem so bad. "What if I just stay in the van?"

In a surprising reversal of roles, Chloe and Owen were waiting in the van when Mel arrived.

They'd explained the plan to me, and it seemed simple enough. They hadn't gone into detail about things—like oh, say, how they were going to kill Norma—but they'd assured me that Mel and I would be safe. Now I had one task: convince Mel to take me back to Norma, so they could follow along, sneak in behind us, and take her out. Chloe's suggestion had been that I offer myself up as a snack, and when I'd questioned the logistics of that plan, she'd pointed out that I was essentially offering myself to Mel as part of a threesome.

I'd stopped questioning her then and considered throwing up.

I was still feeling the nausea as I stood just inside my door, hand on the knob, and took a courage-boosting breath. Mel rang the bell a second time, and I swore silently to myself. Finally I opened the door to find a sight I had not expected.

Mel stood there looking disheveled and uncomfortable. His expression was almost fearful, his shirt unevenly buttoned. The hair on his head looked like he'd tried to cut it, but used two different size guards on the electric razor. His eyebrows were completely gone.

Just … gone.

The missing eyebrows were somehow less jarring than the fact that his fly was down and the front of his left pant cuff was tucked into his sock. He held a plastic-wrapped bouquet of flowers in his right hand. They were lovely flowers, don't get me wrong, but considering the rest of the scene, they were out of place.

We stared at each other with similar expressions of, 'what exactly is happening here?' before I stepped back and gestured to my living room. I opened my mouth to speak, but no words came out. Mel took half a step and then paused.

"Can I—um—come in?" he asked. I nodded and stuttered out an affirmative, my eyes moving to the flowers. They looked expensive—I mean, the bouquet was as big as my torso, for god's sake; what had Mel been thinking?—which confused me even further. I stood there with the door open as he stood awkwardly in my living room.

This was feeling very similar to my first date with Stan. Any second now, my father was going to appear in the room, glaring up at Mel—Dad's barely taller than I am—and demanding he have me back before curfew.

Shaking my head to clear it, I finally shut the door and pointed at the flowers.

"What are those for?"

"For you?" Mel made it a question. Glancing around the room, he held them partially out to me. "I guess?"

"Thanks," I said, grasping them as gently as one would a premature baby. When he let them go and I felt the weight of them in my hands, I looked back up to his face. "I guess I can put them in some water."

"Flowers like that," he agreed without a trace of sarcasm. "Yeah."

Feeling like this was way more uncomfortable than it should have been, I took a deep breath, fairly certain that the discomfort I was feeling was not entirely my own and that I'd managed to ingest his emotions and mix them with mine. Striding past him, I hit the kitchen, opened a few cabinets, and then realized that I didn't own a vase.

I didn't own a vase? Really? Ugh, Gwen, way to be an adult.

For lack of any other options, I pulled my water carafe out of the fridge, stuck the flowers in it and set them on the counter. Taking a deep breath, I focused on the feelings inside me, picking apart my own and pulling them away from the clumsy mess that was Mel's disjointed emotional jumble. It was like trying to pull white pet hair out of white Velcro, but I managed to figure out that I wasn't nearly as anxious as I had been feeling.

When I got back to the living room, I found that Mel was standing in the same position as before, eyes fixed on the wall. He didn't even look over as I walked in, and it made me pause. I'd never seen him be anything less than capable, confident, and arrogant as hell. Norma had really done a number on him. It almost made me feel sorry enough for him to once again consider throwing him some pity sex.

Almost, but not really.

"I have an idea," I said. He turned to me partially and it reminded me of a dog who's convinced the person speaking is about to whack its nose with a newspaper. Pressing on as if he wasn't being quite so pathetic, I cleared my throat and tried to pitch my voice casually.

"Your girlfriend, Norma. Does she like—I mean, she's a—um. She feeds on people, right?"

He turned to me fully and frowned, confusion clouding around him. It took him a second, before he shook his head.

"How did ... What are you saying?"

Continuing to force my tone to stay calm, despite the fact that knew I had literally no idea what was about to come out of my mouth, I took a step toward him.

"I just have—I recognize the way your brain—your emotions? You know?—are feeling. To me." As if it helped, I held my hands out, waved them around my head like a game show girl showing off the prize pack. "I mean, Madeline feeds on people and I've seen it. I've felt what satisfied people are feeling. After. You know, after she feeds. And you're feeling like that. Right? Aren't you?"

His eyes went a bit wide and he stumbled back as if he'd just realized something and he wasn't quite happy being that close to the idea.

"I guess. So—" I cut him off.

"So! You and I should go to her—to Norma, not to Madeline—and she can feed on me. You know? Because I've always felt that—um—Madeline has ..." I was struggling for a finish, but he still seemed pretty preoccupied with whatever idea had come into his head. I continued, trying to get it all out before he could object. I would just keep talking until I confused him into doing what I wanted, if I had to. I'd done so plenty of times with my siblings as a child; a dim, brain-scrambled werewolf couldn't be much harder to persuade. I mean, I was trying to talk him into giving up a succubus and not into doing my chores, but I'm good.

"Madeline's missing, but I want to feel what her customers feel and I think you do too, so you should bring me to Norma and we'll all feel that together. Feel the—how it feels to be with a succubus." I couldn't bring myself to say the word 'threesome.' Saying 'sex' to Mel in an inviting manner had been sickening enough.

Silence dropped over the room like a heavy wool blanket. Even Sonny didn't ring any bells, crunch any seeds, or whistle any tunes. Mel stared at the floor and I poked at his emotions, trying to dislodge whatever was going on in that cluttered psyche of his. I recognized confusion, annoyance, disappointment and, on some level that I'm not even sure he was aware of, outrage. Maybe a part of him knew what was happening to him wasn't natural, wasn't normal, and wasn't the start of a beautiful, long-term relationship ending in marriage and kids.

Marriage and puppies? I don't know what werewolves have, but puppies sounded pretty damned adorable.

Not the point, Gwen, I reminded myself.

"So you invited me here to use me?"

"Well, duh," I said, without thinking. "Uh, I mean. I knew you would have sex with me if I asked and that's a type of using people, right? Just for sex? But then, I mean, but now that you're here, I'm remembering that I've always wanted to see what succubus sex is like. And you know, you can be there, too."

He glowered at me and I felt a stab of insult. I waved a hand placating him.

"With us. You can be there with us, in bed. That's how they feed right?" Again, I felt like I had to cover up my tracks. Changing the pitch of my voice, I pressed on. "You know, because I'm not actually sure."

"So, you're suggesting a threesome with me and my mate?"

"Yes!" I exclaimed, pointing at him. Toning down my excitement over the fact that he seemed to *finally* be getting the idea, I shifted my stance, trying to look casual. "If you two are okay with that. If this is like a marriage, then I don't want to interfere. How about we ask her, though?"

"I can't really call her."

"Perfect!" He frowned at me and I shook my head. "I mean. You—we should go to her. Together. Right now, in fact. You can drive me to her and I'll explain what I want from her—from both of you."

Mel was staring at me with such blatant suspicion that I was reasonably sure this wouldn't even work. I half convinced myself in that moment that I'd completely screwed things up in explaining that Norma was a succubus. Had Mel not realized that? Had I just broken some hard news to the man and we'd—I'd—screwed up our only chance at killing the creature that wanted to possess my sweet ex-husband? Was Witness Protection in Stan's future after all?

I tried to fix a non-threatening smile on my face, but I was betting it was as close to approximating a smile as a dog with its lips stuck up over its gums. Finally, just as I was about to break and start apologizing or barfing out the truth about what I needed from him, Mel nodded.

"Okay. I think that's probably a good idea."

"Really?"

"Well, yeah. Norma has been sort of distant since we made love. I've tried spending time with her but she won't stay. I found her in Tacoma earlier, but she just left. Didn't even say goodbye, like she didn't even see me. I stayed at the warehouse, even though I don't know why she was there. She has a beautiful house—we have a beautiful house together."

"She has a house?" I asked, feeling a tingle of excitement. "Is she there now?"

"Yeah, she has—the house is wonderful and she doesn't even seem to want it." I felt a flood of sadness wash out of him. "But I'm sure she's there now. She got really angry when—when her new friend left. Maybe you'll be her friend? I think she'd like that, actually." His lips tugged up on one side in what could have been a grimace or a smile, I wasn't sure. I nodded frantically, stepped forward and grabbed his arm. Pulling him toward the door, I noted that, for once, he wasn't flexing at my touch.

"Let's go, then! To her house! Come on. Can you drive? Do you know where her house is?"

"Oh yeah. I can drive." Once we were outside and I had locked my door, I turned to find him staring down at me, his expression soft and a little sad. I panicked inside, worried he was about to change his mind.

"Let's go!" I insisted, pushing at his chest. He rocked back slightly at my touch, but then leaned in to hug me. I felt myself go tense, arms squished between our chests.

"Thank you, Gwen. I wasn't really sure before this that we were friends."

"Yeah, okay," I said, my voice muffled against his shoulder. He continued to hug me and I felt his hands shift slightly, moving downward away from my sides. Before he could get a grip on my ass, or whatever he was trying to do, I pushed away.

"We should get going," I insisted, pointing to his car. He gave a distracted nod and let me shove him toward the SUV. When we were finally buckled into our seats, he paused with the keys hovering outside the ignition. I fought off a snarl and tried to be patient.

"Really, Gwen. You don't know how much I appreciate how nice you've been to me. I know it's probably just because you feel sorry for me because I haven't had sex in so long. But, it's just so great to know that you'll be there for me in my time of need."

"Uh-huh. Start the car, Mel. The sooner we see Norma, the sooner we can get this over with."

"Oh, oh right. Yeah, got it."

As we pulled away from the curb, I watched Chloe and Owen do the same in the van.

Twenty-One

Mel spent most of the drive quiet, which I was happy about. Our conversation before had been painfully awkward, and I had no desire to continue it. Luckily, his expression reminded me of someone trying to learn French by listening to the advanced disc without first having gone through the remedial lessons. He looked slightly confused and a little frustrated but, more importantly, he looked that way *silently*.

When we pulled up in front of the house I almost forgot all about him.

It was beautiful. Stone and wood, with a burbling fountain in the center of the roundabout driveway and doors that looked formidable enough to keep out any disgruntled peasants. Mel left the car on for a moment before mumbling something to himself and turning off the ignition. I climbed out of his car slowly, feeling tiny as I dropped to the ground and stared up at the front of the house.

There was a stained glass window above the cavernous entry, full of greens, blues and browns. I couldn't seem to make out an image in the shards, but that didn't make it any less impressive. Mel stepped around the car and toward the front door before pausing with his hand on the knob. When he turned to face me, he looked as if he had just noticed me for the first time.

"She's in here. Are you coming in?"

"Yeah," I breathed, not sure I had the ability to shut my mouth over the shock I was still feeling. Norma owned this place?

Without waiting for me, Mel headed inside. The door stayed ajar and I moved toward it, still marveling at the architecture of even the stone above the deep porch. I felt like I was Lorelai going to ask the Gilmores for Chilton money.

The inside of the house was vastly more modern. It was sleek and uncluttered, without even a single suit of armor or coat of arms. One day I was going to walk into a big house and find a suit of armor, dammit.

Mel had moved through the foyer and disappeared around the corner. I, however, took another few seconds to stand under the high ceilings and feel very small, insignificant, and poor.

The chandelier above me wasn't lit, but I got the impression that it would have positively glittered had it been full dark outside. A staircase climbed along the wall ahead of me, hugging the elegant wallpaper as it curled upward. I leaned over in an attempt to see what it led to, but whatever lay past the iron railing was just too high for my craned neck to do me any good.

I heard Mel's voice and it called my attention away from the million stairs and their hidden end. Concentrating in order to both hear and feel what was going on, I moved away from the steps toward the noise. I perceived annoyance, pain, and the windy feeling of irritation and hunger. Norma was definitely here. I considered the fact that I could probably just run out the front door and hide behind Mel's car until Chloe and Owen got there, and then I scolded myself for being so cowardly. They probably would be there soon enough and I could make small talk with Mel and Norma for a few minutes. I really wanted to see her, I realized. Whether it was the curiosity over this other woman who had caused Stan harm, or something else, I wasn't sure.

Past the curving foyer was a long hall lined with art in much the same color scheme as the stained glass at the front of the house. Blue lakes, green grass, and skies in a variety of gorgeous shades were depicted in paintings and photographs. They all seemed to be of a similar landscape, which changed slightly in each piece the further down the hall I got: trees grew, slopes declined, and water receded.

I found Norma and Mel standing in the living room, the size of which put my entire house to shame. Again, the look here was modern but bare. The furniture was cursory: a couch, a few chairs, and a table with a heavy, rounded iron lamp. The room looked untouched, as if it had been staged for sale and then picked clean of the items that were supposed to make it feel homey. The space above the gargantuan fireplace looked barren, and I thought that it needed a family portrait or another painted landscape.

When I finally stopped scanning the room and focused on Norma, I was just as impressed with her as I had been with the house. She was the same height as Mel, slim and busty, with long blond hair that fell in casual waves to her hips. Her nose was narrow, her lips full. Large blue eyes were currently focused on Mel, and they held a lot of anger. His posture was bent, as if he felt torn between standing his ground and crumbling to the lush carpet to kiss her feet.

She was gorgeous, and even her outfit couldn't detract from that. It was mismatched and unflattering, the orange and yellow button-up top hanging loose over a whitewashed denim skirt. Her socks were two different colors, neither of which matched her top or skirt, and her left shoe had a very noticeable tear along the top. I turned my attention back to her face and watched her lips move as she spoke. When I was finally able to focus, I realized I was feeling a little drunk.

"Mel, I don't want to see you anymore. You need to go away. I have to find Stanley. He's gone and I thought he'd left to buy me presents but I couldn't find him. I always see my pets again when they buy me presents. But he's left and I have no presents." She bared her teeth, wrinkling her nose, and it was the sexiest thing I'd ever seen. "I told him about the house, but he's not come by. I want you to leave before he gets here. You've probably scared him off."

"I took Stan," I said, before frowning and looking to the floor to consider why I'd spoken. When I looked back up, Norma was staring at me. I felt a snap of curiosity against my skin, followed by the scalding wind of her anger.

"You have Stanley?" she demanded. Mel looked between us and then reached out toward her hand. She slapped at him and stepped away, leaving him to look absolutely crushed at the rejection.

"Oh yeah, I've got him. I mean, I took him. I don't have him." What was I saying? "But I used to have him. I'm his ex-wife. You're pretty."

Norma took another few steps toward me before stopping and looking to the floor herself. She seemed to consider something before I felt another burn of anger across my cheeks. I squinted into it and took a step toward her. Maybe she just didn't want to come all the way to me; I needed to do the work and go to her. Her delicate features held a formidable glare as she watched me approach. When I stepped up close enough, I felt warm, like my organs had tiny little space heaters focused on them. It was pleasant, but I had the feeling it wouldn't be if I made her angrier.

"I know you," Norma hissed, watching me approach. "I almost had you once before."

"You can have me now," I moaned, delighted at the prospect. "Can I have a kiss? Can we just make out for a bit?"

"Gwen, that's inappropriate," Mel hissed from behind her. Norma's eyes narrowed before she turned to face Mel. He winced when she did but I decided not to concern myself with him; I just wanted to touch her. My gaze moved from her face to her breasts and I started to really understand what it was that Stan had been talking about. Her boobs were phenomenal.

I had to touch them.

She turned just slightly away and my intended grope turned into a slight brush but she didn't seem to notice. I took this as further invitation and stepped in closer, laying my hand over her left breast so that I could feel her nipple in the center of my palm.

A giddy little thrill ran through me and I closed my hand to squeeze. She still didn't seem to care that I was molesting her. Part of me wondered why this was and considered that she should at least have given me permission to do this, right? The other parts told that part to shut up and in fact considered kicking it in the face and ejecting it from the whole.

Both hands now pressed to her breasts, I gave a little sigh and leaned in, laying my head on her skin. I could hear her voice through her chest and it was so pleasant that I actually took the time to listen to her words as my hands continued their rhythmic squeezing.

"… ex-wife? I would eat her alive for hurting my Stanley, but I must know, does she really have him? Where has she taken him? Was he back in her home?"

"I don't know. I didn't see him. Norma, I didn't mean to—"

"I don't care," Norma hissed. The little space heaters on my organs shot up to full power and I whimpered against her. I couldn't bear to pull away, though the pain made some small part of my brain consider it. "Stanley, did you see him?"

"I don't—she called me and she asked me to bring her to you. There was no mention of this … You don't need him, Norma. You have me. You have me and it doesn't even matter that Gwen knows what you are. I can get rid of her for you. I can—" Mel cut off with a yelp, as if she'd hit him, even though she hadn't moved.

I felt a tension run through her body and I let out a whimper as she took hold of my wrists and pushed me away from her. Opening my eyes (when had I closed them?) I looked up to her face, intending to beg to keep touching her. I wanted her to kiss me and run her hands through my hair. I wanted to undress each other and see what she felt like under the roughness of her denim skirt.

"Who told you what I am? Why are you here? Where do you have my Stanley?"

"I'm here for you," I said, feeling a goofy smile spread over my face. I pushed upward to kiss her but she didn't lean down to meet me, and my lips ended up pressed against her chin. That was okay by me.

"Gwen," Mel whined and I felt him step up close. Like Chloe with the ice cream earlier, I suddenly felt vaguely threatened. I twisted to put myself between Mel and Norma, grunting unhappily. He didn't take me seriously and I felt him try to slip a hand between us. I retaliated by pressing myself harder against her, squeezing my eyes shut and trying to reverse her grip on my wrists. She didn't let go of me and I tipped my head up to plead my case with my gaze.

She was unhappy with me and I felt my world crumble around the edges.

"What's wrong?" I asked as Mel tried to shove himself between us again. She ignored him, continuing to watch me.

"Where is he?" Her grip on my wrists was starting to hurt as she held tight to keep Mel from separating us. "I want him back. What do you want?"

"I want to be with you."

"Gwen!" I felt desperation snap out of Mel as he finally figured out that he was much, much stronger than me. His hand pressed against my chest and I flew back, landing firmly on my back, all the air going out of me. My wrists were sore, raw from being yanked so harshly out of Norma's grip. Struggling against my body and the pain the impact had left along my backside, I waved my arms, trying to get back to my feet.

Mel stood over me, glaring. His entire stance had changed when I'd realized how much I wanted Norma for myself. I couldn't blame him, of course. The fact that he was currently between us was making me think it would be brilliant to grab the heavy lamp from the table next to the couch and start hitting him until he was no longer a threat. Norma and I wanted to be alone, and he was clearly too stupid to realize that.

"That's enough, Gwen."

"Make her tell me where Stanley is," Norma demanded. I wanted to tell her, to give her anything she could ever want, but I couldn't speak. I wheezed at them both, attempting to spout something clever and viciously insulting at Mel for separating us. Nothing came except a painful cough and the sound of a body hitting the floor. Was it mine? Had I fallen over again? I didn't think so. Mel was still standing, and I'd gotten my arms under control so I was nearly sitting up. Just one more step to my feet and then I could hit Mel, pick Norma up off the floor and we could—

Hang on.

"Mel," I wheezed. He stepped forward, teeth bared. I pointed behind him. "Norma."

Coughing, I slapped at my chest, trying to dislodge the pain there and free my voice. Mel blinked down at me and then turned to face the woman I loved. When he saw that she'd collapsed to the ground and was currently bleeding all over the nice rug, he let out a strangled cry. He dropped to the ground alongside her, clearing my field of view. Chloe and Owen stood at opposite sides of the room, both aiming handguns at Mel and Norma.

I realized in that second what had happened, and it made me so spitting mad.

I took a gulp of air and finished pushing myself to my feet, stumbling to the side before I caught my balance completely. Mel was still on the ground, grasping at Norma's body gently, as if worried he'd make the hole in her head bigger with too much jostling.

"What did you do?" I demanded. Chloe's eyes flicked to Owen and I followed her gaze. He'd been behind this. He'd been here in Seattle solely to kill Norma and he'd gotten me to help him. She was dead because of me but, more importantly, she was dead because of him.

Ignoring the pair of guns that swept up toward me, I stepped around

Norma, grabbed for the lamp on the end table and tried to make my way toward Owen. The curving iron was heavier than I expected though, and I got it just off the table before my arm felt like an angry Sasquatch had appeared to yank it out of socket.

"Dammit," I hissed, sweeping my arms so that I could grab the lamp with both hands. Irritation lashed out of Owen and I saw Chloe's aim shift rapidly back to Norma, as if she didn't see me as a threat. She was stupid, then, because she had no idea how much damage I could do in the name of my one true love. As I crossed the room, much slower than I would have preferred thanks to the leaden lamp, Owen jerked a chin toward Mel.

"Watch him, I've got her."

Lifting the lamp proved harder than I would have thought and it gave Owen the chance to lower his gun, holstering it under his arm. He hopped back, nimble as a jungle cat, when I swept the lamp as high as I could—roughly waist level—and tried to hit him. Before I could heft it up again, he lifted a leg, kicked at the lamp and knocked it out of my hand. The abrasive metal tore at my skin as it scraped out of my grip, but I just stumbled and changed tactics.

Bringing my hands up like I'd seen people do in movies, I threw my fist at his face, pushing the whole of my body toward him. Owen let out a small laugh and I felt his irritation change to humor as he dodged my punch, grabbed my wrist and twisted to shove his shoulder into my chest. He rolled his body along mine, and the next thing I knew, I was on my back. Wincing at the pain of once again having the wind knocked out of me, I struggled to get back to my feet and continue my attack.

Owen lost interest in me as soon as I was on the ground, but I felt that, like Chloe with her gun, he was being pretty stupid. I don't know much about fighting but in that moment I was convinced I could take out an entire army. Norma was dead and with her my last chance at happiness. Something surged up in me, rushing through my limbs in a tingle. My empathy seemed to flare over the room, sharpening every feeling within my range. Hell, even outside my range. Generally, I can sense those around me in a sphere about the size of Owen's rental house. I can shift it, pushing my power out like spinning a hula hoop around my body. It takes concentration and I get strained if I really force it, but it's possible.

The anger inside me, the demand that I avenge my succubus mistress, seemed to double my range, strengthening my power until I could see the feelings of everyone and everything spread across my vision like spilled paint over glass. Mel's despair was slimy, flooding out over the room like an oil spill and, as much as it disgusted me, I understood. I'd lost Norma, too.

Within the despair was anger. That, I could appreciate. That I could understand. That I wanted for myself and I considered taking it, closing in to suck it out and add it to my own. I'd never in my life considered going after someone's negative emotions on purpose but, in that moment, the idea seemed flawless.

I was on my feet and I didn't remember getting off the ground. Then I was right behind Owen, even though I didn't remember closing in. I could feel some anger in him, too, though it paled next to the glowing rage at Mel's core. I paused, turning my attention to the two humans in the room, and wondered for a moment what their emotions were worth.

Chloe was standing near Mel, her gun still aimed down at him, though her stance was loose, distracted. I could feel the greasy pool of pity in her gut, cold and thick against my senses. I had a vision of pulling the knife from the sheath at Owen's hip and slicing her open to spill it out over the ground. Pity would do me no good.

Owen noticed me as I grabbed for his weapon, twisting to face me, surprise naked on his face. He caught my wrist as I reached, the surprise bleeding into irritation. Pity here, too. I hated it.

"What are—"

"Stop," I hissed, lifting my free hand to press against his face. I shoved my empathy inside him, reaching for the pity, aiming to tear it out and fling it wide. I could feel everything now that we were touching, all his emotions both past and present. I recognized everything he'd felt with me over the last few days, saw it all like a timeline packed with notations. As fascinated as I was by this new ability, I couldn't reach into his past and pluck out what he'd felt before. I needed to focus on the now, on what I could steal and capture for myself in the moment.

There were other notions there inside him too, things I'd never felt before. Anger, jealousy, love, those I knew well. These feelings weren't new to me, and I understood them immediately by touch. The others, though, the more—I liked the way they felt. Ambition, drive, the desire to live itself. I could feel it all and, if I wanted, I could rip it out. I could take it for myself, make each one a part of me and leave Owen empty on the carpet of Norma's beautiful home.

I had the pity, could feel the slippery glide of it in my grasp, and it made me gnash my teeth in revulsion. Pity was weak.

Owen's eyes were on mine, wide with confusion and surprise. There was no fear, no panic, just shock. I was just about to suck away the pity, to pour it out into the ether, when I felt a hand on my jaw. Nails dug into my skin, the pain a tingle against my throat, and I felt my head turned away. Chloe was close, her face filled with concern.

My empathy pulled back from Owen, fascinated by what it saw deep in her past. There was guilt churning, roiling like pool of lava buried in the earth. It was ancient, an echo of something past. I knew from the touch of it that she had let go of it years before, and I instantly wanted to know where it had come from. What had this fascinating woman done to deserve such a well of remorse?

"Gwen," Chloe said, her voice soft. "Don't let it control you." I blinked, the thing surging in me pulling back, retreating at the feeling of her love for me.

"Probably shouldn't touch her," Owen said. There was a shaky edge to his voice I'd never heard before, but before I could get a hold on what caused it, he knocked my hand away from his face. I barely noticed as he adjusted his grip on my wrist to twist it up and back, forcing my arm into an impossible angle. The pain roared through me, all I could feel for a moment, and before I knew it he had me on my knees, his face serious over mine. Through the tears in my eyes, I could see both him and Chloe watching me, concerned.

"Ow," I whimpered. "Stop."

Owen did, bumping his knee into my chest just hard enough to knock me onto my back. He flicked his gaze to Chloe in what looked like an 'I got this' signal, before reaching into the pack strapped along his hip and thigh.

"This is not how I pictured it going the first time I tied you up, let me tell you," he said. His tone was conversational, casual, but I could still feel worry inside him, a faint disquiet over what I'd done. He snapped plastic loops around my wrists, yanked them tight, and then grabbed me under my arms, pulling me away from the center of the large room. He propped me up against the far wall, bound my ankles, and then we both froze as Mel let out a roar of pain.

"Shit," Chloe said, her free hand going to her gun. Owen got to his feet.

"Yep," he said, as if resigned.

I fought against my bonds, but it was no good. When I tried to kick at the backs of Owen's ankles, he just glanced briefly back at me before drawing his gun.

"We can't kill him," Chloe said. I felt Owen's exasperation at her words, but I wasn't sure if I agreed with him or her. On the one hand, Mel seemed to be the only one left to avenge Norma. On the other, he had tried to steal her from me.

Perhaps I would kill him after he killed them. I liked that idea.

Owen stepped sideways through the room, drawing Mel's ire away from Chloe, putting his back to the massive fireplace. As he moved, I got a good look at Mel for the first time in several minutes. He was standing over Norma's body, and his eyebrows had grown back, along with the uneven hair on his head. His teeth were bared but his jaw looked misshapen, like it was pushing outward under his skin. He was breathing heavily, and a little growl slipped out with each exhale. His focus entirely on Owen, he didn't notice that Chloe was slipping up behind him, gun still aimed at his back. Owen didn't betray her movement, keeping his gaze directly on Mel.

"Get them!" I called. Mel jerked his gaze to me briefly and it was all

Chloe needed. She holstered her weapon and yanked a long, needle-thin gold chain out of her pocket. Using the couch as a springboard, she launched herself onto Mel's back, wrapping the chain around his neck and tugging. He grunted and I felt his shock as he twisted in an attempt to face her. I caught sight of the hair at the back of his neck growing down his shoulders and under the collar of his shirt to join the thick hair on his arms.

He did two complete turns with Chloe clinging to his back before he seemed to get smart. Owen had holstered his own weapon and opened another pocket on the leather pack strapped to his thigh. Before he could pull out whatever it was he was reaching for, Mel clipped him in the shoulder with his furry hand. Owen grunted but seemed to move with the impact, catching himself before he face-planted into the stone of the fireplace. Mel ignored him for the moment, grabbing back for Chloe.

She surprised me with her agility, holding the two ends of the chain with one hand as she produced a small knife with the other. As Mel reached a clawed hand back toward her head, she leaned away and jammed the knife into his palm. Mel screamed, and I felt myself whimper at the enraged roar of it.

I was still rooting for him to win, but the rage inside me had faded slightly. I was losing the reckless gumption I'd been feeling right after Norma's death and it was being replaced by the strong desire to pee my damn pants.

Mel jerked his hand away from Chloe in an arc, spraying blood across the room. Without hesitation, he yanked the knife out of his palm and threw it to the side. Chloe had gone back to doing her best to suffocate him, but Mel's neck seemed to be getting broader the furrier he got. He had a muzzle, and the entire shape of his head had changed to include tall, fur-tufted ears.

I had managed to gloss over the sound of joints cracking and clothes tearing up to that point, but when Mel twisted his head in an attempt to bite Chloe's arm, I saw that his nice, misbuttoned shirt had ripped at the seams to reveal deep black fur on his shoulders. Chloe pressed further into him and, while his head was turned, I saw Owen dive forward, syringe in hand. He dropped to his knees under Mel's swinging arms and jammed the syringe up into Mel's groin.

I don't even have testicles, but that hurt to watch.

Mel let out a sound that started as a roar of anger and trailed off into a howl of pain. His bulk shifted to the side and Owen twisted to shoot his foot out, sweeping Mel's legs out from under him. The wolfman dropped to his side and Chloe let out a grunt as she hit the floor shortly after. I watched in shock as Owen pushed to his feet at the same time as he drew his gun, aimed it at Mel, and stepped to the side, out of range of Mel's long limbs.

Chloe rolled away, leaving the chain around Mel's neck and coming up in a crouch. She'd produced another knife and she held it out in front of her.

"Next time warn a girl," she muttered. Owen's grin was quick and wicked, but he didn't move from his spot until it had been a full minute of Mel laying still, barely outside arm's reach of Norma's corpse.

"You son of a bitch!" I yowled, fighting against my bonds. My struggle felt human, though, weak and ineffectual. The clarity of my empathy had faded, leaving me with only the rage Norma's death had sparked.

Chloe glanced over at me and the pool of pity in her solidified, going cold and hard as though ice chips were forming along the edges. She was annoyed with me. Despite my best efforts, I was unable to get to my feet and continue the fight. Owen holstered his gun, satisfied that Mel was down for the count, and turned to face me. Grinning across the room, he watched me struggle for a bit before he chuckled.

"She's pretty cute when she's mad."

"Yeah, but she bites," Chloe said conversationally, getting to her feet. As she moved toward Mel, Owen came closer to me. I tried to kick out with both legs but missed entirely. Waggling his eyebrows, he dropped down over me, sitting on my knees and reaching into his pack again. I tried to punch him again, with both fists this time, but he just he swept my arms out of my way with his right hand, leaning close as he did.

"Hate to do this to you, sweetheart, but you've really made a mess." Pressing his lips to mine, he ignored the growl I let out as he lifted his left hand. I saw it sweep closer in my peripheral vision before I felt a pinch in my neck.

The world went black.

Twenty-Two

I woke up in the arms of a woman, comfortable and content. My head was cradled in the crook of an elbow, and it was so dim in the room I could barely see who was above me. My first thought was that Norma had come back to life for me, that now we could be together. I lifted my hand to the arm draped over my chest and smiled.

"Love," I murmured, hunching my shoulders up around my neck like a child happy to be tucked in snugly, before I turned so I could lay my cheek on her breast. The woman shifted and the lights came up. I realized it wasn't Norma I was with, but Madeline. She was stunning.

The ruddiness of her cheeks had cleared up, leaving her skin flawless. Her lips looked full, her eyes soft and inviting. When she smiled, her teeth were perfect and, when she brushed my hair off my cheek, I noted that the dark hairs along her arms seemed to have lightened and thinned.

"You've come out of it," she said softly, laying her hand on my cheek. "I wasn't sure I was getting through."

"Madeline?" I asked, though I knew it was her. I recognized the feeling of being this close to her and, though she looked different, she wasn't entirely foreign. Like seeing someone made up by a professional make-up artist next to their own gawky high school picture. "Where are we?"

"My bed," she said. Her hand on my cheek was warm, like she'd pressed it to a hot oven before touching me. I frowned, and it made her laugh.

"Why am I—" I cut off, suddenly uncomfortable being draped in her arms like we were lovers. I sat up, scooted away from her as she trailed her arms along my body until I was out of reach. "Why am I in your bed?"

"You needed help. You and Mel, though I'm not sure where he got off to. Chloe and Owen said he disappeared before they could round him up."

"Disappeared from where?" I looked about the room, realizing I had no idea what had happened in the last few hours. "What time is it? Are we dating? I thought I was straight. What's going on?"

Madeline laughed, tipping her head back as she did. Her hair fell over her shoulders like a waterfall. I found I wanted to reach out and run my hands through it. When she caught my gaze again, I felt myself blush.

"Everything you're feeling now, everything you felt with Norma, it wasn't your fault. You'll pull through. Now come, sit in my lap. We have a bit more until you're right as rain."

My gaze fell to her hand as she reached out toward me and I thought about the contentment I'd felt upon waking. I realized I missed it, and that all I had to do to get it back was put my hand in hers. When I did so, she tugged, gently pulling me close. I looked up to find her slipping a hand behind my head and leaning in close as she tipped my mouth to meet hers. Her kiss was like a tornado in my mind, whirling my thoughts up and outward, leaving me blank.

It seemed it had become habit for me to get knocked unconscious by something supernatural and wake up in bed with a man. Last time it had been Chloe's bed and Mel; this time it was Stan and the bed was mine.

Sitting next to my hip, Stan smiled down at me, and I felt happiness flutter out of him. It took me a few brainless seconds to comprehend exactly what him sitting over me meant.

"You're okay!" I breathed, pushing into a sitting position and grabbing for his shoulders. He let me pull him into a hug and held on tight as dizziness took hold. I groaned as I felt the world slip out from under me. He hugged against the side of me that was suddenly magnetically attracted to the bed; instead of letting me topple, he kept me against him and ran a hand over my hair.

"Why am I hungover?" I mumbled against his sweater. He let out a soft laugh, ran his hand down my back and shifted closer, letting me straighten my spine marginally.

"Madeline had to fix you. You tried to kill Chloe and Owen."

"I tried to kill Chloe?"

"Yes, but it wasn't your fault."

I opened my eyes, staring at myself in the floor-length mirror across from my bed. I looked terrible. I noticed the bruise along my right wrist and felt the fuzzy memories trying to surface. Everything from the moment I'd stepped into Norma's house was a cloud of sensations, emotions, and flashing visions. One memory was clear, though, rooting to the forefront of everything else: I remembered Mel getting stabbed in the balls.

Stan pulled back slightly when I started to giggle, the look in his eyes matching the alarm he felt at my state of mind. He glanced over at the doorway before calling out for Chloe. I pushed myself upward, keeping a steadying hand on Stan's shoulder as I looked to the door. Chloe came in, followed closely by Owen. He smiled as he saw me, stopping next to the bed to regard me. I was still giggling and Stan gestured to me with his free hand.

"Is she okay?"

"She's probably just thinking about Owen stabbing Mel in the crotch," Chloe explained. Disapproval fanned out of Stan, hitting me in the face and making a snort slip its way into my giggling. Owen barked out a laugh at the sound, and I reached out to him. He took my hand, gave it a squeeze.

"Thank you for that mental image. You don't ever owe me any birthday presents, for that was truly the greatest gift of all," I told him. He winked at me and I could tell there was a bit more behind it than mutual amusement at Mel getting tranq'd in the junk. After a second, I felt curiosity get the better of me. "Where is Mel, anyway?"

"We're not really sure," Chloe admitted. One of the fuzzy memories shuffled up, trying to remind me of something about Madeline and the warmth of a dark room. "He just up and disappeared. I'm sure he's fine, though. If he could walk, he's alive. We didn't really hurt him."

"Ah," I murmured, wondering if I should send a fruit basket or something to apologize for what we'd put him through.

"So you're okay, then?" Stan asked, distracting me. I turned back to him and nodded.

"I think I feel okay. I don't want to kill any of you, or make out with any succubi. Succubusses?" I wrestled with my groggy mind. "Succubi, right? Like when there's more than one Elvis?"

"Something like that," Chloe agreed, winking at me. "I had to change your clothes because you had chocolate squeezing out of the back pocket."

"Hunh?" I asked, glancing down at myself. I was wearing loose pants and a sleep-tee. Looking back up to Chloe, I tried to figure out what she was talking about. She jerked a thumb toward my bathroom.

"The candy you stole from Mel, you left it in your pocket and it melted. You're either gonna need to toss those pants or find a really good dry cleaner."

Owen was smiling, glancing between us to see my reaction as Chloe spoke. When I recalled the chocolate she was talking about, I felt my face settle into a pout. That had been pretty good chocolate and I'd wasted it on pants. Dammit.

Deciding changing the subject was for the best, I tried to pull myself out of my lost-sugar funk.

"Is Norma actually dead?"

"She is. Owen took care of it."

"I can't believe you just shot her in the head and that was it."

Owen shrugged, though there was something there he clearly wasn't saying.

"They're not hard to kill; I didn't consider the fact that it would make you and Mel so mad, though." Another fuzzy memory tried to force its way forward. A flutter of panic held it back and I moved on before I could realize what was making me so nervous.

"And yet you just had syringes full of tranquilizers lying around?" I asked, feeling the discomfort inside Stan double.

"They come in handy more often than you'd think," Owen explained. "Like our first date, for instance."

"Ah," I said, biting my lip. Stan was no longer the only one feeling uncomfortable. "Can I have a few more minutes alone with Stan?" Chloe and Owen nodded, turning to leave as suddenly as they'd come in. Chloe shut the door behind them, but I caught her eyes lingering on me, full of suspicious concern.

"What happened at Madeline's?" I asked. Stan's cheeks went slightly pink and he cleared his throat, shaking his head.

"With me or you?"

I blinked and shook my head. "Both, I guess."

"Nothing untoward."

"Well, that's good at least. She kept her promise." When his gaze drifted to the headboard behind me, I nudged him with my knee. "I don't remember much. You?"

"There was some touching. Nothing inappropriate."

"All outside your bathing suit area?" I asked, thinking of Owen's remark. Stan nodded.

"Yes. I'm not entirely certain but I think we can assume she was, well …" He trailed off and I lifted my hand to gesture vaguely.

"A perfect gentleman?"

Stan smiled and nodded. "More or less."

"Is there really no term like that for women? Is it only men who can be either beast or man?" Stan looked troubled by my words and I wondered for a moment if he was thinking about the way our marriage had ended. I hadn't been just beastly, but monstrous. I know I couldn't forgive myself and I sort of hoped he never could either.

I realized then that it was very dark in the room, except for the one lamp on the far nightstand keeping things dimly lit. I glanced through the open doorway at the clock I kept on a shelf in the bathroom and balked at the time. I'd lost several hours.

"Jeez." My bladder took that moment to explain the consequences of ignoring it for so long. "Ah, excuse me for a second." Swinging my legs out of the bed, I hurried to the bathroom, slamming the door.

After I'd washed my hands and run a brush through my hair I went back out into the bedroom. I perched on the foot of the bed and Stan turned to face me, lifting a knee and laying it in front of him on the bed. Something had occurred to me in the bathroom and it was eating away at my brain, an experience Stan and I now shared that I wasn't sure anyone else would quite understand. Fighting off an embarrassed smile, I watched him in the mirror while I spoke.

"Norma was pretty."

"Oh. Yes. Well." The distress I'd felt in him earlier peeked out and I swallowed, pushing through the doubt that I couldn't help feeling within both of us. Had she been beautiful? Had Madeline?

"I kind of couldn't help but just grab her boobs," I admitted after a bit. Stan's eyes went wide and he met my gaze in the mirror.

"You too?"

"Yes!" I exclaimed, turning to face him for real. He gave a short laugh and lifted a hand to touch his own cheek, like he was hiding from the memory. I reached out and touched his hand. "I am so sorry."

"It's not your fault."

"I feel like it is. You wouldn't have been here, alone, prone to her wiles if I hadn't gone off in the middle of the night." Cutting myself off before I went too far into why I'd been gone, I rubbed my palm over the back of his hand. "How did she get you?"

"She just came to the back door and knocked. Next thing I knew, we were in this nice family sedan with a baby seat in the back, driving out to that warehouse. I was too smitten to really ask any questions."

"It was that fast for me, too."

"Gwen, this really wasn't your fault. She had my home address. If I had left Seattle on time, she would have met me there and you and your friends wouldn't have been around to save me."

"Yeah, I guess that's true," I said with a nod. "Then you would have been succubus food."

"Probably not a bad way to die, I'd guess?"

"I think, judging by how pathetic Mel was in the end, that may not be true."

"Oh," Stan said simply. We sat in silence for a bit longer before I shifted to straighten myself out. I left my hand on his.

"When do you leave?"

"I pushed my train out until tomorrow—today. Around two."

"Have you slept?"

"No, but I'm not tired at all. Chloe suggested we all go out and get some breakfast. She said you'd probably be hungry when you woke up."

"We've got a few hours until anything opens up, though. I'm going to see if they want to crash here, to nap or something. Are you okay?"

"You need to stop being so concerned for me."

"No, I don't," I said. Smiling at him, I leaned forward, pulled him into a hug. We stayed that way for what felt like a long time. I think we needed to hold each other, and not just because we'd both lost control with a beautiful monster. I pulled away slowly and, without thinking about it, kissed him. He kissed back and our lips parted, but the kiss remained chaste. As we pulled away, we watched each other's eyes, some piece of our history passing between us, settling in a way it hadn't before. Feeling like closure had been achieved in some form or another, I smiled and got to my feet.

"Why are you looking at me like that?" I asked when Chloe's concern got too annoying to ignore.

"I'm not looking at you at all," she said, glancing away from the pan of vegetables she was cooking. "Well, now I am."

"Okay, but your head's looking at me. I mean," I corrected, trying to clarify. "Your feelings. Your emotions are looking at me."

"Are they being creepy? Peeking at you from behind a fence while you're trying on bras?"

"You're already force-feeding me vegetables. I don't need your sass, too, young lady."

Chloe laughed and it eased the anxiety that was grasping at me like a kid pulling on mommy's shirt and begging for a candy bar.

"Why are you so worried about me?"

"I'm always worried about you," she explained. "You're basically diabetes on two legs."

"No," was my only argument. She laughed again, harder this time, turning to lean against the stove and smile at me. She regarded me for a few moments before her smile faltered and nervous concern gripped the edges of her psyche with iron fists.

"What do you remember from the night we stopped Norma?"

"Mel getting stabbed right in the balls," I announced, giddy that it had been a week and the image hadn't deteriorated in my brain one bit. Mel had been missing, but I wasn't terribly concerned. He was a strong, independent werewolf. After what he'd been through with Norma, I imagined he was probably off drowning his sorrows in coconut-covered boobs and coconut oil-covered butts.

Stan had gone back to Portland, Owen had left the next day, so it was just Chloe and me back to our regular lives. Since I'd woken up with Stan sitting at my bedside, though, there'd been an undercurrent of anxiety running through her.

She was still watching me, her expression calm and curious despite the shaky feeling behind her soft smile. Deciding to indulge her, I thought about her question for a moment, trying to bring to mind whatever answer she was looking for.

"I don't know. There isn't much left in the old noodle. I remember having—being *forced under duress* to ask Mel to have sex with me—"

"I gave you ice cream!" she argued.

"*Under duress!*" I repeated, pointing at her. Her anxiety cracked a little and I grinned at the relief that started to leak through. "After that, I don't remember much. There was a fancy house and … I think I got fresh with Norma. It gets blurry after that."

Truth was, I wanted it to stay blurry. When I thought too hard about anything after checking out the fancy foyer, my thoughts seemed to ice over. If my brain had knees, they would have started knocking any time the subject was brought up. I shook my head, waving away the incident.

"You don't have to … I'm fine. Is that what you're worried about? What are you worried about?"

The tension in Chloe's shoulders relaxed a little and she went back to poking and stirring the colorful mix of food she'd put together.

"So Madeline did a good job, then?" Her gaze rolled to me, but the action was slightly hesitant, like she wasn't sure she wanted to meet my eyes. "She got it all … It's gone?"

"What's gone?"

"The …" She was quiet for a second and I felt dishonesty start to boil up from the recesses of her mind. It burbled back down to nothing after a moment and she licked her lips before speaking the truth. "Norma was in your head, like she was in Stan's. You didn't take her death well and I didn't like seeing you that way." Fear jittered through her, chased by the ghost of guilt. "I didn't like what it made you do."

I thought back to Stan's comment about how I'd tried to kill Chloe and I jumped to my feet, closing the distance between us so I could hug her. She stiffened slightly when my hands touched her bare arm, but then relaxed almost instantly into the hug.

"I'm sorry if I tried to hurt you. But at least you didn't have to stab me in the balls to stop me, right?"

"Stab you in the balls?" Chloe asked, leaning away just enough so she could catch my eye. "Honey, I've got news for you about the birds and the bees."

I laughed and stepped back. We smiled at each other for a moment longer before she turned to the food and lifted the pan to flip the contents like an expert.

"Is that why you've been coming over to make me broccoli every night since it happened? Is this punishment for me trying to whack you?"

"Yes," Chloe said. "And had you killed me, I would have come back to haunt you shaped like a giant eggplant."

"Yes, just what I need whenever Owen comes back into town, a giant purple, dong-shaped ghost going, 'wooo-ooo-ooooo!' while I'm trying to get him to take his pants off."

Chloe's whole face wrinkled with laughter for a few moments before she was able to speak again. "Just don't try to kill me and things will be fine."

"Likewise," I joked. Her expression went tight and I wondered as she turned the burner off and set the pan aside if the faint wisp of guilt she was feeling was real or imagined.

As she piled our plates high and told me to pour us some water to drink with dinner, I decided it had to be imagined. Chloe was one of the best people I'd ever met. She couldn't have had anything to feel guilty for.

About the Author

Olivia is a vegan thirty-something living in New Mexico with a clowder of cats and a stink of litter boxes. She enjoys vexing her kitties, cooking, watching action movies, and making up collective nouns for things that don't already have them (like a "stink of litter boxes"). You can find her and all information about her different series at OliviaRBurton.com.

Gwen Arthur Novels

Visit OliviaRBurton.com for more information

www.ingramcontent.com/pod-product-compliance
Lightning Source LLC
Chambersburg PA
CBHW072135170626
46813CB00004BA/1570